Indecent Protection

Irish Honor, Volume 4

Amara Holt

Published by Amara Holt, 2024.

Prologue

Elaine

Past

The cold metal of the locket sliding between my fingers contrasts with how my blood boils beneath my skin.

They say time can soothe everything. Calm the anger, make us forgive, lessen or even erase the hatred in our hearts.

Maybe that's true, but it can never erase the pain of loss.

We are all born knowing that our journey on this planet will come to an end. No one in their twenties, however, expects it to come around the next corner or during a commute, as it happened to my sister.

There's the illusion that we have a whole lifetime to live because we think ourselves almost immortal.

"I would give anything to have you back, Elysia. You would be so proud of our Jax. He's getting more handsome every day."

Despite my words sounding gentle, rage still flows through my body like a river whose waters cannot be contained. It's a kind of wild fury that, when I let it surface, makes me want to hunt down the one who killed her—the monster who took Elysia from me. A faceless demon, because she never wanted to tell me who Jax's father was. And yet, I hate him. I know he found her and ended her life.

I feel her loss every day and my heart longs for justice, though I know that pursuing this faceless man means putting my nephew at risk.

Besides, what is justice? Not the kind of justice from men, certainly. Even though I don't meddle in Irish mafia matters, my employers, I would trust my life to them rather than to the police, the so-called "regular justice."

I wipe away an unexpected tear and look at the gravestone that marks where my sister is buried.

How can an entire existence be summed up by a stone and an inscription with her name?

I look around the cemetery, knowing I shouldn't stay too long. In fact, if I were thinking clearly, I wouldn't have come in the first place, because I don't know if that man knows about me or Jax, but on days like today, when I wake up, I need to visit her. Remind myself why I can never give up: because my nephew needs me.

He will grow up protected, no matter what I need to do to ensure that.

Chapter 1

Odhran

Seattle

The darkness of the night seems to help make our humanity disappear. In the shadows, we are like ghosts lurking.

I don't like peace, the absence of noise, or anything that suggests calm. I thrive in the storm. Storms and the unexpected are my elements.

Today, however, the element of surprise is crucial, even though I appreciate the spectacle a grand entrance can create, as well as the fear on the enemy's face.

Some believe that I fulfill my role within the Syndicate with such enthusiasm because I am loyal to my brother, Cillian, our Boss. That's partly true. Yes, I would die a thousand deaths for him, but I also enjoy war, whether it is started by an enemy or initiated by us.

I watch my men waiting for orders to invade. There are only three of us today. I could have come alone, actually, but Cillian would have a fucking heart attack if I didn't bring a few soldiers.

"When?" one of them asks me.

"In five minutes," I say. "I don't want to scare him or risk him putting a bullet in his own head. Cillian's orders were clear. The bastard will serve as an example. In the future, when any of you bastards think about raising a hand against your own wife, you will

3

remember this night. We are Irish. We honor our women, not abuse them."

Abuse? No, what Eoghan O'lly did to his son's mother cannot be called anything other than *massacre*. And worst of all, he brought shame to our people and made my aunt Orla cry when she saw, on every news channel, the footage of the torture he inflicted on the woman, since the bastard even posted the video online.

I am far from being an emotional guy. To be honest, I'm not even sure if I have feelings and emotions inside me.

Common concepts to the rest of humanity such as guilt, remorse, anguish, are foreign to me, yet I was sleepless the day the footage was leaked around the world.

Seeing what he did to his wife made me lose even more of the little faith I had left in humanity.

No, faith is not the best word. I have never had faith in humans; there are only a few I have handpicked to trust.

When I finally give the signal, our entry is swift, calculated with surgical precision.

Since the videos were leaked around the globe, the FBI and even bounty hunters have been after Eoghan. However, because our world exists in the underworld, we have access to information that the "heroes" cannot reach.

Everyone leaves a trail and, for the misfortune of the police and the FBI, and our luck, we don't need a warrant issued by some fucked-up judge to investigate, capture, judge, and punish. No one tells us if we can invade Eoghan's house and dig for information until we find his whereabouts, and that's why while the authorities are chasing their own tails, going in circles, we are here, about to send the miserable bastard directly to the arms of Satan.

The fear on his face when he sees me makes me despise him even more, if that's possible.

He is facing me, standing, still holding the milk bottle, which he apparently grabbed from the kitchen, in his hand, but his eyes slightly drift to the left.

I raise my weapon and with a precise shot, I make the milk explode, spreading the white liquid, without hitting the bullet, though. A shot at him would be too easy. That's not how he's going to die.

The jerk screams, scared.

"It was just a warning. You won't grab the gun," I say, guessing he was looking in the direction where he had left it. "I have plans for both of us."

"You don't understand, boss. She was a bitch and deserved it!"

"Spare yourself the attempt to delay your death. Nothing you say will change the fact that you disrespected your own home. You made the most important woman in Cillian's life cry with your little show for your followers, who, to start with, you shouldn't even have, you idiot."

We are not fucking celebrities, but apparently, the idiot thought it was a good idea to create a YouTube channel and show his "physical evolution" through working out and a lot of steroids, of course. That's where he also uploaded the video in which he tortured for hours and, finally, killed his own wife, just because she wanted a separation.

"I was angry, boss. Maybe I overdid it with the steroids."

"I don't care about the reason behind it. You have a fucking brain. There was time to think about what you were doing. You killed her consciously. The act itself wouldn't have been forgiven, but making my aunt cry? You dug a painful death for yourself, you bastard."

"Can I at least choose how I die?" he asks, opening his arms dramatically. "A bullet between the eyes."

"Why would I show you any mercy when you had none for your son's mother? Killing her was too little. You wanted to humiliate her in her final moments. I consider myself a fair guy, but not in a good way."

"What does that mean?"

"I believe in an eye for an eye, a tooth for a tooth," I say, handing my weapon to one of my men. "And in your case, that saying will be taken literally."

I've seen many men tremble. The fear of others doesn't give me pleasure; I'm not a sadist, but in this situation, I smile when I see him wavering on his feet, as if his knees were weak.

"What's wrong? Isn't it as much fun when the fight is against someone your size?"

"Why don't you just kill me? We both know that's what's going to happen in the end."

"Because, my friend, you will be the proof that no one stands against the Syndicate and lives to tell the tale. Every coward like you, who is one of ours and thinks of raising a hand against his wife, will remember your death."

I usually don't wear gloves or long sleeves, not even in winter, but today I came prepared because his beating will be filmed and distributed among our subordinates. Every action he took with his wife will be repeated. Including the end.

I walk up to him leisurely.

"I'll give you a chance to react. You'll get the opportunity she didn't have, you bastard. The difference is that now you'll fight someone who weighs the same as you, not forty kilograms less. Let's make this *interesting*. You start," I say, making a "come here" gesture with my finger. He hesitates, knowing he has no chance. "The longer you take, the longer I'll delay your death."

Eoghan finally approaches, both arms raised in a defensive position. I am faster and angrier, though. The first punch I land on his ribs is because, suddenly, the disfigured face of his wife comes to mind. The image breaks the dam of the beast within me, and once I start, I can't stop.

I feel the blood inside my gloves, but my anger is still not assuaged.

Twenty minutes later, his face is an unrecognizable mass, but that's just the beginning. I still spend hours using my torture tools on him. All properly documented.

Even though my arms and hands are covered and my face doesn't appear in the footage, it will still be edited by Kellan. My brother has the soul of a hacker and loves to play with technology.

"Sit him up," I say, almost at dawn when there are no more tools to use on him. "I want him in the same position he put his wife in when he delivered the fatal shot."

My men have work to do to follow my order. Eoghan weighs about a hundred kilos and is completely out of it.

They finally position him as I instructed. I grab a bucket of ice-cold water I've used throughout the night and wake him up again.

"Film it," I order my men. "Look at me, bastard. You wanted to put on a show for your followers. Now it's your turn to be the prey, not the predator. Messages to Satan in our name."

I finally blow his head off with a shot, and immediately a sense of peace spreads through my body.

Death, in my world, is work. Today, however, it was revenge. My favorite word.

Chapter 2

Elaine

Boston

God, I'm already late!

As I struggle to dress my Jax, who has recently decided that bath time means playtime, I glance at the clock on the bedside table. I can't afford to miss work today. I was transferred to Boston just recently to literally "play at work."

"Hestia, could you give him his dinner? I'd love to, but I have to rush if I want to get to work on time."

"Mama, *dinner* for Jax, *dinner* for Jaxxxxxx!"

Jesus, he's full of energy today.

"Yes, that's right, his dinner."

Even in my hurry, my heart melts for my boy. He's just turned two, and looking back, I can't believe how fast the time has passed.

Jax doesn't resemble me or my deceased sister at all, so I assume he must take after his father. Although he also has brown eyes, his skin is softly golden, like a kind of natural tan, unlike mine, which is much lighter. Moreover, his eyes are almond-shaped and his hair is straight. I, on the other hand, like my sister, have a wavy mane.

"*Dinnerrrrr!*"

I look at Hestia and smile as she shakes her head.

"I guess there's no helping it, my dear. You'll have to feed him."

I try to pick him up to carry him to the kitchen, but he escapes and climbs down from the bed by himself. At two years old, Jax is very independent, like a little king, and thinks he can manage most of his short life without help. He doesn't want me around to feed him, just to watch him eat.

Watching him grow and become a beautiful boy is a unique experience because only I know what we went through to get here.

"Food!" he says, clapping as he enters the kitchen and breathes in the aroma.

Hestia and I laugh, probably both remembering the week he insisted on pretending to be a sniffing puppy because he saw a cartoon where a boy did that. He spent about three days crawling around the house. My boy has some quirks.

As I lift him to put him in his high chair, I think about how it sometimes frustrates me not to be home to follow his progress, but Hestia is wonderful and sends me videos of all his daily achievements.

In addition to my job at the Irish Syndicate fights, as one of the girls holding the signs during the breaks, I have several other temporary jobs. I do whatever it takes to ensure that Jax never lacks for anything.

Half an hour and a lot of mess later, I know I can't wait any longer. A bit of crying can be overcome, but unemployment in what is my main source of income cannot.

"Hey, sweetie, Grandma Hestia is going to give you your dessert, okay? Mama has to go to work."

"*Sad*. Mama *sad*" he says, perhaps because he senses how upset I am to miss these moments with him.

How can someone so small be so sensitive? He notices the slightest change in my face.

"Mama always feels sad when she has to leave because she misses you a lot."

"Don't be *sad*, Mama."

"I'm not. I just wanted to watch cartoons with you."

His eyes shine with amusement, and I achieve my goal because nothing is better than seeing him smile.

"So, are you going to stop with the flattery or am I no longer needed?" Hestia says, sounding a bit jealous.

Despite the sourness of her words, I know she's just teasing me. She's the most selfless person I've ever had the chance to meet. Life blessed me with a neighbor who became like a mother to me. Wherever I've moved since Elysia's death, Hestia has come with us.

"Yes, indeed, and very much. Thank you for being my support. Now I have to run or I'll really be late."

"I don't like you working in fights," she says for the thousandth time.

Hestia has no idea that it's not just fights, but underground competitions organized by the Irish mafia. If she suspected this, I'm sure she would be terrified.

The need to be semi-nude among men who kill for a living doesn't please me, but I'm a practical person, not a dreamer. I have both feet on the ground, and as long as I'm not committing crimes myself and the money is coming in, I'm okay with it.

Some might say my morality is somewhat gray, dancing to the tune, but the truth is, it's easy to judge someone when you live in utmost comfort.

Have a child and be the sole provider for feeding, clothing, and, in Jax's case, caring for his health, and then tell me if you can judge me.

I kiss my boy and breathe in his delicious scent before giving a smile to Hestia.

"Good night to both of you. I'll try to come back as early as possible."

"Don't worry about it, dear, we'll be fine."

"Don't forget to check if the doors and windows are securely locked," I say, trying to keep my voice neutral to avoid showing fear.

Hestia doesn't know the full story about my sister's death or that I suspect Jax's father might have been responsible for Elysia's death. I didn't think there would be any benefit in telling her, except to make her scared, so I believe she thinks my paranoia about security is just pure exaggeration.

She's wonderful, and I can't help but thank the heavens once again for having her in my life. We three work well together, and it's a blessing to have someone trustworthy to leave Jax with.

I PARK THE CAR THAT has seen better days—no, actually, I bought it falling apart—and enter through the back door of the warehouse where the fights will be held tonight.

There's no one here yet except for the Syndicate's bodyguards and a few other girls who will be doing the same job as me—entertaining jerks during the fight breaks.

"Good evening, everyone! Is everyone excited?" I ask, forcing myself to sound cheerful when, in reality, I hate every second of this job.

From a girl who dreamed of having a shop specializing in bridal bouquets to someone earning a living by showing her body in a corset and garter belt to a bunch of guys, there's a big difference.

"You bet your sweet ass, girl!" one of the women replies.

I know she's been working in the fights for a decade, while I've been in the "business" for just a little over a couple of years, which, from my perspective, feels like a lifetime.

I started shortly before I ran away with Elysia and I thank God for having this job. The fights happen all over the country, and there's always work. Wherever we moved, it was mainly from this Syndicate "activity" that I made our living.

"I'm already thinking about the clothes I'm going to buy next weekend with the money I'll get today," she continues.

I shake my head and can't help but smile. The woman is several years older than me, but I feel like an old lady next to her.

It's amazing how priorities shift when you become responsible for someone other than yourself. I don't even know how long it's been since I bought something for myself.

I let my gaze fall on my worn jeans and the plain white T-shirt I'm wearing.

I'm fine with it.

I need very little for myself. Nothing is more important than keeping Jax well-fed, clean, and safe.

On top of that, I have rent, Hestia's salary, and occasional issues with my second-hand car that's seen many years of use.

A new purse is definitely the least of my needs right now.

Chapter 3

Odhran

The moment I step into the warehouse where the fights will be held tonight, the energy of the place brings a good feeling to my chest.

The adrenaline-charged atmosphere combined with the loud music is a scene I've known since I was young. We all fought for a while, not out of necessity, but from the desire to unleash the wildness we keep contained at all costs.

The competitions are noisy, and you can feel a primitive type of violence in the air. Here, we make our own rules, and that's one of the reasons I feel viscerally connected to the fight environment.

The place smells of beer and food. Wherever you look, there are groups of bastards like me, eager to see some blood.

A group of three *ring girls* walks past me, and when I give them a nod, they smile and whisper to each other. I can guess from the way they looked at me that there's a chance I've been with one of them, or even all of them.

I don't remember names, but I never forget bodies.

I leave Juno, my brother Cillian's protégée, who will debut tonight as a *ring girl*, in Maria's hands after she gives Kellan a hard time for staring at her ass without even trying to hide it. Juno has a bit of a rough edge to her, and if you ask me, our Boss is in for a surprise when he finds out his little girl has grown up into a sharp-tongued woman.

13

I step away from them and head to the locker room to find my cousin Lorcan, who will be fighting tonight. At least every two months, he steps into the ring to exorcize some of his demons.

"Finally, you bastard!" Lorcan says, hugging me as I enter the locker room.

He tells everyone to leave, and I know why. He wants to know about Eoghan O'lly.

We're far from being sensitive guys. Death is on the menu almost daily, but what that bastard did to his wife was something I've never seen before.

Apparently, he had been beating her for years, and when she tried to escape, finally mustering the courage to leave him, he kidnapped her, spent an entire day beating and torturing her until he killed her with a shot. Every second of the woman's torment was documented and then uploaded to the internet. After that, he fled.

We had been searching for him for months, along with the feds and the police, but unfortunately for them and Eoghan, we found him first.

With the police or the FBI, he would have gone to jail. With me, he took a slow and painful walk to hell.

"I wish I had been there," Lorcan says once we're alone.

Lorcan is one of the most protective people when it comes to women that I've ever met. Just like my brothers and I would rather lose a hand than raise it against a woman, my cousin feels the same. What happened to Anati O'lly, that poor bastard's wife, is something none of us will forget anytime soon.

"You had your own shit to deal with. You're not omnipresent. That's a privilege of your grandfather Ruslan."

I can now joke about the fact that Ruslan Vassiliev is Lorcan's relative, but when we discovered it a couple of years ago, I was fucking shocked.

Lorcan is one of my older brother's trusted men and, at the same time, the grandson of the former Pakhan of the Russian mafia. There was no way that shit would work out, since Yerik and Cillian hate each other, I thought. But somehow, peace was maintained.

It's not that Cillian is thrilled every time he knows that Lorcan and his grandfather met, but my brother respects Ruslan, and more than anything, respects the blood.

Lorcan is loyal and doesn't need to pick a side. He may have Russian blood running through his veins, but the Syndicate, and we mainly, are his life.

"How was it? I hope you made him pay, assault for assault, for what he did to his wife."

"Don't doubt it. I practically followed a *script*. Watched the video several times. Memorized it and did to the bastard what he did to Anati."

"I wonder how many of our soldiers do the same to their wives behind closed doors."

I shrug.

"The world is shit. We're not heroes, and even if we were, we couldn't save all the abused women on the planet."

"I wanted to bring him back to life just to kill him again. I could have done that for months," he says, sounding disgusted.

"Forget about that shit. Let's talk about tonight's fight. Besides, at this point, Eoghan has already made his way to hell," I pause, "in pieces, of course."

Lorcan, being the sociopath he is, laughs.

"What is there to say about the fight? I'm going to win," he asserts, with a predatory gleam in his eyes.

"Do it, I bet big on you today."

Half an hour later, I sit near my brothers to watch the fights. Lorcan will be the last to step into the octagon.

I lift my eyes to the ring, waiting for the spectacle to begin. I feel reassured by the brutality that is about to unfold.

I don't know if it's because of the environment I grew up in or if it's just part of who I am. I can't imagine myself in a regular family, with a mom and dad working nine-to-five jobs. I enjoy the warlike atmosphere, the schemes, and, most of all, the heat of the battles we face. I believe I'd be bored to death if my life boiled down to being a fucking CEO of some company or any other so-called *normal* profession.

The announcer steps into the octagon, and the crowd cheers, eager for blood.

As my mind wanders while waiting for the matches to start, I glance around, not paying too much attention, to see if there's any of my women who makes me want to take her with me tonight.

I see beautiful faces, some of them smiling when they notice me looking their way, but no one grabs my attention because deep down, I know who I came for.

The pretty girl with cinnamon-colored eyes who turned Kellan down about two weeks ago. She was recently transferred to Boston, and as far as I know, she hasn't been out with any of the guys yet.

The only time we made eye contact, unlike most of the female population regarding me, she quickly looked away.

Challenges are what motivate me, and her apparent disinterest caught my attention more than a smile would have.

I know she's here tonight, and I fully intend to start the hunt.

Her name is Elaine. The woman who has been haunting my thoughts unusually. The girl who doesn't yet know, but will soon be in my bed, where I'll extract every gram of pleasure from that beautiful body.

Chapter 4

Elaine

"**C**an you walk in those heels?" Maria, the woman responsible for providing us with the "uniforms" for our fight appearances, asks a statuesque blonde with legs for days.

I don't remember seeing her here before. I doubt I could forget someone like her. She's stunning.

"There are high heels in Ireland." I hear the girl reply with a tone of false sweetness that I recognize all too well. "Besides, I'm half American. I have a pretty good idea of how *civilized* people dress."

I lower my head to hide a laugh. I don't even know the blonde's name yet, and I already like her.

Sharp-tongued and ironic—she's my type of girl.

"Don't mind her, darling. She always seems to be wearing her panties inside out," I say, approaching her after Maria leaves. "I'm Elaine, by the way."

"Hi, I'm Juno, and I'm not upset about her bad mood, but about this"—she says, showing the outfit she's holding.

"Oh, you're the newbie, right? I thought you had been transferred."

I know that for the girls on their first day of work, our corset, high heels, and garter belt uniforms might seem like they belong in a *strip club*, but even though they show a lot of skin, I pretend I'm at a lingerie fashion show because I know the Syndicate Boss, Cillian, would never allow us to be touched against our will.

He, his two younger brothers, Kellan and Odhran, along with their cousin Lorcan, are not people you want to mess with, or so they say. I think the respect the patrons show us, keeping their distance unless they are "welcome," is due to the fear they have of the Irish boss's family.

"Transferred?"

"Yes, there are places like this all over the country where... huh... the Syndicate operates."

I've only recently arrived in Boston myself. I've traveled almost the entire country, coast to coast, to keep Jaxton and me safe.

Something in Juno's face makes me want to hit myself as soon as I finish speaking. Damn big mouth. Why did I open it? I have no business commenting on Syndicate matters. And what if the girl is related to them?

"I have to go," I say, grabbing my own outfit. "Watch out for tripping when you get into the ring, Juno." I start to walk away but turn back. "And don't worry about the catcalls or rude comments you're sure to hear. They won't touch you unless you let them."

"I have no intention of letting them."

I shrug and smile.

"You never know. There are some pretty hot members, especially the boss and his relatives."

"You think... um... Cillian is good-looking?" she asks, sounding curious.

"Never seen him?"

"Not in person," she replies, and I get the sense that she's not telling the truth.

I only know the Boss and Lorcan, who is their cousin, blonde and long-haired, Kellan, and Odhran by sight.

As for the youngest of the O'Callaghans, I've only seen him once, and that was enough for me. The man is devastatingly handsome, and it's not the kind of beauty you can look away from because, combined with it, the Irishman has *sex appeal* too. His blue eyes promise things that make us women want to rip his clothes off with our teeth.

"I am immune," I tell myself. *"I wasn't born to be a mobster's pastime."*

He was traveling, as far as I know. I heard some girls talking in the locker room that "Mad Lion" is back. The one time we crossed paths, despite the hypnotic effect the man had on me, I ran, just as I did with all the other Syndicate men who looked at me like they wanted to strip me naked. Only Kellan, arrogant and lethally handsome, came at me full force. If my attention hadn't been stolen by Odhran, it would certainly have been directed at Kellan.

What the hell am I saying?

No stolen attentions, Ms. Elaine. Besides being mobsters, they're womanizers!

I don't need that kind of trouble in my life.

From what I've heard, Odhran, of all people, is the most temperamental. No one can make eye contact with him for long, according to the gossip, because his gaze is chillingly cold.

"Good-looking? No, he's ridiculously handsome, but if you want advice, keep your distance," I say, forcing myself back to the present. "If you're going to choose one of the elite members, go for the two younger brothers, or even their cousin, Lorcan. They're womanizers, but much less intimidating than the Boss, or so they say."

That's not entirely true. Yes, of course, Cillian is intimidating with that godlike pose, but Lorcan, Kellan, and especially Odhran are not men I'd want to have as enemies.

I wouldn't advise anyone in their right mind to get involved with a mobster, but I know how appealing dating one can be for girls, if you can even call two nights at most in their bed dating.

"No, you misunderstood... I..."

I decide that this conversation has gone on long enough. I'm not interested in other people's dramas; I have my own problems to deal with.

"I have to go, Juno. Good luck. See you around," I say, bidding farewell because I came here tonight to work and not to waste time chatting, even with someone as nice as her.

Twenty minutes later, I'm dressed and ready to step into the octagon.

Just seconds away from starting my walk among the mobsters, I take a deep breath because, as always, my heart feels like it's about to explode out of my chest.

The arena is packed, and the noise from the fans is almost deafening.

The tight fabric of my outfit clings to my body, accentuating every curve. Here, I am not Elaine the survivor; I am a spectacle for the audience.

Heavy rock blares throughout the place, and the blinding lights barely let me see the people who came for the bloody show.

Not that I want to look at anyone in particular. I'm focused on not falling, which could get me fired. The heels we wear should be illegal. Climbing into the octagon multiple times with them should come with a life insurance policy.

As I walk with my arms outstretched, holding up the sign announcing the first fight, adrenaline courses through my veins.

I hear catcalls and invitations for an "unforgettable night," which is code for maybe great sex but with no strings attached.

No, thank you.

Despite some of the explicit remarks directed at me, I maintain a fake smile, trying to project a facade of confidence.

I won't let them intimidate me.

When I'm in the octagon, at a safe distance from the crowd, I let my eyes roam over the audience.

I wouldn't be able to say what made me turn my head in a specific direction, but I did, and when my eyes lock onto another pair of blue ones, it feels like all the air has been sucked out of my lungs.

Intense eyes watch me, as if he's a hunter who has just found his prey. Normally, this kind of blatant lust would anger me, but inexplicably, I can't stop staring back at him.

No, the feeling I had when I first saw him wasn't an illusion. There's something about the man that deeply affects me.

He wears a black leather jacket over his huge body, with a broad neck where tattoos are visible. His almost-black hair is all tousled, with curls going in different directions. The man's mouth could only be described as an invitation to sin.

He's a dangerous mix of beauty and a sexuality so aggressive it makes my knees wobble.

Momentarily, I forget where I am, and he seems to notice because a smug smile spreads across his face, though his eyes remain serious.

My heart races wildly. The crowd's enthusiastic cheers fade away until it's just the two of us.

For a brief moment, I forget the spotlight and the crowd watching me. I even forget that I'm at work.

Someone beside him demands his attention, but even though he doesn't look away from me, he responds, and when I glance at his companion, I realize in a split second that it was Kellan who called him.

I force myself back to reality.

Even if I weren't averse to dating mobsters, which I am, this particular one has a terrible reputation for using women and then discarding them. I've seen more than one girl crying in corners for having been given the boot from "Mad Lion's" bed, according to their own words.

I will never subject myself to that. I won't be a name crossed off his list, no matter how drop-dead gorgeous the Irishman is and how his gaze made me melt.

Chapter 5

Elaine

At first, I think I'm going crazy when, standing in front of a closed door, I hear a female voice say:

"I don't know what kind of woman you're used to dealing with, sir, but I'll repeat one more time: I'm not a prostitute. Now, get out of here."

"Speak to me like that again and you'll regret it, bitch."

I was looking for Juno, the newcomer, and asked Maria where I could find her because I felt bad about the way we parted. Besides Hestia, I don't have any friends, and the blonde seemed really nice to me.

However, now that I hear this conversation, my protective instincts kick in. I don't care who's in there; no woman should be forced to do something she doesn't want to.

"You can't touch me. I'm under Cillian's protection," the voice continues.

I only think of my sister and how much I wish someone had taken care of her against men like this idiot in front of me.

My anger grows when, after what she says, I hear the attacker's laughter.

"Cillian is a businessman like me. He wouldn't get involved with me over a little whore."

I open the door with such force that it slams against the wall with a bang.

23

Inside, I see Juno with a shoe in her hand, trying to hit a bastard any way she can, while he holds her arm tightly.

I don't think before jumping on his back and locking in a chokehold with both arms, trying to make him leave her alone while I scream at the top of my lungs for help.

I know if there are any security or even the Boss and his relatives around, we'll be safe.

Juno, realizing what I'm doing, kicks the son of a bitch in the balls.

She keeps hitting him as best as she can, and just when I think we have the upper hand, he slaps her, making my new friend fall unconscious.

Then, he throws me off his disgusting body, flinging me to the ground.

The man comes towards me, and I panic because I know I have no chance against him now. Then, suddenly, the bastard disappears, and I hear a cry of pain that I'm sure came from him.

I couldn't say how much time passes, but the middle brother, Kellan, kneels beside me.

"What happened?"

"This man attacked Juno. I was coming to talk to her, and when I saw she needed help, I jumped on his back, but as you must have noticed, I wasn't good enough to stop him."

"You were amazing, girl. Do you think you broke anything?" he asks, apparently holding no grudge over the brush-off I gave him. Or more likely, he doesn't even remember me. With so many women around, he might have only noticed me because I'm relatively new to the Boston unit.

"No. I just want to know if she'll be okay."

I see, out of the corner of my eye, a man who looks like a doctor entering.

"She will be. Juno belongs to Cillian, so you don't need to worry about her. Now, if you're sure you're okay, you need to leave. I'll make sure she gets home," he says, his eyes discreetly scanning my body.

It's nothing offensive, but I feel at a disadvantage and get up immediately.

"You don't need to."

"I'm not giving you a choice. Change clothes and someone will take you home."

I look at the couch where they've laid Juno.

"And her?"

"As I said, the girl is my brother's responsibility. Don't worry. Juno will be fine."

"Can you at least give me her cell number? I'd like to call tomorrow. Maybe the girl needs a friend to talk to about this."

He studies me as if he's considering what to do, and only then do I remember something he said.

Juno belongs to Cillian.

Jesus, was I casually talking to the Boss's wife?

"What's your name, sweet thing?"

"Elaine," I reply, now sure that he has no idea who I am.

"Elaine what?"

"Ramsey."

"Listen to what I'm going to say, Elaine. I'll give you her phone number because I think she'll want to thank you, and after today, the chances of my brother letting her return to the fights are zero, but if anything happens to a hair on her head because of the information I'm about to give you, you won't live to celebrate your next birthday."

"You know what? Don't bother. I'm not a..." I stop just in time to avoid saying: *"I'm not a dangerous killer."*

It's the dumbest thing to say to someone whose job is to send others six feet under. But it's the first time I've been threatened with death, and my brain isn't working right.

"Not a what?" he challenges me.

"I just wanted to know she'll be okay," I say, looking again at the still unconscious Juno.

"I'll give you her number, but don't forget what I said. Be smart, Elaine, and nothing bad will happen to you."

I pretend I'm not trembling as I get up. Acting tough is my specialty, or I wouldn't have survived among dangerous Irishmen.

I still look at Juno and feel like going to her, but I'm neither crazy nor suicidal.

Kellan's warning was clear; she has an owner, and I wouldn't want to be in the skin of the bastard who attacked her when the Boss gets his hands on him.

Chapter 6

Elaine

The adrenaline drops from my body so abruptly that I feel like I've been kicked in the chest by a horse as soon as I realize what I've done.

I don't like my job in the Irish Syndicate fights, but they pay well, and in a way, being among the mobsters gives me a sense of security.

Yes, it's stupid, perhaps, because they are far from being princes. I know that each one of them is a killer and operates on the wrong side of the law.

Although, if what they say is true, and so far I have no reason to believe otherwise, that the Syndicate Boss, Cillian, and the rest of the relatives don't tolerate cowardice against women, then I am safe.

My story in the fights began when a friend I worked with at a supermarket in a small town near the Canadian border told me that they were looking for women with attractive bodies to be "ring girls" in underground competitions.

At first, I ignored it, but when I saw how much they were paying, I couldn't say "no"; so we moved to New Jersey.

Gradually, my life with my older sister was "falling into place." We weren't even middle class, but we had plans for the future. I would work making flower bouquets for weddings. She would become a nurse.

And then, suddenly, we had to run.

One day, she came home and told me to pack as little as possible, and that we couldn't stay in the place that had been our home forever.

Elysia tried to protect me by not revealing details about why we were fleeing, but I'm not stupid. She had been dating the same guy for months, seemed serious, although, in my opinion, a bit toxic too, since I had seen her come home with swollen eyes from crying several times. And considering the man didn't even live in the United States, according to what she told me, but somewhere in the Caribbean, that's a big red flag.

You see your boyfriend occasionally, and he still makes you cry? My advice would be: kick him to the curb as soon as possible, girl!

The problem is that my sister was never one to share information, so I knew very little about this relationship. Still, I suspected that the reason for her sudden desire to disappear was related to him.

It coincided with my sister wanting to leave with a situation that occurred at my job, and I always wondered if one thing was related to the other because, as far as I know, her secret boyfriend could very well be a gang member or even the boss. There are wealthy individuals connected with these gangs too, who use their "services" for criminal tasks.

The fact is that a few days before Elysia wanted to leave New Jersey, I told her about the girl who worked with me in the Irish Syndicate underground fights, Janice, who disappeared. Some time before, her sister had been kidnapped by the Salvadoran mafia, known as "M" for Muerte.

The life story of both was very sad.

The woman who was my coworker, Janice, said that her sister was taken from a mall in New Jersey by the Salvadorans.

They sent her to a mansion in South Carolina, where she was made *available* to several men, who took turns abusing her. They profited by "renting" her out to perverts, and when they thought she was no longer useful for their purposes, they dragged her to a swamp to execute her and then throw her body to the crocodiles, which seems to be their usual method.

The girl knew she was going to die, so she jumped into the water before they could shoot her.

She narrowly escaped. Or rather, she survived. I don't think anyone who goes through such violence can fully recover. The wound will always be there, ready to bleed again.

She was brave enough to testify. Only two guys were convicted and on lesser charges because, according to the authorities, there wasn't enough evidence.

Incompetent sons of bitches!

The injustice and the constant threats from the Salvadorans to get her again made her take her own life months later because she couldn't cope with her own pain and fear.

The story shocked me deeply, and it got worse when the girl who worked with me disappeared into thin air without any warning or farewell. Among us, it was rumored that she had moved to the other coast, but I don't believe that. She also vanished from social media.

The accounts weren't deleted; they have been inactive since her sudden "move." I think the Salvadorans killed her for revenge because Janice's sister testified against them.

I spent days brooding over this and eventually told my sister the whole story, which I hadn't done before because she was very scared of these things.

Elysia was a bit naive about the real world, despite being older than me.

I told her that I thought the people who made Janice disappear were the "M" for Muerte, a gang that was always committing horrible crimes in the streets of New Jersey, and also responsible for the kidnapping of my coworker's sister.

The moment I mentioned the Salvadoran mafia, something changed in Elysia. I had already noticed that she was showing signs of nervousness and talking about ending the relationship with the rich guy she was seeing without explaining why, but a few days after this conversation about Janice's disappearance, she said we had to move.

It wasn't a move. She never said it outright, but what we did was hide. I begged to be transferred to the fights on the other coast at her request, and shortly after we arrived, Elysia discovered she was pregnant with Jax.

I saw my sister, in a few months, reach her limit. Thin, stressed, and scared; even then, she didn't tell me the reason we were running, no matter how much I insisted.

After Jax was born, she finally, slowly, started to show the happiness she once had. She gained weight, began to take care of herself, and got a job.

And then, one night, she went out to work and never came back. They found her body days later.

They said it was a drug overdose, but I know it's a lie, or at least, if there was drugs in her system as the autopsy indicated, she didn't use them willingly.

Her father was an alcoholic, and because of that, she never even touched a cigarette.

I take a deep breath to control the wave of pain that hits me. Even after all this time, I still can't come to terms with the injustice of my sister's death being ruled as a suicide from an overdose.

My intuition tells me this is not only related to Jax's father but also to the "M" for Muerte.

The bastard who contributed to my nephew's birth, as far as I know, is unaware of his existence.

I will do whatever it takes to make sure he never finds out. I'm terrified that he might come after us. I have a suspicion that my sister discovered something about the Salvadoran mafia and that Jax's father was involved in that mess.

Elysia never told me anything, but what if he thinks she did? I can't let anything happen to me. I need to live to take care of my boy.

In fact, I don't even know if Elysia ever mentioned me to him, but I trust my intuition, and it tells me that this man is dangerous and that I should never let him come near us.

Since very early on, even before what happened with Elysia, I've been a survivor. I've always stayed away from trouble. She used to say that I was the more suspicious one between us, but the truth is, life's odds have always been against us. I wanted to change the narrative. Prove to the world that I could succeed.

And that's why I will never get involved with a mobster. I haven't stayed alive these past few years to become just another piece of meat for the Irish and their associates.

In here, when it comes to men, I act like a robot.

I go in, barely make eye contact with any man, do my job, and return to the safety of my home, to the boy I raise as my own. Jax is the reason I get up every morning and never give up, even though I'm terrified that sooner or later "he" will find me.

What happened today was total madness.

For starters, I shouldn't have gotten close to the newcomer, Juno, who I now know is a protegé of Cillian. I keep myself completely detached from what happens with the Syndicate men. The fights are a means to an end: to give a better life to Jax.

I blame loneliness and my nomadic life, never putting down roots in one place, for making me approach her, who seemed lonely too and somewhat out of place.

So, I pulled out my "sympathy" card, which I offer to only a few people, and decided to get closer.

Mission accomplished; I had no intention of forming deep bonds with the girl, but the moment I saw that bastard attacking her, I went insane.

I went completely berserk with my protective instinct activated.

I'm not sure if I'd have killed him if I'd had a weapon in hand. I never thought I was capable of doing something like that, but that was before what happened to my sister.

I stretch my arms up, and immediately, I feel pain in my rear and back. The bastard didn't hurt me more only because Kellan arrived just in time.

I look in the mirror and see a scratch on my right cheek. I thank God that Jax is still so young and doesn't understand what's going on, but Hestia, I have no doubt she will notice.

I close my eyes for a few seconds while I mentally prepare to leave the corridor.

One of the Syndicate men knocked on the bathroom door a little while ago to confirm that someone would be waiting to take me home, but when I open it and encounter complete silence, I realize I might have taken too long trying to calm down.

Chapter 7

Elaine

I think if someone were to define me in just two words, they would be suspicious and alert.

As for the first, it's not because I lack faith in people, but because they need to convince me that they are *good*, because since what happened with Elysia, I need much more than smiles and instant friendships to relax around someone. The second is due to the circumstances.

Needing to protect Jax, I never allow myself to relax, and right now, all my instincts are activated, alert to any danger, as if an unknown, hidden evil is lurking around me.

When Kellan came into the room earlier and intervened in the chaos between me and that bastard, I still didn't let my guard down. I pretended that mounting the back of a troglodyte twice my size to save a stranger and then being thrown like a tennis ball through the air was no big deal. The truth is, I'm still shaking, and the growing sense of danger at the moment intensifies my fear.

I take uncertain steps down the empty corridor, looking around because I am a fugitive by nature and have learned to always check every place I am in.

I almost sigh with relief when I turn a corner and can see the exit, praying that the man Kellan mentioned is indeed waiting for me, when without any warning that I am no longer alone, someone grabs my arm.

I scream and start scratching, kicking, and pushing whoever is trying to stop me, because in my mind, it's that man who has come back to hurt me.

My survival mode kicks in as I continue to fight against the wall of muscle holding me captive, even from behind.

The wildest thoughts cross my mind.

The Boss sided with the man who attacked us, and now I will be punished for hitting him.

They will take me somewhere and end my short life, leaving Jax completely alone in the world.

The main thought, however, is the certainty that I won't let them do to me what they did to my sister. They will have a hell of a time trying to get rid of me.

I continue to struggle, but it's like being trapped between steel claws, and seconds later, I am exhausted. And then, when I think all is lost, that my end has come, I hear a rough laugh near my ear.

"Calm down, wild cat. I'm not going to hurt you. At least today, I'm here to protect you."

Something in my brain shuts off, and as if my body knew before my mind that I'm no longer in danger, I go still.

"Much better this way," my captor says, turning me towards him, and the moment I look at him, I nearly have a heart attack seeing that it's Odhran.

"You're the Boss's brother," I say like a fool, and this time, I catch him off guard when I take a step back, managing to free myself from his hold.

Or maybe, he chose to let me go, which I have to admit, is the more likely scenario.

I have no doubt that he would only need one arm to keep me captive.

"And you, the crazy one who thought you could fight someone fifty kilos heavier."

"And what should I have done? Let that idiot use me and Juno as punching bags?"

One corner of his mouth was lifted in a half-ironic smile, but after what I said, his expression closes.

"It wasn't supposed to happen. You should be safe here."

"There are assholes everywhere. And if that was your attempt to apologize, I accept. Now, I need to go."

"It wasn't," he says, taking a step closer.

"What?"

My heart is completely irregular.

Jesus, what is it about this man that makes my body react this way?

I don't like mobsters or womanizers, and Odhran O'Callaghan is a combination of both.

"Calm down, fool!" I demand of myself, trying to convince myself that he is just another sexy Irishman among the many I've seen from afar over the years.

"I wasn't apologizing," he says.

"Then what's the reason for this conversation?"

"I didn't start a conversation with you, princess. I'm doing a favor for my brother, who asked me to take you home."

"Kellan asked for that?"

"Do you know each other? I thought you'd turned him down," he says, sounding suspicious.

My God, what a crazy conversation.

What does this man care about my relationship with his brother? And how did he memorize my face, knowing I was the one who said "no" to Kellan when he asked me out, if even Kellan himself seems to not remember?

Confused and overwhelmed, I decide to give him what he wants to get away from Odhran as quickly as possible.

My intuition tells me that the man represents a threat, and it's not just because killing is as routine for him as breathing, but because he affects me in an unexpected way.

I shrug, pretending not to be affected by his presence.

"I've been working in the fights for a while. Everyone knows who you are. I hadn't seen anyone from your family before coming to Boston, except for the Boss, but since I've been in town for a few weeks, I figured out who you and Kellan were even before he... um... asked me out."

"How?"

"What?"

"Who told you who me and Kellan are?"

"Are you always this suspicious?"

"Answer."

"Your eyes are identical to the Boss's. When we first saw each other, you stared at me and..."

"*Stared?*" he mocks.

I feel my face flush with embarrassment, and I never thought I could blush, but if he thinks he's going to have the upper hand, he doesn't know who he's dealing with.

"Oh, so you weren't the one almost burning the corset off my body the first time we met? Didn't you do that again today? Sorry. My mistake. Maybe it was some other *pervert...*"

Jesus, what am I doing?

I manage to stop myself just in time, remembering who I'm dealing with.

The gorgeous bad boy isn't just another rowdy Irishman, a common member of the Syndicate; he's the boss's younger brother.

He steps forward and now I'm trapped between his body and the wall. Given what happened earlier today, maybe I should be afraid, but that's not what's happening. I feel like I've been hit with an electric shock.

"Maybe it was some other *pervert* you were going to say?" He doesn't wait for me to answer, brushing a bit of hair from my neck and lowering his head, letting his lips graze my skin. "Perversions aren't really my thing, but we could try if it excites you, beautiful. My brother asked me to make sure you got home in one piece, but I've just changed my mind. Come with me."

I was focused on his chest because I was afraid to look him in the eye and show how his proximity affects my body, but the mobster's offer—one I'm sure, if extended to almost any girl working here, they'd be rolling on the floor fighting each other to accept—brings me back to reality.

I'm not a liar. There's a part of me, a devilish voice, that says: what if, just for one night, you forget everything and dive into an adventure? You'd have a few hours of pleasure in the arms of this gorgeous man and then just move on.

It's a pity, or maybe a stroke of luck for me, that I can't throw myself into life without measuring the consequences.

I can't afford to get kicked out of this job if the youngest O'Callaghan decides he doesn't want to run into me at the fights anymore, discarding me like he's probably done with so many others.

"No, thanks. I have someone waiting for me at home."

He doesn't need to know that this someone is two years old and calls me "mom."

The man takes a step back as if suddenly discovering that I have a contagious virus.

"Are you married?"

"I have a commitment and it's a 'forever'"—I'm telling the absolute truth, though in a misleading context.

His expression changes immediately and even against my will, I can't help but admire the fact that Odhran won't intrude on another man's territory. Not many guys step out of their way when they want a woman, whether she's free or not.

"Come on, I'll take you," he says, with a closed expression and not moving closer again.

He turns his back to me and starts walking out of the warehouse, making sure I'm following.

There are two cars parked on the lot, I notice as we approach a motorcycle.

The faces of the men are not unfamiliar to me.

They work for the Boss, and by the way they look at me, as if at any moment I'm going to pull a knife from my bag and attack Odhran, tells me they are his bodyguards.

I see Cillian's brother grab the only helmet on the bike and hand it to me. I take advantage of his distraction and observe him more closely, beyond his physical beauty.

Odhran doesn't seem like the type who needs someone taking care of him. On the contrary, I'd say anyone who has him as an enemy should always sleep with one eye open.

"Get on and hold me. Don't worry, I won't do anything except fulfill my brother's request and get you home safely. I don't sleep with another man's woman, not even for one night, Elaine."

I was about to put on the helmet but stop, shocked, when he calls me by name.

Kellan, who tried a move on me, didn't even remember who I was, and yet the youngest O'Callaghan knows who I am?

Because after his conversation with his brother earlier today, Kellan must have informed him, you fool. Don't see things where there are none.

If I were smart, I'd just finish putting on the helmet and get on the bike, but the man's arrogance in thinking that if he decided to stay with me, I would accept without a second thought drives me crazy.

"Why?" I ask, even though I know it's the wrong thing to do. "If you have no commitments to anything or anyone, what difference does one night of betrayal make?"

"To me, betrayal is betrayal, no matter the context. Besides," he smiles as he gets on the bike, "I was going to ruin you for your man. I doubt he'd continue being your 'forever' after I had you for a whole night."

Chapter 8

Elaine

Weeks Later

I thought I liked plans. With my life as a fugitive, they're necessary, actually. A matter of survival.

I can't deny, however, that I'm glad fate surprised me.

The night Odhran took me home, he quickly said goodbye with a nod as soon as I got off his bike, without even saying a word. I muttered a "thank you very much" and received no response.

I told myself I wasn't disappointed. I'd have to be really stupid to want anything with that cheeky Irishman, so I did what I do with everything that bothers me and shoved it to the back of my mind.

The next day, I went looking for Juno. We went out to share a burger in neutral territory, where neither of the criminal organizations owns, but when I saw her surrounded by bodyguards, I understood that Kellan wasn't kidding when he said the blonde belonged to his brother.

Now, weeks later since I met her, and although she doesn't talk much about it, I don't need proof that it's pure truth, because when they're near each other, you could get shocked by the tension in the air.

The fact is that, to my surprise, Juno turned out to be an amazing girl and the hours we spent together at that dinner turned into the start of a friendship.

A slow-moving one, because like me, she isn't one to trust easily or talk about her life. I know we all have skeletons in our closets, so I never push or force the issue.

I think Juno doesn't tell me anything about her past because of the Boss. If she is indeed his woman, and I suspect she is, the girl would also be Cillian's Achilles' heel, his vulnerability, and must have been trained to keep her mouth shut.

What we know about each other, despite our mutual affection, is very superficial.

I told her about Jaxton, but Juno thinks he's my son, not my nephew. Maybe someday I'll reveal the truth, but I'm not ready yet.

Several days after our meeting, she invited me to see the bakery she was setting up. The woman has magic hands when it comes to sweets, especially cupcakes. I tried a few and they tasted like heaven.

When I arrived to meet her at the still-under-construction shop, Odhran was there, but acted as if he had never seen me before, treating me with indifference.

I also pretended he was a *nobody*, though that's a lie. Just being near the Irishman made my body tingle.

Seeing the gorgeous man, however, wasn't the highlight of that day; it was the fact that I got a permanent job at Juno's shop without having to give up the fights; but mainly, now I have health insurance for Jax.

I've already taken him to a cardiologist because he was born with a little heart problem. He can't have surgery yet, but doctors say it might be necessary at any time.

Tomorrow will be the opening of her bakery and tonight, we're doing the final "rehearsal" before we finally open the doors to the public.

The bakery is full of Irish people, including the Boss's aunt, Orla, who also came, but it's a particular man who's making my whole body tense like a guitar string stretched to its limit.

Odhran still doesn't speak to me. In fact, he acts as if I'm the same as a wall, because his expression remains blank, completely neutral, when he looks at me. However, his eyes never leave me for a second.

Is this what it feels like to be prey in front of a predator? I get the impression he's going to pounce at any moment and strangely, it doesn't scare me. If I were completely honest, I'd confess I even yearn for the attack.

"Your son is the cutest thing in the world, Elaine," Mrs. Orla says. "Juno showed me a picture of him yesterday eating a cupcake here. I could just gobble him up. I can't wait for my boys to fill me with grandkids."

I discovered, by overhearing conversations, that although the Boss was an adult when his parents died, everyone considers her a mother, especially Odhran.

Orla is a miniature version of her nephews. Direct and intimidating. But as we get to know her better, we also realize how loving she is. Slowly, I'm feeling something I've never experienced before — being part of a large family.

"He is, and now that he's discovered Juno's sweets, he asks me every day for the '*aunt Juno's goodies*'."

Orla laughs.

"Does his father not visit him?" she asks, with her usual indiscreet manner.

"He doesn't even know Jax exists," I say, though I'm not willing to share more.

"Jax is the only man in your life, then?"

Jesus, doesn't the woman know the meaning of boundaries?

I'd be upset if it were someone else trying to dig so deeply into my private life, but I know she means no harm. It's part of her personality to want to know every little thing about those she cares about.

"Yes, Jax is the only man in my life."

"Your *forever*." I hear a guttural voice say behind me and feel a shiver run through my body because I know who it belongs to.

It takes me only a few seconds to realize I've been unmasked, but I'm not willing to lower my guard for him, so without turning around, I say as if still talking to Orla.

"He is my forever. The only trustworthy man on the planet," I say, and she laughs.

Without even acknowledging the Irishman, I flee to the bakery's kitchen, feeling my heart racing in my chest.

Seconds later, when the door closes behind me, I know who's here with me.

Did I unconsciously want him to hunt me down?

"I never thought you were a liar, Elaine."

I turn around and see him casually leaning against the door, the leather jacket outlining every delicious muscle. I've seen this man in the ring, fighting, so unfortunately, since that day, he has become my only sexual fantasy.

Odhran's body is the kind that even makes a saint think naughty thoughts.

"A liar, me? I didn't say anything but the truth. I really had my *forever* waiting for me at home."

"But not a husband."

"And what does that matter?"

"To me, it matters. I want you."

My God, this man should be forbidden from saying things like that.

"Just because I'm unavailable. What's up? Have the options run out in the fighting world?"

Normally, I wouldn't confront someone from the Boss's family like this, but right now, I feel on equal footing.

And it's not just that; deep down, I'm a little disappointed too, because Odhran doesn't even seem to be putting much effort into convincing me to go out with him.

Yes, he's gorgeous, and maybe women faint when he gives that cheeky smile, which shows a lovely dimple in his chin always with a five o'clock shadow, but I'm not looking for a one-night adventure.

"My options are endless," he smiles, not looking annoyed at all, which makes me even more angry, "but I take one at a time, Elaine, and now, it's your chance."

I pretend to think about it.

"No, thank you. I'll pass."

He moves toward me, and without realizing what I'm doing, I back up until I feel the sink counter against my back. He presses me, placing an arm on either side of the counter, but without touching me.

"You're not just a liar, you're a coward too, but here's the bad news: I never repeat an invitation, beautiful. You'll spend the rest of your days wanting."

Chapter 9

Elaine

Months Later

It's like a game of cat and mouse, but with the prey—I—knowing that sooner or later I'll fall into temptation and throw myself into the arms of my predator by choice, the Irishman who occupies my thoughts every night when I lie down in bed.

We haven't spoken since the day before Juno's store opening, except for the occasional nod, but even so, the tension between us grows uncontrollably.

I thought knowing I had a child would drive him away, but he still looks at me like a walking temptation nearly two meters tall.

Today is her graduation day, and I'm feeling strangely uneasy. Part of it, I know, is because I'll see Odhran more than for just a few minutes. I'll have to be near him at the reception Orla is hosting afterward as well.

However, it's not just that. I've learned to follow my instincts, and they're telling me that I'm no longer safe in Boston. On a few occasions, we had the feeling that we were being watched at Juno's store. The first time it happened, she was so nervous that I convinced myself that whoever was there had something to do with Cillian's business.

I don't get involved in the Syndicate's affairs, but I know there was someone following her because, a while back, I overheard conversations between her and the Boss.

Additionally, there was a time when they asked to borrow the place where I live to, as they told me, "catch a rat in a trap."

Juno didn't go into details, and I didn't ask. The fact is that I, Hestia, and Jax went to Orla's house.

When my friend arrived there, hours later, she was dripping wet, and Cillian's aunt locked herself in one of the guest suites with her, where they talked for a long time.

I noticed the tension on Juno's face when she finally joined me, Jax, and Hestia, but still, she didn't open up.

When I entered my apartment two days later, I expected to see some sign that something bad had happened, but everything seemed perfectly in place.

Juno never brought up the subject with me again, and I respected her silence, especially since I don't want to know about Cillian's enemies, if that's the case. Ignorance, where the mafia is concerned, is a blessing. The more I know, the more dangerous my life becomes.

"Juno Cavanagh" the announcer calls my friend, and she climbs the stairs to receive her diploma.

Cillian isn't here.

She told me the Boss would be waiting for her in the car.

I never thought, from a woman's perspective, about a long-term relationship, what it would be like to live with a mobster, but today I'm getting a small taste of it. He isn't an ordinary guy and can't walk around holding her hand in public, for example.

Everything has to be private, secret, and carefully planned, because Juno is the first lady of the Irish mafia.

I smile when I hear her aunt, Eimear, who came from Ireland especially for her niece's graduation, shout Juno's name proudly as she sees her receive the diploma.

Orla is also with us and claps her hands.

I whistle, excited, and Jax, on my lap, who I'm sure doesn't understand anything, smiles and cheers, enjoying the commotion.

He's smitten with Orla and without any hesitation, throws himself into her lap.

"Oops, sorry about that."

"Don't worry, he's so cute!" Cillian's aunt says, and my son grins from ear to ear, knowing he's pleasing her.

"Official sweet-maker now," Juno says, waving her mock diploma at us.

I'm so happy for her, but suddenly, I have the feeling that I'm being watched. When I look in the direction I think the person is, I see only a suit out of the corner of my eye, but not the man wearing it. Even so, an overwhelming sense of unease hits me, making me feel nauseous.

Panic, an old companion, makes me want to run, and I think Juno notices.

"What's wrong?" she asks.

"I... think I saw someone. It must have been my imagination."

She pulls me to a more secluded corner.

"You're pale again, just like that day at the bakery when you told me we were being watched."

I look at my friend, unsure if I want to involve her in this, but I decide it's better to tell half the truth. If I'm not going crazy, and the person I thought was watching me came for me and not because they're an enemy of Cillian, I might need to run at any moment.

"I think I saw someone from my past."

"What do you mean by someone from the past? An ex? Jax's father?"

No, God, please don't let it be him, because if it's true, I'll be lost, as it means he knows who I am.

In that case, my sister must have told the man about me.

And about Jax? Did he find out about him too? Why didn't he come looking for him before?

I feel on the verge of fainting.

"No. Nothing like that," I lie, because I'm not really sure.

How can I explain to her that Jax isn't my son, just like that? To do that, I'd have to tell the whole story and, most importantly, that I don't even know who his biological father is.

"Girl, you're really scaring me. Do you want me to talk to Cillian?"

"No. Not yet."

Should I do that? Ask the Irish for help? Maybe. If my intuition is right and Jax's father has some connection with the "M" of Muerte, the Irish might protect us.

But what if they're associates? I don't know anything about the Syndicate's business. What's to guarantee that the Salvadorans aren't in some sort of partnership with the Irish?

"Okay, but let's agree on this: if that 'ghost' you think you saw shows up again, you have to promise to let me know. Promise me."

"You have my word. I'll tell you."

Chapter 10

Odhran

Cillian and Juno's Wedding

Somewhere in the Caribbean

"Can you hold him for a moment?" my aunt asks, handing me the almost-asleep boy in her arms.

"What?"

"He doesn't bite, Odhran. Jax is just a wonderful little boy."

"Isn't he a bit big to be held like this?"

I'm sure the boy can walk, although I have no idea how old he is. Matters involving children don't interest me.

"Jax is dying of sleep. I'll be right back; I just need to go inside for a moment to prepare the outfit Juno will change into, because she wants to enjoy the party and the wedding dress is too long and heavy."

I barely have time to respond before she hands me the "little package" in a suit and tie. The boy immediately clings to my neck and rests his head on my shoulder.

The feeling is both pleasant and strange. It's like holding a miniature person.

I don't spend time with children. I don't remember ever having held one in my arms.

"Training to be a dad?" I hear Kellan ask, teasingly, beside me, and even then, Jax doesn't wake up. On the contrary, he adjusts to get more comfortable.

"I'm doing a favor for Orla."

"Not for Elaine?"

"Go to hell—" I cut off the sentence, as I'm sure my aunt wouldn't like to hear me swear near the boy. "Mind your own business, Kellan."

"That's exactly what I'm trying to do," he says, not ironically. "She's not like the women we usually date, Odhran."

"And how would you know that? Elaine turned you down. You never managed to—" I was going to say "take her to bed," but again, I leave the rest of the sentence hanging because it seems wrong to talk like that about Jax's mother while holding him in my arms.

"She turned me down?" he asks, genuinely confused, and I roll my eyes.

"You don't even remember?"

He smiles with irony.

"I think the point here isn't that I don't remember. There's a chance I was just bored when I met her, so it's lucky that the girl said 'no,' but the real question is: how do you remember that?"

"Mind your own life."

"Our new sister-in-law will rip your balls off if you hurt her employee. When I said Elaine isn't like the women we're used to dating, I meant she's a mother, has responsibilities none of us want. Besides, she's alone in the world."

"What?"

"Didn't you ever think to look into her background?"

I won't tell him that I never make my relationships with women personal because that's obvious.

"Don't be a hypocrite. Do you check the past of the women you sleep with?"

"No, but I've never been obsessed with a woman the way you apparently are with Juno's employee. But here's the thing: we all want what we can't have. You know your interest in Elaine won't last."

I can't deny it. I've always been sure that long-term relationships aren't for me.

"Tell me more about her being alone in the world."

He looks at Jax, who remains completely asleep.

"She only had one sister, who died of an overdose," he says, lowering his voice and, in the end, only moving his lips on the last word, surely to spare Jax from hearing, if there's a remote chance he's waking up.

"And what else?"

"I don't know much more, but after she showed interest, I checked her background. Elaine is a good girl, Odhran. Much less tough than she believes herself to be, and if all you want with her are a few nights, leave her alone and move on. There are several here today, more than willing to jump into your bed."

"I don't—"

"What? Didn't you come intending to be with her? I'm not an idiot. You two have been eye-fucking each other since you arrived on the island. You know I never interfere in your business unless it involves your safety, but I'll tell you something you can take or leave: there's no chance this ends well. I can foresee the end as if I had a damn crystal ball in front of me. You're going to hurt her, and Juno won't forgive you. With so many free women, you want to stir up trouble with our brother's woman?"

I know he's right, and it irritates me even more.

As if drawn by her gaze, I see Elaine across the garden, talking to Juno.

The two are focused on us as well, and while my sister-in-law smiles, I notice Elaine is looking at me in a way she hasn't before, seeing me with her son in my arms.

For the first time in my life, as far as I remember, the awareness that my desires aren't above everything and everyone hits me, and even though it goes against my instincts, I accept that Kellan is right.

I divert my gaze and do a sweep around the party, knowing exactly what I need to do to end any potential between us once and for all.

I may not be able to extinguish my desire for her, but the reverse, I'm sure, will be true.

"Hand him over to Orla," I say to Kellan, passing the boy to his arms.

As soon as he takes him, I head straight for my target. A blonde who is part of the staff that organized Juno's party and whose father is a member of the Syndicate.

She smiles when she sees me approaching, and I give her a nod.

That's enough for her to come my way.

I usually don't touch a woman in public, but at this moment, I'm on a mission.

I drape an arm deliberately around her waist, pulling her body toward mine, and start walking with the blonde, heading toward the guesthouse where I'm staying on the island.

I've always been detached and never had the sensitivity to care about other people's feelings, but a voice in the back of my mind tells me I'm making a mistake.

I silence it because it makes no sense. I'm free. Elaine and I have nothing, and the sooner the girl understands how I live my life, the better for her.

Chapter 11

Elaine

"I'm going to kill him," Juno says beside me.

"Who?" I ask, pretending I don't have a lump in my throat.

I keep looking straight ahead, focused on Kellan holding Jax, because I refuse to turn my head in the direction Odhran just left with a blonde who, I know, worked as one of the wedding organizers.

"Elaine, you don't have to pretend with me."

"He and I are nothing to each other, Juno." I finally give up pretending I don't know what she's talking about.

"You two looked hypnotized every time I saw you together."

"I find him attractive, I've told you that before, but it's not enough to make me want to be a temporary distraction for that lecherous jerk."

"Now, that's my girl! Don't feel bad for falling for his charm, Elaine. I knew things were evolving between you two, even though you barely talked. I thought it was only a matter of time before that stubborn mule of my brother would see that..."

"See what? Don't romanticize or confuse the fact that Odhran wants me with something more. I'm sorry, but I don't want to talk about this anymore. Enjoy your wedding, dear, because your Irishman is coming our way and he looks like a man on a mission." I force myself to smile. "Don't do anything I wouldn't do, girl."

I give her a kiss on the cheek and walk over to Kellan to get my boy.

"I'll take him now, thanks."

"Do you want me to take him to the room?"

The lump in my throat hasn't dissipated, so I avoid eye contact.

"No, thanks."

I take my son and, without saying goodbye, start to walk away.

"Elaine?"

I turn around.

"Yes?"

"It was better this way."

"I have no idea what you're talking about. Good night, Kellan."

I pass by all the guests, stopping only to say goodbye to Orla.

"Don't leave yet, Elaine. You look so beautiful in that red dress!"

I smile.

"It was a gift from Juno. I felt like a princess," I say, and then feel anger for showing that there's a romantic fool inside me.

I couldn't believe it when I was invited to the wedding. Yes, I'm an employee, and we've become relatively close since I started working at the bakery, but we're not confidants. An invitation to the wedding of the Irish Syndicate boss is a huge honor.

"So, that's what I'm saying. Stay. Have fun. Don't worry about my nephew."

Oh my God, am I that transparent?

"I've had enough fun, thanks. I'd rather stay with Jax. He's not the only one tired. I'm exhausted too," I lie about the last part.

Thank God, she doesn't press further.

The night is warm and the air is filled with the scent of the sea. The sound of the waves calms me a little, but not enough to make the anger—part of me, part of Odhran—go away.

God, how naive of me to think the dirty Irishman was interested only in me.

Why would he choose a single mother when he could be with any woman he wants, free of concerns?

As I walk with a completely unconscious Jax in my arms, I take a deep breath, saying goodbye to this paradise I arrived at two days ago. I had thought about staying a little longer because Jax loved playing in the sea, but I don't want to see Odhran with the blonde, or even with another woman who might be available tomorrow.

Is it a cowardly exit? Definitely, but also completely focused on my self-preservation.

Maybe I've started to feel a much stronger connection to Mad Lion than I've admitted so far.

I thought there was some sort of connection between us.

So stupid, Elaine!

The wind blows a strand of my hair over my eyes, and the sensation is pleasant. I could easily live on an island. There are beaches in Boston, but nothing remotely like this.

In Massachusetts, I like to go to Cape Cod, which is a little piece of heaven, but it's far and expensive for me. Since I moved to that state, I've only been there once.

Besides, I have a feeling I'll be safer in a big city in case Elysia's ex finds out about Jax and decides to come after us. I wish she had told me more about their relationship because I have no idea if other people knew they were together or who those people might be, if they even exist.

I look at the stars and wonder if, at some point, the fear of someone taking my child away will pass, if there will come a time when I can relax and just enjoy life with him. The fact that Jax's father doesn't live in the United States is a real blessing, but I still don't want to take any risks.

I have many unanswered questions.

Did he kill her because Elysia left him, or because he found out she had hidden the child from him? Did my sister reveal details about me to him, or does he have no idea I exist?

All the energy I felt at the beginning of the party has left my body, and I feel tired now.

"You need a bath and a glass of wine," *I tell myself.*

I'll change Jax's pajamas, even though he's asleep, then soak in the tub for half an hour, and when I'm nicely relaxed, sit on the bungalow's porch to watch the sea and plan.

I never have time for that. Usually, I come home too exhausted, and whatever energy I have left, I dedicate to my son.

Today, with my head confused and my heart tight, maybe it's a great opportunity to think about the direction my life is taking.

The image of Odhran leaving with the blonde comes to my mind, but I push it away once more.

Hell, I don't want to feel hurt because of that bastard.

Haven't I spent all these months telling myself he was no good? Why am I shocked when I finally have proof of it?

I always knew I shouldn't get involved with someone like him, but between logic and desire, there's an abyss.

Those blue eyes full of promise and that dangerous, always mocking smile are a threat to any woman's sanity.

Despite the whirlwind of emotions bubbling inside me, I smile when I hear music and applause.

Juno's party was beautiful. Limited to a few guests but like a fairy tale.

The Irish know how to celebrate, and their contagious energy is impossible to ignore.

Today, I know there were no soldiers here besides the bodyguards. Only the high-ranking members of the Syndicate were invited, according to Juno.

Men I've never seen before and who look powerful.

I walk slowly because the path leading to the bungalows, which are separate from the main house, is wooden and slatted, and I'm wearing very high heels.

Suddenly, the feeling of being watched, the same one I had at Juno's graduation, makes me look up.

A few steps away from me is a tall man in a suit, staring at me. I can't see his face because he's in the shadows. The way he's positioned blocks my path.

"Excuse me?" I ask, forcing a polite tone, even though every hair on the back of my neck is standing on end.

Every drop of my blood tells me I'm in danger, even though it makes no sense. In the middle of the Irish Syndicate boss's party, who would dare to harm me?

"No."

"I don't know who you think I am, sir, but you must be confusing me with someone else. I just want to go to my bungalow and put my son to rest."

"I went to great lengths to find you, Elaine, and I'm not going to let you go so easily. If you're so concerned about your boy, you're going to give me what I want, or I'll make you regret it."

He steps forward, emerging from the shadows and revealing his face.

When I see his features, especially his almond-shaped eyes, my knees lose their firmness because I immediately understand that the person talking to me is Jax's father, and also that, as my intuition has screamed all these years, he is not a good person.

I have no idea what he wants from me, but I know I need to escape from this man as quickly as possible.

Chapter 12

Elaine

I am determined to keep walking because even though the man called my name, I don't want to believe it's true, that Jax's father not only found me but I've just had confirmation that he was looking for me.

Our brain finds ways to escape reality when it can't handle a crisis, and right now, I am completely overwhelmed.

Instead of thinking about the danger I'm in, I try to imagine how my sister's ex might be at the Syndicate Boss's party.

"No, he isn't Jax's father," *I deceive myself.* "He's certainly just a jerk who became interested in me."

But what he said earlier leaves no doubt that we are not face to face by chance.

"I went to great lengths to find you, Elaine, to let you go so easily."

Soon after, I recall the other part of what the man said.

"If you're so worried about your boy, you'll give me what I want, or I'll make you regret it."

He doesn't know who Jax is, thank God!

Whatever the reason he's pursuing me, it isn't about discovering he has an heir.

I decide to play dumb and take a step to the side to bypass his body, but the man doesn't seem ready to give up, moving to intercept my path.

I try again to go in the opposite direction, and he mirrors my action.

I lift my head, ready to tell him to go to hell or even start screaming, but I know I can't do that or I'll wake up Jax.

A cold sweat spreads across my neck and back.

I prepared for this moment since Elysia died, but in my naive plans, I would see him coming. I would have time.

Maybe he thinks I knew all about their relationship and could link him to my sister's death.

Now, more than ever, I think this is a real possibility. And considering the fact that I'm sure he is part of the Syndicate's high ranks, or he wouldn't be here, I'll have to leave this life I was beginning to feel comfortable with behind and move as far away as possible. And even further, I can no longer work for the Syndicate's fights anywhere in the country.

"Run!" my instinct screams, but I am at a disadvantage.

On an island, in heels, and with my child in my arms.

I think quickly about what to do.

I didn't grow up in a fairy tale, overprotected. I'm from the people and improvisation is my middle name.

I can't afford to be afraid now, even if I sense that as soon as I'm alone, all the contents of dinner will end up in the toilet.

"What's his name?" he asks, gesturing towards Jax, and I feel the panic spread through me because the threat in his tone is unmistakable.

Whatever this man wants from me, he's hinting that my son is in danger.

"That's none of your business. Now, please, move aside."

As if fate were testing my sanity, Jax wakes up and lifts his little head.

The stranger in front of me approaches, and even in panic, I force myself to bring all my rationality to the forefront.

"I don't know who you are," I say as firmly as possible, "but if my husband sees you with me, he'll complain to Cillian. I doubt the Boss will like to know you harassed his wife's best friend."

"Husband? You're married?" he mocks, and I'm sure he knows I'm bluffing.

Has he investigated me? So why didn't he try to approach me earlier, at the party?

Because I was with Juno or Orla the whole time. He wouldn't dare come up to me in front of them.

"You're lying, Elaine. When Elysia left me, at first, I didn't care. I didn't want her anymore anyway and was thinking of a way to get rid of her. Only much later did I find out that miserable sister of yours stole from me. — Elysia stole from him? I don't believe it. She wasn't a thief. — Since then, I've tried to guess who she left what belonged to me with, until they found out for me that she had a half-sister. And guess what? She's single."

It doesn't escape me that he doesn't confess to having reconnected with Elysia, but now, I have no doubt that he did. He went after her, believing she stole from him, and when he didn't get what he wanted, he killed her.

"I'm going to ask again to let me pass."

"Still, I couldn't find you anywhere because you two, like the bitches you are, have different last names," he continues, as if I hadn't said anything. He smiles maliciously, ignoring my request. "I could hardly believe it when one of my men, a hacker, managed to track you down through facial recognition after finding an old photo of you with Elysia on the internet. Isn't technology wonderful? The only thing that didn't quite make sense to me was you being an employee of the Syndicate and also working with the Boss's wife."

"Let me pass or I'll scream. Juno will get here so fast he won't even have time to blink."

"Is there a problem?" I hear Lorcan ask behind me, and I almost sigh with relief.

"No, no problem, just this gentleman mistaking me for someone else."

"I'll walk you to the bungalow," Lorcan says, giving the guy a friendly pat on the back. "Go back to your wife, Trevino, and stop bothering Juno's friend."

The man still glares at me one more time but soon bids Lorcan farewell.

"What just happened here?"

"As I told you, the guy mistook me for someone else. I think he's drunk. Who is he?"

"He works for us. Trevino Cabrera, a lawyer. Why?"

"Nothing. I just don't want to cross his path again. He was persistent."

"Did he do anything inappropriate, Elaine?"

Yes, I think he killed my sister and now he's after me because he believes I have something Elysia stole from him.

God, and I thought Elysia wanted us to flee because she discovered a connection between her boyfriend and the "M" of Muerte, the Salvadoran mafia, when, in fact, Trevino Cabrera is a Syndicate lawyer!

"Um... No. I think he was just looking for adventure and thought I was someone else."

"Son of a bitch," he says, and only then do I realize that when he said goodbye to Trevino Cabrera, he told him to go back to "his wife."

Did Elysia know she was seeing a married man?

No, I don't think so.

Like me, my sister would never get involved with someone else's partner. It's more likely he lied.

"Did he really do nothing to you, Elaine?"

How do I tell the Boss's right-hand man that a trusted Syndicate member might have killed my sister?

What would Cillian do?

He'd probably never believe me.

No, I can't stay near the Irish anymore.

"Lorcan, can I ask you a favor?" I ask, minutes later, already at the door of my bungalow.

He offered to carry Jax, but I refused.

"Speak, girl."

"I need to leave. That's why I was going to the bungalow," I lie without remorse. "Hestia, the woman who takes care of Jax, just called. She isn't feeling well. I'd like to leave at dawn. I was going to leave in a few days, but I don't want to leave my friend alone. Is there any way I can leave earlier than planned?"

He looks at me strangely.

"What's going on, Elaine?"

"Nothing. Just life's responsibilities. Hestia has been like a mother to me, and I feel guilty leaving her alone."

"You're not telling the truth. Is it because of Odhran?"

He looks uncomfortable about his cousin.

God, can it be more embarrassing? Now the whole family thinks the bastard broke my heart.

And didn't that really happen?

Of course not. The fact that the Irishman was the only man to catch my attention in a long time doesn't mean I feel more than desire for him.

However, he just gave me a good way out.

"I just don't want to stay here anymore," I say, without needing to force my voice to sound sad.

"So your friend isn't sick?"

"No. I'm sorry for lying."

"I don't like liars, Elaine. To survive in our world, keeping secrets is not a good idea."

His voice sounds flat, emotionless, and that makes it even more frightening.

"I didn't mean to, but I didn't want to play the fool. I don't even have a reason to be upset with Odhran." I decide to fully commit to this excuse.

"I'll leave as soon as daybreak. You can come with me on the boat to the neighboring town to catch the flight back to Boston. I'm not going there, or I'd give you a ride. Just make sure you can change the ticket."

"Thank you very much. Don't worry about it. I'll figure it out."

I quickly say goodbye to him after we set the time to meet. As soon as I close the bungalow door, I change Jax's pajamas and, after making sure he's asleep, spring into action.

An hour later, I'm dressed, the bags are packed, and I've double-checked that the doors and windows of this guesthouse are locked.

I sit rigidly in the armchair, every cell of my body on high alert, and when around one in the morning, I hear the doorknob turning, I'm sure I'm going to have a heart attack.

I barely breathe, cell phone in hand, ready to call Orla if necessary.

And then, everything goes silent.

I wait a while longer before moving. I go to the window and look through the blinds into the darkness, but I don't see anyone.

I'm heading back to the armchair when I notice a piece of paper under the door.

Shaking, I take it to read in the bathroom.

When I open it, I feel dizzy.

"Do you think you can run from me, Elaine? We have matters to settle, and the more you try to escape, the worse our reunion will be. Wouldn't it be a shame if your son grew up without a mother?"

Now, more than ever, I'm certain there's only one way out.

Run.

Chapter 13

Elaine

Somewhere in the central United States

Two years later

"**M**ommy, can I play in the yard?" Jax asks, and Hestia and I exchange a glance.

In hers, I see a warning, as if saying: "You can't keep him in a glass bubble forever, dear."

I know she's right, but it's hard to be sensible when my intuition tells me that danger is lurking outside.

The day I left the island, I acted like a fugitive. I got home and told Hestia, without giving details, that we needed to leave because Jax's father threatened to take him from me, even though that's a huge lie.

Even though, upon discovering he had a child with Elysia, Trevino Cabrera wanted him—which I doubt—legally, I am his mother.

When he was born, my sister insisted that I adopt him. She said she would feel safer that way. At the time, I didn't understand, thinking it was because she had fragile health, but now I'm not so sure. I think Elysia knew she was in danger.

I don't like hiding anything from Hestia, but what was I supposed to say? Reveal that Jax's father is a psychopath who thinks

I have something his sister stole from him and seems willing to end me if necessary to get it back?

God, I can't go on like this or I won't make it to thirty. I live in constant fear.

Did Elysia know he was part of the Syndicate? I don't think so. Something else made her uneasy about her boyfriend and made her run. No matter what Jax's father said, I will never believe the story that she stole from him. My sister was one of the most honest people I ever knew.

She probably found out that Trevino was married, wanted to break up, and he wouldn't let her end their relationship.

But deep down, I know this explanation doesn't make sense. If it were just that, why would he be after me now? No, the man truly believes that Elysia took something that belongs to him.

And to think I was sure that the coincidence of our escape aligning with my telling her about the disappearance of my coworker meant that Jax's father had something to do with the "M" in Muerte.

Of course not! The timeline was just a coincidence. A high-ranking Irish mafia member could never be connected to the "M" in Muerte.

When we prepared to leave Boston, it wasn't hard to gather what little we had. The rent was paid month to month, without a lease and always in advance, so all we had to do was notify the landlord that we wouldn't be staying anymore.

Since I started working with Juno, I had saved up a good amount of money, which helped us live comfortably right after our escape, until I could figure out what to do.

I didn't want to disrupt my friend's honeymoon, and the day after we left the state, I called Orla and briefly explained the situation: that I had run into Jax's father, who threatened to take him from me, so I needed to leave.

Orla, with a temperament similar to the Boss's, initially said she would handle everything and that we should "go home." I thanked her and firmly refused.

In that note she left me, there was a threat, and I wasn't going to put my son's or Hestia's lives at risk.

Like a good coward, I push the anxiety to a distant place within me. That's how I survived the last two years; otherwise, I would have breathed fear twenty-four hours a day.

Orla had no choice but to accept my decision, and I asked her not to tell Juno because I intended to do that when she returned from her honeymoon.

And so it happened. I resigned all at once from my "plate girl" job and the bakery. With a short and precise phone call, I said I had left Boston and had no plans to return.

Juno insisted that I tell her the truth about Jax's father, but I revealed nothing beyond that he was after the child and that I didn't want to take any risks.

I love Juno, but the truth is that even after spending months together, we didn't know much about each other's lives. By intuition, I'm sure her past wasn't a bed of roses, just like mine, but we never exchanged deep confidences.

With that in mind, I couldn't suddenly show up and say: "Look, Jax isn't actually my child; he's my nephew, and his father, coincidentally, happens to be one of your husband's trusted men! The same man I believe killed my sister. Oh, and I can't forget that he accused Elysia of stealing something that belongs to him and now thinks I have it."

Even though I refuse to believe his accusation, there's that voice saying: what if it's true?

In that case, it would be unlikely that even at Juno's request, Cillian would side with me against his trusted man.

He is protective of Juno and Orla, but who am I, besides being the wife's employee?

Between a high-ranking Syndicate lawyer and a "plate girl," a simple bakery attendant, who would he choose to believe?

I preferred not to stay to wait for the answer. It's not about my protection, but about keeping my son out of Trevino's clutches, as his threat was clear.

I remembered, right after leaving Boston, that when I said we had to flee, my sister mentioned that I should stop working in the fights, but without knowing why, I said "no." How could I agree with that when the fights were where I made most of our living?

In the end, she had no choice but to accept my decision.

Didn't she tell Trevino that I was one of the plate girls? No, from what he said, he only found out later that Elysia had a half-sister.

"I can't help but worry," I tell Hestia when, at last, I allow Jax to play in the yard.

This is the fifth time we've moved. We arrived here only a couple of days ago, and I've been seriously considering leaving the country because I can't stand running anymore.

In every place we've been, Trevino or someone acting on his orders has almost caught up with us.

However, the escape from our last home was the most traumatic for me.

The town we were in, in South Dakota, was tiny and almost off the map. It was where we stayed the longest—eight months.

I managed to realize a dream I had cherished for years: starting a small flower bouquet business. Until then, I had been doing various odd jobs, as always, but as time passed in that small town and no threats emerged, I felt safe enough to finally set a definitive course for my life.

I never imagined there were so many brides in South Dakota, and gradually, I gained a reputation among the farming families, whose daughters only wanted to get married holding the bouquets I arranged.

I went to Boston a while ago for a course, and like a reckless fool, I decided to go to a bar considered neutral, outside the territory of all gangs and mafias, to play pool and have a beer.

As if fate were playing a joke on me, I ran into Lorcan's men there, Keiron and Rourke, two Neanderthals as hot as hell who, apparently, were eyeing a very beautiful blonde.

She was young too, with an innocent face, which made me go up to the girl and give her advice to stay away from the mobsters.

Neither of them was very pleased with my interference, but I felt it was my duty to let her know what she was getting into.

Did they tell Lorcan or any other Syndicate member that they saw me? Maybe.

I don't allow myself to think about Odhran. I've erased him from my mind since I left that island in the Caribbean, and it's likely that the opposite is also true.

I met a guy, about two years older than me. Handsome, honest, honorable. There was no magic between us, but I felt good with him to the point of thinking for the first time about something more than just friendship.

Claim Dustin, the owner of a used car dealership who had come to the small town where we lived to visit his farming parents, seemed to be enchanted by me at first sight. He didn't give up until I accepted his invitation to go out.

Five months later, he made it clear that he wanted more than a fleeting relationship and started talking about marriage.

It wasn't something I had thought about before, but even so, the idea became tempting the more he talked about his plans.

A permanent home. A family for Jax. Never having to run again.

And then, one day, it all ended when I received a phone call from Claim in the middle of the afternoon.

Chapter 14

Elaine

He told me that some men broke into his store during the night and smashed all the vehicles.

I had been uneasy in recent days, with the familiar feeling of being watched. So, when Claim told me that, I decided to partially tell him the truth, because I thought he had the right to know what was happening, after all, we were planning a future together.

I mentioned it might have been related to Jax's father, as he was a dangerous man.

In a split second, the man changed towards me.

He told me, bluntly, that he didn't want trouble for himself and that it would be better if we broke up.

At first, I was so disappointed that I couldn't believe it, but soon after, anger took the place of hurt, and then I thanked God I hadn't made the mistake of getting involved with a coward.

The man who swore me love and wanted to marry me, runs away at the first sign of trouble?

Yes, that's exactly what he did. He sold the store days later and vanished God knows where.

I did too, of course. Used to living on high alert, I quickly packed up my things and moved to another state with Hestia and Jax, but I feel like the noose is tightening.

For some time now, she knows almost the whole truth. The fact that Trevino, a trusted man of the Irish mafia, might be Jaxton's father. However, she has no idea about the accusation he made about Elysia stealing from him.

"You can't live like this forever, Elaine."

"I know."

"If you think we'll be safe out of the country, let's do it."

"Would you come too?"

"Where else would I go? You two are my family. Have you thought of any place?"

"Yes, I've considered several possibilities. The problem is that flying out of the country will leave traces."

"What if we cross the border into Canada by car?"

I had thought about Mexico, but maybe she's right, and the northern part of the continent might be safer.

"I'll plan carefully and give you an answer next week."

Odhran

Boston

"IS IT EVER GOING TO end?" Kellan asks Cillian. "I can't believe this shit will never end."

This time, even my older brother, who no longer goes on missions because his security is also managed by the Syndicate, came.

In the early morning, on the outskirts of Boston, in a place forgotten by God, we are gathered around a table while our men are outside dealing with the bodies of the enemies. The "current" enemies, would be a better way to put it.

In our line of work, there aren't many peaceful days, and the verb *trust* is basically limited to family.

Cillian, who is the most strategic of the three of us, rarely loses control, but tonight he seems close to breaking point.

I'm fire, he's ice. Kellan is our planner.

I enjoy the execution. The pleasure it gives me to destroy every damn person who crosses our path.

Tonight, however, we had a special mission. We eliminated the descendants, as we have been doing for years, of those who killed our parents.

A lot of time has passed, and the sons of bitches still haven't learned their lesson. My family was killed in an attack, breaking an honor code within the Syndicate itself, in an act of betrayal by my father's and uncle's trusted men, the former Boss.

The culprits were not only punished, they became an example, but from time to time, a descendant from hell appears who thinks they can seek revenge. That was the case tonight, and now they are all literally about to turn to ashes.

"It's over, finally. There's no one left. I made sure of that," I say.

Cillian looks at me, and I can tell that, like Kellan, he is fed up with this shit. It's a chapter we all want to turn because every time a descendant of our parents' killers appears, we relive the day of their death.

My older brother just wants to forget. Kellan, to fulfill the promise we made at their graves. As for me, in a twisted way, I enjoyed every second I spent facing them again. Too bad it's over for good. Eliminating them eased some of my hatred.

I was the one of the three brothers who, as a child, saw my parents fall dead on the sidewalk beside me. And if I didn't meet the same fate, it was because one of the bodyguards was quick enough to save me.

I wasn't grateful. At that moment, I wanted to die too, because I will never forget that scene.

In the first few days, I didn't even stop to mourn their deaths. I was just a boy, but I wanted to go after the killers because, practically from the moment we were born, we were taught to seek revenge and only then allow ourselves to grieve, if necessary.

Revenge is our escape valve in a universe where death can occur on any random day, when least expected. We are not invincible, but we make it clear to our enemies that if they attack us, they better kill us, otherwise, there will always be retaliation, and not something pretty, but something that will last for generations. No offense will be forgiven, and second chances do not exist.

"I hope these were truly the last ones," Cillian says, and I know it's because now it's not just us that's at stake, but his family too.

Married, with a young child, my brother doesn't want anything that might threaten his wife and heir.

Not that there is security in our world, but it is much easier to deal with a present enemy than with someone coming after revenge.

"As far as I'm concerned, I could keep killing the descendants of those sons of bitches until my time comes to walk to hell," I say.

Despite the tension in the air, my older brother smiles.

"Pick new enemies, kid. I don't want to hear about those damned ones anymore. I'm taking your word that it's over."

A few minutes later, in the hallway, I see Keiron, one of the men directly subordinate to Lorcan, coming towards me.

We rarely see each other, especially since Rourke, his best friend, moved in with a former Russian mafia soldier.

I still can't believe it. Both Lorcan and Rourke are now tied to women who were born on the enemy's side. The former with the sister of a Ruslan goddaughter, whom my cousin saved and whose involvement nearly caused a war between the Syndicate and the Brotherhood, of which Yerik is the Pakhan. As for Rourke, he asked for Tulia as a gift—which means, in our world, permission to be with her on a permanent basis—after saving Lorcan's life.

The negotiations for both deals were tense and almost ended in tragedy, if not for Ruslan's intervention and because now the two organizations Cillian and Yerik lead are united to fight a common enemy: those damned Sicilians.

"Is everything alright with tonight's operation?" I ask, because he seems like he wants to tell me something, and I know he's about to leave to dispatch some cargo to Mexico.

I like Keiron. In a way, we have a lot in common.

"Everything is going according to plan."

"Are you really thinking of leaving?"

I heard some rumors that he wants to spend some time in Ireland.

"Yes, but I'm not sure if I'll stay there permanently. I like Boston."

"Ireland is still your home."

"Not so much anymore. Boston is my place."

"Then why leave?"

"I need to breathe some fresh air," he says, without elaborating further, although I suspect it has to do with the rumor that he and Rourke shared women.

With his friend now in a serious relationship, I doubt that arrangement could continue. You don't need to be a love expert to realize that Rourke is extremely territorial about his Russian woman. Besides, I don't think Keiron wants anyone permanent in his life, and just spending two minutes near Tulia, Rourke's girlfriend, you can tell that the girl dreamed of a prince *in the singular*, not *in the plural*, because that definition of prince would never fit the best friend of her man. I think to use that label, Keiron would need to manage to be faithful.

"Did Rourke ever mention to you that some time ago, when we met Tulia, we ran into Elaine in a bar?"

"What?"

"The ex-girl from the pla..."

"I know who she is," I growl, in a bad mood.

I know who she is?

No, that's a very mild version to explain that even though two years have passed, I still think obsessively about the woman.

On Juno's wedding night, despite my *little show*, I didn't sleep with the blonde. Being with a woman just for pleasure is something I've always done, but I never fucked one while thinking about another, and I knew that it wasn't the Irish woman my cock wanted, so I said good night and told her I had changed my mind. She didn't even get to enter my bungalow.

I got up the next day, hoping to casually find Elaine at the pool since Orla had told me she'd stay on the island a few more days, but to my surprise, my aunt said she had left on the same boat that took Lorcan to the neighboring city.

And then, when days later I went to the bakery pretending I needed to do some shit, but actually just wanted to see her, came the bombshell that she had moved away for good.

She ran away from me? Maybe.

The fact is that she's been missing for two years. I could have hunted her down, but I didn't, because I knew Elaine deserved more than I had to offer.

I thought that over time, I wouldn't even remember her name, but that's not what happened.

Elaine is like an unfinished job. The kind that leaves me with the feeling that I let something slip, but even though I still desire her, I kept my distance, not inquiring about her whereabouts. However, I know that if she ever comes back, I won't be as generous as when I let her run away. I'll take everything I want from her.

"No, Rourke didn't tell me about it."

"Aren't you going to say anything?" he asks, and I guess he's smiling.

It's become something of a joke among those close to us that Elaine was the only one to reject both O'Callaghan brothers in the same year.

Technically, she didn't reject me. I could have made a move on the beautiful woman at Juno's wedding and I know we would have spent the night in my bed, but in the end, I decided to think about someone other than myself. In an incomprehensible way, since sensitivity is not a concept that applies to me, I prioritized her and Jax over just what I wanted.

"Elaine is none of my business," I say and walk away without looking back.

Chapter 15

Elaine

A sound that resembles scratching pierces the night, breaking through my already restless sleep.

I'm sure it came from outside the house.

I sit up in bed immediately, my body tense. I look over and see that Jax is still sleeping soundly.

He usually doesn't stay in the room with me, but he had a nightmare tonight.

I wonder how much my sister's fear during pregnancy affected him. They say that babies, even while still in the womb, are sensitive to their mother's emotions.

I get up slowly and when I reach the hallway, Hestia is standing there, but even in the dim light, I see the apprehension on her face.

"I think they found us," she whispers.

I feel my heart pound.

"How do you know that?"

"I'm almost sure I saw someone outside."

"My God."

"What are we going to do?"

I always have escape plans. Throughout this time we've been hiding, I haven't just sat around waiting for them to show up to think about what to do. I've created small strategies, which we've used more than once when we thought we were at risk.

They are never a long-term solution, but at least they give us a chance to breathe for a while.

"If there's someone out there, our only chance of escaping is following plan 'A.'"

It means calling the police and reporting a threat of invasion. They arrive in a few minutes, which is enough time for us to escape relatively safely, as the sirens always scare off my pursuers. We've done this before, and it worked.

"And where do we go after that?"

She seems more scared than usual. Hestia is not a nervous person. She is calm and centered.

"I don't know yet, but I'll figure it out, as always," I say, perhaps trying to convince myself more, even though I know the net is closing in and the options are running out.

Five minutes later, I end the call with the police, but we remain standing in the same spot.

There are no windows in the hallway, and at the moment, it's the safest part of the house besides my room, but I don't want to wake Jax.

"WE DIDN'T FIND ANYONE, Miss Wehde. Are you sure you saw someone outside the house?" one of the officers, who is very friendly, asks me.

Wehde is one of the fake surnames I used during our two-year escape. I have three sets of fake documents for each of us, made by experts and never arousing the suspicion of the authorities. The problem is that they are expensive to make, and with the recent move from South Dakota, which made me lose all my clients, my savings are running out.

"I am sure," I lie, because I believe Hestia when she said she saw someone prowling around the house. "Would you mind waiting while we pack a bag? I'll feel safer spending the night in a motel with my son and my mother."

"That's a sensible approach. Feel free to take your time. We'll be in the patrol car."

Less than half an hour later, we gather the essentials.

I look at the house, saddened to be leaving everything behind once again. Hestia is already in the truck, waiting for me with a semi-awake and grumpy Jax, who hates having his sleep interrupted. At four years old, he already shows signs of what he'll be like in the future. Despite being a loving child, he is also stubborn and proud. Quite mature for his age, sometimes the things he says shock me, as he seems like a miniature adult.

The feeling that I'm harming his development, preventing him from making friends like a normal child, nearly suffocates me, but I stop myself from thinking about it at the moment.

"I'll be right back," I tell Hestia and give a nod to the officers, who are in the patrol car a few meters away. "I forgot my work tools. I can't afford to buy new ones anytime soon."

These are the materials I use to create my artworks, my beloved bouquets, and they were expensive.

I start walking toward the small external room, an annex to the house, that I use as a workshop.

One of the reasons I chose this property to rent was precisely because of this small room, where I could work at night. I suffer from insomnia and sometimes stay awake almost all night.

I open the door and reach for the light switch. A feeling of dread, a kind of chill, passes through my body, as if warning of a malignant presence, but when I turn on the light, no one is there.

However, as soon as I approach the toolbox, I feel like I'm going to vomit. There's a single white flower, leftover from an order I delivered today, on the counter.

It's covered in a sticky red liquid, and when I take a deep breath, I know the ochre smell is blood.

I lean on the counter to keep from falling and only then see there's a note next to it.

"Next time", it says simply.

My brain short-circuits, and I know my journey as a fugitive has come to an end.

Now, I'll take an alternative route. Seek protection in the wolf's den.

It's my last chance. The final card.

I'll have to trust that my friendship with Juno will save me from Trevino Cabrera's clutches.

Chapter 16

Elaine

"You can't come in," one of the Syndicate men growls, blocking my way.

I break into a cold sweat.

I know he's right. There are only three ways you can attend Syndicate fights: if you're working there, as a guest, or if you're part of the elite surrounding Cillian.

I don't fit into any of these categories.

I stare at the giant blocking my way. He must be new, or transferred from somewhere, because I'm sure I've never seen him before.

"I need to speak with Odhran," I say, not believing that I'm actually uttering these words.

I thought I'd never see him again, and yet, now he's my only hope.

The first thing I did after arriving in Boston was to settle Jax and Hestia into a small hotel. Then, I went in search of Juno.

It was no surprise to find that his phone number had changed. What did I expect after two years of no contact, except for when I said goodbye, saying I was leaving?

But I'm not a quitter, and I went after Orla at the restaurant. I could hardly believe it when I hit the door again.

According to a waitress, who thankfully recognized me, the matriarch is traveling with her nephew and family.

Total vacation, no phone calls or interruptions, was what the girl told me about the orders she received.

That left Lorcan, who would have been my first choice, but I have no idea how to find him. Kellan, who I don't know if would help me, and finally, the last man I would wish to encounter again.

Mad Lion.

Odhran O'Callaghan, the arrogant, bastard jerk.

I was surprised to realize that even after two years, my anger towards him hadn't diminished, but I'm out of alternatives. I'm not going to take a chance to see if the message with the bloodied flower was serious.

"Are you deaf? Get lost, babe."

"Wow, what the hell are you doing, idiot? Is this any way to treat a lady?"

I turn around and come face to face with Keiron. If there's someone more despicable than Odhran in the Syndicate, it's him.

I remember our last meeting at the bar and how he and Rourke got angry with me, but I swallow my pride and give my most perfect—and false—smile, hoping it works.

"I need to speak with Odhran," I say.

"Really? And I'd love to have an audience with God to see if he could get rid of some assholes on this planet, but we can't have everything we want, Elaine."

"I'm not joking, Keiron. It's urgent."

"Honey, you left. They're not going to hire you back. There are no second chances with us."

"It's not a job I want. I need to talk to him. I'll beg if I have to, but can you at least tell Odhran that I'm here and have something to say about my son?"

For the first time, the mocking expression fades.

"Odhran is the..."

He doesn't finish, but I understand.

Is Keiron thinking I came because Jax is Odhran's child?

How can he assume something like that? If I've learned anything about the Irish, it's that they value family greatly. I doubt any of the Syndicate guys, no matter how terrible husbands or boyfriends they are, would deny a child.

I should deny it, clear up the confusion, but I'll use any weapon at my disposal to achieve my goal.

"He won't like to know that I wanted to talk about Jax and you stopped me."

Keiron looks me up and down.

"Why don't you just call him then?"

"I don't have the number."

He looks thoughtful, as if deciding, and I hope it's in my favor.

"Don't leave. I'll be right back."

I know that all the warehouses where the fights are held have an office, and I assume that's where Keiron is going. The competition is still two hours away, and if Odhran has already arrived, which I hope he has, because I don't even want to think about him being outside Boston as well, he must be waiting for the fights to start in the office.

I step away from the surly giant and begin to pace the courtyard.

I'm very anxious, but in the last few days, since we fled, I've felt like I could suffer a sudden illness and die at any moment.

God, help me. I have no other options. I'm not even scared for myself anymore. It's all about Jax.

Odhran

"WHAT DID YOU JUST SAY?"

"Elaine is outside and says she needs to speak with you about Jax."

There's an accusatory tone in his voice, and also an implied question.

Does he think I'm the boy's father?

If I were someone who explained my own life, I'd clear up the misunderstanding, but that's not the case.

"Let her in," I finally decide.

I tell myself I'm just curious. There are few things that have the power to surprise me, and Elaine's visit is completely unexpected.

"Do I need to search her first?"

I mask a smile.

"No, I'll do it myself."

Elaine

"YOU CAN COME WITH ME," Keiron says a few minutes later, and in a foolish way, I feel like sticking my tongue out at the giant jerk who blocked my entry.

Yes, logically, I know he was just doing his job, but it's like being barred from the door of your own home. I worked in the fights for years, damn it!

"Did he ask why I came?"

Keiron raises his hands in front of his body, as if surrendering. "I don't get involved in other people's wars, princess."

Chapter 17

Odhran

There was only one thing until today that could make me anxious: the minutes before attacking an enemy.

Not even when I fought, before stepping into the ring, did I feel any adrenaline coursing through my body.

Until the moment the door opens and I see the woman who left about two years ago, killing was my favorite drug.

For I have just added another one to the list. When I look at her doll-like face, her long lashes almost covering those honey-colored irises, and her sculptural body, I know this time I won't let her go without making her mine.

I focus on her full lips, and all I can think about is having them around my cock while I grab her hair and thrust until I hit the back of her throat.

My cock hardens with the thought, the scene playing out in my mind like a damn movie.

A better man would send her away because I know I'm poison and Elaine is too good for what I want with her, but I'm not that man. I'm a hunter and here is my prey.

I scan her from feet to the now waist-length brown hair, which contrasts with the shorter cut she used to have that barely reached her shoulders.

She wears jeans, short boots, and a black top that makes her generous breasts almost spill out of the neckline. Even the little jacket she has on top can't contain my desire.

I've always liked the way she felt confident in herself. It's certainly something that caught my attention. The clothes she wore were sexy, but the confident attitude drove me crazy.

A woman who feels good about herself is a turn-on.

Once, on the few occasions we exchanged a few words, I asked her why she didn't agree to come with me that night I invited her, on Juno's first day of work.

She smiled and said she was too smart to get involved with a mobster. I can't deny that I'm the worst possible bet for a good girl, but I knew at the time that she was lying. If I hadn't listened to Kellan's advice on the day of our brother's wedding, I would have made her mine right there on the island.

Or even after that, if she hadn't left Boston for good, as sure as the damn sunrise, we would have happened.

I've been with more women than I can remember and have never felt so obsessed with one. There's no way to have her within reach and just let it go. I fought against the desire because I don't accept being controlled by anything or anyone, but now she's back and I'm saying fuck the old rules.

I want her and nothing will stop me from having her in my bed.

"What do you want to talk to me about that's so important?" I say, without getting up from my desk.

There's something in her eyes that's not just about the way she looked at me before she left Boston, but a mix of desire and apprehension.

I try to focus beyond her appearance and soon notice how her body seems tense.

Because of me?

No, or she wouldn't have come.

She seems like someone on alert, ready for war.

Even more wary, even more distrustful, even more hurt than when she left.

Yes, hurt. Even before Kellan told me she was alone in the world, I could see a dark side to her soul.

Is that why the woman attracts me so much? Because beneath the sexy goddess facade, I can see her internal scars?

"I didn't want to talk to you, but to Juno or Orla. They're not in town and..."

"So I'm the last option? You're breaking my heart, Elaine."

"You don't have one, Irish," she says, in a combative stance, and I think her anger still relates to what I did at Cillian's wedding.

"You're right, there's nothing here inside my chest. What do you want?"

I was deliberately brusque because even for me, who welcomes the unexpected, the whole situation seems surreal.

The Elaine of the past would have told me to go to hell and said she had changed her mind, but she doesn't move and that piques my interest.

I stand up and approach her, stopping only a few steps away.

I can smell her fear and it's not just of me.

"What did you come here for, Elaine?"

I see her chest rise and fall as she takes a deep breath, as if uttering a response costs her a great effort before finally confessing:

"I need help."

Elaine

"I WANT TO LEAVE."

In fact, I think I've never wanted something so badly in my life, not because I think Odhran might physically hurt me, but because it took me a fraction of a second to understand that the attraction I felt for him hasn't diminished one bit, and judging by the way he's looking back at me, the feeling is mutual.

And then, I remember him leaving with the blonde from the wedding and the anger returns with full force. It's a shame I can't land a kick to that bastard's balls.

"What kind of help are you talking about, Elaine?"

He seems almost bored asking, and his tone immediately brings me back to reality.

What am I thinking? I'm not facing some ex-fling, but the brother of the Irish mafia boss.

"Jax's father wants to take him away from me." I spill the lie, knowing it's my only chance to get his help, and as if I can't stop myself, I continue with some half-truths. "He's not actually my son; he's my nephew, but my sister asked me to register him as her child as soon as he was born. I legally adopted him, but this man is after both of us, and I can't let him take my boy."

"Why not, if he's the father?"

What am I going to say? Claim that I think one of the Irish mafia's lawyers, a trusted man of Cillian's, killed my sister?

There's no way I can accuse a high-ranking member of the Irish Syndicate without proof.

"He's married. He doesn't care about Jax; he just wants to hurt my sister, even after her death."

He doesn't say anything, and his silence makes me even more nervous.

I take a few breaths before continuing. I know what I have to do, and yet, I'm in a panic. The no is almost certain, but I came all this way thinking of a solution, and the only possible way for that horrible man not to hurt us is to shield ourselves from the lawyer.

To do that, I need someone even more powerful than Trevino Cabrera to take on Jaxton. If he agrees to my plan, we'll be protected. I know it's risky. I haven't forgotten the warning Lorcan gave me, back in the Caribbean, about lying to them, but right now, I find myself with no choice.

"I need you to pretend to be Jax's father, Odhran. That's the only way that man will leave us alone if he thinks Jax isn't his child."

Chapter 18

Odhran

"Hands on the wall. Face away from me."

"What?"

"You heard me, Elaine."

"Odhran..."

"Believe me, this is my gentle version."

"Are you going to search me?"

"You bet your pretty ass I am. You came here. You knew how we operate. This isn't a walk in the park, girl. For all I know, you could be carrying microphones or weapons."

"Have you gone crazy?"

"You have five minutes to obey me or get out."

I cross my arms over my chest, and she knows I'm not going to give in.

Although I don't think Elaine is suicidal enough to come here trying to deceive me, the proposal she made is so absurd that it can only be part of some scheme. She was sent by someone.

All risks I take are calculated and personal. I'm not afraid for myself, but I can't compromise the Syndicate's security.

"I can't leave without your help."

"Then do as I said."

"What are you looking for?"

"Weapons, listening devices."

"I can prove I'm not carrying anything without you having to touch me."

"How?"

She is backed into a corner, almost at the door. Without breaking eye contact, she begins to undress.

At first, I'm surprised by her audacity. Then, completely obsessed with her beauty.

The real version of her is much more delicious than the one I've been fantasizing about for nearly two years.

Elaine looks at me with her chin up, and when she's only in lingerie, a ridiculously tiny black silk and lace set, she does a full three-sixty-degree turn around herself.

"See? No weapons or listening devices."

Is she teasing me? Does she know how seeing her almost naked and so combative makes me want to press her against the wall and fuck her until neither of us has any strength left?

"Why the hell did you do that?"

She places her hands on her hips.

"No one touches me against my will. Want to check if I'm armed or have listening devices? You can look, but touching is only when I say so."

Her words irritate me, and I don't react well when provoked.

"Do you think I need to abuse you? If I wanted to touch you, I would have done it a long time ago. Now put your clothes on or I'll throw you out of the room as you are."

It's just a bluff. I would never let anyone see her like this, but when I notice her eyes widening, I feel satisfied.

Elaine picks up her clothes from the floor and, at lightning speed, is dressed again.

"Do you really think I came here to betray you? To do something against the Syndicate?" she asks, a few steps away from me.

"I don't trust anyone who isn't family or those I consider family. That being clear, can you tell me what the hell you were talking about regarding me taking on Jax's paternity?"

"I don't know how to tell you this."

"I'm listening, Elaine."

"There was a reason I ran away. On the day of Juno's wedding, I encountered someone at the party who threatened me."

I feel my blood boil.

"Did someone from the Syndicate try to abuse you?"

"Yes and no."

"Clarify."

"Jax's father is Trevino Cabrera."

I strain my memory, trying to connect the name to a person, and it takes me a few seconds to recall that he is one of the lawyers working for the Syndicate. His base of operations is outside the United States, and if I'm not mistaken, he's Honduran.

A loyal man to the Syndicate, he's been working with us for years.

"Go on."

Elaine tells me that her sister, who was in a serious relationship, although she never revealed the boyfriend's name, suddenly decided to run away.

I sense she's not telling me everything, just the main points. I've interrogated people before, and the pauses she makes while narrating are because she's obviously thinking carefully before revealing each little detail.

"Elysia fell into depression, seemed terrified after we ran away, then found out she was pregnant with Jax... — Another pause. — Actually, I'm not sure if she discovered she was pregnant before we left. The fact is that after she gave birth, she started to improve. One night, she went out to work and never came back."

"Are you implying that Trevino Cabrera killed your sister?"

She pales.

"No, I wouldn't say something like that without evidence."

"If Elysia never told you who the boyfriend was, how did you come to the conclusion it was him?"

"The resemblance between him and Jax is striking. Maybe not to a stranger, but I see my son's face every night. Besides, at the party, he said my name and knew I was Elysia's sister."

I still study her face unhurriedly because something tells me she's only telling me what she needs to.

"Say something. Will you help me?"

"I don't make decisions based on emotion. Continue talking about why you left the wedding."

Elaine

I KNOW I NEED TO MOVE the pieces of this game carefully. Be direct enough to convince Odhran that my fear of Trevino Cabrera is real, but only regarding the bastard wanting to take Jax from me, not because I think he killed Elysia.

"I was scared. He wants my son."

"That would be natural, Elaine."

"*Natural?* He's married."

"And didn't your sister know that?"

"I can't be sure, but I don't think she did. Anyway, once Jax was born, she gave him up for adoption."

"Why?"

"Despite us being very similar, we're not daughters of the same father. We share only the mother. At the time, I thought she gave Jax up for adoption because my sister had a health problem, still a child, with her heart. It seems that her paternal family had a hereditary heart condition. The fact is, Elysia's health was always a concern, and I believed she wanted to ensure that if she were to die, Jax wouldn't go into state custody."

"Why not give him to the father?"

"I had no idea why, but my theory now is that Elysia discovered Trevino Cabrera was married. No woman would accept raising her husband's child with a mistress."

"What did Trevino say to you at the wedding? You said you think he only wanted Jax to hurt your sister, even after she was dead. Why?"

"Elysia ran away from him. I don't think, being a proud man, he liked that — I say, not mentioning the note he left under the bungalow door. — The fact is, he wants Jax. I don't believe it's out of love. Bringing home a boy who's the result of an affair? I researched him, Odhran. He has five kids with his wife. Why would he care about a little boy with no connection to him?"

"So you ran away."

"I went into hiding. Jax is mine. Parents aren't those who give birth, they are those who give love, and that boy has had every drop of mine since he opened his eyes for the first time in this crazy world."

I run my hands over my head.

"I don't want ties with anyone. Not even in a pretend scenario."

He's brutally direct, but in a twisted way, I appreciate this honesty.

"I'm willing to work for the Syndicate for free if you help me. I would do anything not to lose Jax."

"I'm not a saint, Elaine. If you're looking for a knight in shining armor to save you, you're at the wrong door. Anything I do in life is a negotiation."

"I'm not sure I understand."

"I don't want kids, not even in a false context, but I'm willing to let people think the boy is mine, under one condition."

"Condition? I have nothing to offer."

Odhran

SHE DIDN'T COME BY choice, but in search of protection; otherwise, we wouldn't have resumed our interactions.

Elaine was forced to come to me, as if she weren't afraid, I wouldn't see her again.

The idea, in a way that completely defies logic, drives me crazy.

I stare at the woman who insisted on occupying my thoughts, even during the time we spent apart.

It's time to put an end to this obsession.

I'm not a damn superhero. I can keep her safe, but in return, she'll be mine for as long as I want.

"I want you."

"What?"

"You asked me for a favor, and this is my price. You'll be my woman until I tire of you."

Chapter 19

Odhran

"You must be going crazy."

"For wanting you?"

"For blackmailing me and thinking I'll accept something like that."

"There's no way out."

We both know I'm right, and I see flames burning in her eyes. At this moment, Elaine hates me.

"I'm not going to sleep with you. You can't stay faithful to a single woman, and I'm not risking my health."

"Jealous?"

"No, call it *self-preservation.*

"Is that the *only* reason you're saying no?"

"What?"

"If I give you my word that I'll spend some time *only* with you, will you agree?"

"I'm not an idiot, Odhran. I may have been in Boston for just a few months, but I've been working in the fight scene for years. I know your reputation. You never stay with the same partner for more than half a dozen times."

"I'm single and I like to fuck. I'm not going to apologize for that."

"And I'm not asking you to. It's none of my business who you sleep with."

"If that's your answer," I say, walking over to the table and picking up my phone. "I'll ask Keiron to escort you out."

"No, let's negotiate."

"I don't force women into my bed."

"I hate you."

I smile.

"Why, Elaine? Is it so hard to admit that it would never be forced? We both know that the attraction we feel won't die until it's satisfied."

I expect her to retort, to yell at me, but instead, she says the most unexpected thing in the world:

"Kiss me."

"What?"

"You're right about our attraction, but until now, everything has been a "maybe." It could be that the moment we touch, no spark will happen, and if that's the case, not even this indecent protection agreement will make me accept your proposal."

I put the phone down and sit at the table, crossing my legs at the ankles.

"I can seduce you with just a few words. I can make you beg to come just by saying how I'm crazy to taste your pussy with my tongue, but let's play a fair game. Come to me, Elaine. You want a kiss so badly to be sure my touch won't be repulsive, little liar? I'm here, at your service."

Elaine

I'M TREMBLING AS I walk towards him. There's nothing I can do or say to stop Odhran from noticing it.

Right now, I hate him, and it's not about the indecent proposal to become his mistress, but because he seems to know the right words to say—dirty, indecent words—that make my body crave each of those promises.

"You think you're irresistible."

"Not really. But I'm experienced. I know you want me, just as I want you."

"I don't get involved with mobsters."

"You've said that before, and yet, you're still here, knowing my terms."

"I want to hit you so much right now."

"Not the first time," he says, but then adds, "You said you don't get involved with mobsters. So who do you get involved with?"

The question surprises me because it sounds like... no, of course not. Odhran isn't jealous of anyone, let alone me.

"I had a boyfriend," I say. "A good man."

I don't add that he was a coward who, at the slightest hint of danger, ended things without a second thought.

Sure, having his agency's cars destroyed wasn't exactly "trivial," but the man I want for myself one day won't run away when a threat appears. I want someone by my side to face whatever life throws at us.

"And where is that good man now?"

I force myself back to the present.

His expression is neutral, but his eyes emit danger. Still, I keep walking towards him.

"It's over. Where's your blonde now?" I say before I can stop myself.

"I didn't sleep with her," he says, not even trying to hide that he doesn't know who I'm referring to.

"I don't believe you."

"That day, I wanted to show you that I'm not what you need, Elaine. And I still am not."

"So why did you change your mind?"

"Because I've been obsessed with you for over two years and I don't like the feeling."

The honest answer, completely free of any irony, not only catches me by surprise but also makes my blood boil.

"A kiss," I say. "An experiment to find out what this madness is between us."

He uncrosses his legs, letting me get closer. I press our bodies together and wrap my arms around his neck.

"Maybe we don't even match."

"Maybe," he says softly, completely different from his usual demeanor, and I feel the warmth of his breath against my lips. "Or maybe you won't be going home tonight."

I know it's dangerous to even consider his proposal, but Odhran attracts me like a magnet.

It's ridiculous how feeling my heart race makes me completely excited.

I've never experienced this except with this Irish bastard, which only shows that my intellectual and emotional intelligence don't go hand in hand.

I should run, but I know that even if the building exploded, I wouldn't back down, because all I can think about is how much I want his mouth on mine.

He wraps a strong arm around my waist, making me feel small and vulnerable, eliminating any chance of escape, but even though our lips are already brushing against each other, Odhran doesn't kiss me.

I lean in and give a light bite to his lower lip. I had closed my eyes, but I open them again and look at him.

"I don't even know how to start seducing you."

"Start? Just breathing near me makes my blood boil, Elaine."

The insecurity disappears, replaced by desire, and in the last second before starting the kiss, I find myself thinking that I'm making the biggest mistake of my life.

But it will be the most delicious one as well. That, I have no doubt.

I wanted to prove to myself that the chemistry between us isn't that strong, but I'm now sure that being with Odhran will be a point of no return.

"Still want to run?" he asks, after I touch his lips and pull away slightly.

"No, I want more of you."

It's as if my answer is his trigger, as his hand moves to my neck and he claims my mouth in an intense and passionate way.

Every cell of mine feels his heat and strength; Odhran's breathing is rapid.

I give in to the kiss like I don't remember ever doing in my life, letting the overwhelming desire envelop me in its tempestuous wave.

I know he's wrong for me, but I also know I don't want to be in anyone else's arms but his.

The dangerous Irishman has awakened something I didn't know existed, a hunger and need that leaves my body on fire.

As our mouths consume each other in wild caresses, I allow myself to live this madness, letting lust consume me completely.

Chapter 20

Odhran

"I'm assuming we have a deal," I say, my voice coming out like a growl, because the desire this woman has stirred in me is fierce and has brought a barbaric side, which I keep relatively hidden, to the surface.

"Hummm..." she moans as I bite her neck.

"Answer me."

"We can discuss the terms later, but yes, we have a deal."

I almost smile at her audacity.

Elaine is feisty even when she's crazy with desire.

"There's nothing to discuss; you're mine until I say otherwise."

Her body stiffens, but she doesn't try to escape, because she's smart and knows she doesn't hold the best cards right now.

Elaine desires me, but she also hates me.

Unfortunately for her, she needs me.

"I accept your indecent proposal as long as you don't go with anyone else while we're together. If you 'get tired' of me tomorrow or the day after, we still have a deal. You'll continue pretending to be Jax's father and protecting us," she pauses and looks at me, the challenge shining in her eyes, "until I say enough."

"We could expand our terms, but I assume you don't want to share me," I say, more to provoke than because I'm thinking about being with someone else.

She's right when she says I don't stay with the same woman for a long period, but I never wanted one I couldn't have, and Elaine has been escaping my bed for two years.

"We only share or not share what belongs to us. You're not mine, just as I'm not yours. What we're doing is a mutual agreement of protection versus pleasure."

"You're a liar, Elaine, and I'm going to prove it to you. In our deal, you'll have my protection, but I'll force you to admit that you want this as much as I do, which means it will be for your pleasure as well."

She opens her mouth, and I know something thorny is coming, so I don't give her time to protest.

I spread her legs further and turn her back to me, making her ass fall onto my hard cock.

I don't want to fuck her in this office, with several assholes just a door away, because when I have her under me, thighs and pussy open to receive me, I want to hear her moans of pleasure.

I can't leave here right now. Of the family, I'm the only one in Boston today, and the fight will begin soon.

However, I know I can't just let her leave without making her come.

I grip her neck with one hand and force her to turn her face towards me, my tongue invading her mouth as soon as I reach it. My other hand slides down her abdomen to her breasts. She didn't put the jacket back on, so I have free access to the breasts that left me drooling when she did the unexpected striptease.

I grip one, then the other, my thumb rubbing against the hard nipple. Elaine gasps, pushing back, and perhaps unconsciously, she rubs against my shaft.

I squeeze the hard bud until I hear her moan in a mix of desire and pain.

Her breasts are heavy with desire, and without stopping kissing her mouth, I slide my other hand in front of her jeans, between her thighs. The jeans are so tight that I feel the outline of her pussy and press my middle finger against her clit, until I hear her moan my name.

Her breathing shifts into a gasp of pure desperation.

"Does it hurt, baby? Do you need to come?"

"I hate you."

"But you want me."

She's trembling in my arms, her surrender awakening my madness. I barely touched her and Elaine responds with such raw desire to my assault that makes me yearn to fuck her right here, like a damned inexperienced teenager.

I don't stop kissing her as I use one hand to lower the strap of her top and pull down the bra until the deliciously soft skin is at the mercy of my touch.

I undo the button of her jeans, and she stops kissing. I can feel the battle between tension and the need for the pleasure I can give her.

"You don't have to be a good girl with me. I'll never judge you. It's all about our desire, princess."

"I'm not like that."

"Like what? Delicious?"

"Are you joking with me?"

"No."

"What I meant is that I'm not casual, Odhran. Your proposal is wild, but I'm not a liar, I want you too. But not here."

"I just want to give you pleasure. As a gentleman, I can't let you go home with your pussy throbbing with desire. Let me make you come."

"You're not a gentleman. A gentleman would never say something like that."

"I'm the one who's going to give you everything you've never had in bed, Elaine."

"Is this a test?"

"What?"

"If I say no, our deal won't be valid?"

"It's not about the deal. I want to feel you. The agreement is already made, I'm not backing down now, so stop thinking so much and let me give you what you're craving."

She spontaneously turns her face back and kisses me, and I take it as a yes.

I finish lowering the zipper and pull her pants down a little, but not the panties, because I can still feel her tension.

What's happening between us now is new to my world. I never stay just on foreplay, and when I'm with a woman, 100% of the time, she's more than willing to let me do whatever I want with her.

Elaine's sudden shyness, the way she gradually surrenders, surprises me as hell and only heightens my desire even more.

She deepens the kiss, as if she's starving.

"Suck my tongue. Suck it nice."

She does so lightly, but when I slide my hand inside her panties, Elaine becomes wild, sucking with enthusiasm.

"Don't provoke me. You have no idea how much I'm holding back."

"Mmm..." she moans, not realizing the danger she's in.

I touch her clit, playing with the hard little button, caressing it lightly, but when Elaine bites me hard, I slip my fingers to her entrance.

She's soaked, and when I insert my index finger, her legs tremble and she presses even more against me.

She moans into my mouth, and when my other hand moves up to caress her breast, she loses control completely.

"You're a turn-on, baby. So wet for me. Ride my fingers, Elaine. Show me what you want."

I could make her come very quickly, but perhaps I've discovered a masochistic side of me, because I like watching her pleasure.

She spreads her thighs as much as her pants allow, giving me more access, and as I start fingering her, she rides my hand, her teeth marking my lips as her desire intensifies.

I go back to touching her clit, and one of her arms rises, reaching my neck. She grips my hair, trembles against me, whimpers my name until her body succumbs to pleasure, leaving my hand completely soaked with her orgasm.

"I need to lick that pussy."

I kiss her mouth once more, determined to lay her on the desk to quench my thirst, but as soon as I have her in the position I want, I hear Keiron's voice calling me from outside.

"Not now!" I shout, pissed off, but by this time, Elaine is already up, getting dressed, her face flushed, I think both from pleasure and embarrassment.

She looks on the verge of a panic attack.

"No one's coming in without my permission."

She doesn't say anything, and I decide to see what the hell Keiron wants, because I know the moment is lost for now.

"Don't leave here. I'll be right back."

Chapter 21

Elaine

I locked myself in the bathroom after Odhran left the office, shame spreading through every drop of my blood as I realized that after fleeing from him in the past, I ended up in exactly the same role I promised myself I would never occupy: just another name to be crossed off the extensive list of the Irish mobster.

I wished there were a window in the bathroom because although it was humiliating, I would escape through it without a second thought. Anything is more dignified than facing Odhran and seeing in his arrogant gaze the certainty that I'm no different from all the women he's had before.

I wash my face and try to calm myself, preparing to face the inevitable, when a knock on the door startles me.

"Elaine?"

"I'll be out in a moment."

I look at myself in the mirror and to my surprise, I don't see anything different from what I imagined. I'm still the same Elaine as always, maybe a bit flushed, my eyes still shining from the recent orgasm, but other than that, I'm the same person.

"Open the damn door or I'll break it down."

I comply, but I don't look at him. I focus on his broad chest.

"Don't you know the concept of privacy?" I ask, bringing anger to the forefront, as I prefer it to the shame.

I'm ready for a fight because I don't want Odhran to see my vulnerable side, but as soon as I look at him, I know something is very wrong.

"We need to get out of here."

"What?"

"You've entered my world, and not only that, you want a role, even if temporary, within it, so it's time to face reality."

"What does that mean?"

"I'm not going to give you details, just that we're about to suffer an attack from an enemy organization."

I don't even have time to panic because maybe seeing the shock on my face, Odhran gives me no choice, grabbing my hand and already starting to lead me out of the room.

On the way, he grabs my bag, and then we head to the back of the warehouse.

When I arrived, the place was already full. Normally, about three hours before the fights, people start arriving to chat and drink. Now, however, the atmosphere feels ominous. Only a few men are scattered around, and all, without exception, have weapons in their hands.

"What's happening, Odhran?"

"I've explained what I could. Understand one thing. Regardless of our deal and your status in my life, the Syndicate's matters will never be shared between us."

I swallow hard. For the first time since I've known him, it's not the Mad Lion who's in front of me, the hot Irish bad boy with a reputation for having an unpredictable temper. It's Odhran O'Callaghan, one of the men who belongs to the Irish Syndicate's royalty, a cruel and frightening killer.

As we grow up, we're taught to fear monsters, but what about when we have to choose between the bad and the worse?

Because I have no doubt that I'm not running from a monster to the arms of a hero. I'm fleeing from evil to seek refuge with a villain.

I let him lead me, although seeing the weapons in his men's hands makes me feel a bit dizzy, as if I'm part of a virtual reality.

It's incredible that even after spending years in the Syndicate's fight world, I had never seen one of the O'Callaghan's men armed, and I've just concluded that I'm not as tough as I thought.

"Elaine?" Odhran calls me, and only at this moment do I realize that we're already outside.

"I..."

"Now is not the time to disconnect from the world around you," he says, urgency evident in his voice. "You need to pay attention and do everything I say."

"I'm listening."

"Keiron will go with you to get your son. He'll take them to a safe place. I'll get there as soon as I can."

"Safe place? But why? No one knows who I am!"

"We have a deal, and if you want me to protect Jax, pretending he's mine, it will be on my terms. Make up your mind."

I know I don't really have a choice, but the point is: do I *want* to? I've been running for a long time and I'm tired of being scared.

"We have a deal. I'll do whatever you say."

"Keiron!" he shouts, but without breaking eye contact. "Don't leave his side until I get there."

"I can't leave Hestia behind!"

"Who is Hestia?"

"Jax's nanny, and a good friend too."

"Is she trustworthy?"

"Completely. She's like a mother to me."

"Alright. Take the three of them to my building, Keiron. I'll send another half dozen men to watch over them."

SINCE THE MOMENT WE left the warehouse, I've felt like I'm in an action movie.

After giving me a helmet, Keiron told me to hop on the back of his motorcycle. Instead of taking the road, he drove into a trail through the forest at the back of the warehouse, which made it clear that this was an escape route, already prepared for a situation like today's.

I had to wake up Jax, but Hestia was already awake, probably waiting for me.

We hadn't even unpacked, so we only had to gather a handful of belongings before we could leave again.

When we arrived at the building's entrance, a van was waiting for us, and as it drove through the streets of Boston, I kept my sleeping son pressed against my chest, my heart racing, praying to God that I had made the right choice for all three of us by asking Odhran for help.

Chapter 22

Odhran

We all knew this would happen sooner or later.

From the moment those damned Sicilians crashed a meeting between us and the Russians, organized by Ruslan so we could find a way to keep the peace since my cousin Lorcan got a Russian mafia princess pregnant, Yerik and Cillian had formed a temporary alliance and war with the Sicilians was declared.

Thus, my only concern was getting Elaine out of here, as when Keiron called me, he had already canceled the fights for the night and left only the soldiers in the warehouse.

The Italians think they're so clever, but what they might not realize is that we have spies embedded in the Cosa Nostra. We weren't sure when the attack would happen, but last week, before going on vacation, Cillian had warned me about the possibility they'd try something while I was alone in Boston.

As soon as I saw Elaine leave on the back of Keiron's bike, I prepared for what I was sure would be a massacre. I don't intend to leave more than one damn Sicilian alive. Just the one I'll interrogate, and after I get what I need from him, I'll send him back to his boss in pieces.

The air inside the warehouse is charged with the electricity of impending tension, everyone ready to counterattack the Sicilians.

My men are moving frantically, loading their weapons, checking ammunition, and inspecting knives.

We're used to violence, to brutality, but this time we're facing an adversary who dared to step onto our territory, determined to destroy us.

What they don't know is that we are never unprepared and never underestimate an enemy either.

I look around knowing that every man here with me will only stop fighting if he's dead. Surrender will never be an option.

When Keiron told me he got the information from Kellan that we were going to be invaded, he had already, even before talking to me, organized everything.

If we make it out alive today, I have no doubt Cillian will promote him.

I know that tonight, regardless of the outcome, marks the beginning of a war. A lot of blood will be spilled from both the Italians and our men, and if there isn't an agreement in the end, in a few months, we'll all end up dead on both sides.

My secondary phone rings. It's only used to talk to my brothers and Lorcan, so I know I need to answer.

"I'm arriving in Boston in half an hour. Try not to die before then. How did Kellan find out?" my cousin asks.

"That doesn't matter right now. They'll be here any moment."

"Yerik needs to be notified. We made a deal to face the Sicilians together."

"I know. Cillian isn't happy about it, but since the sons of bitches decided to attack both organizations at the same time, it seems fair that they get double the retaliation."

"Odhran, if it's not possible to kill them, don't play the fucking superhero. Get out of there, and then we'll get them back."

"I'm not leaving until there isn't a damn Sicilian left breathing. Hurry up or you'll miss the party, cousin."

"Crazy bastard. Cillian will tear your head off if he knows you're playing the suicidal hero."

"He'll only be able to do that if I'm still alive. I need to go. I'm hearing movement outside."

Seconds later, as if to confirm what I said, the sound of gunfire erupts, and I crouch behind boxes that have always been strategically placed for a potential invasion.

Ten minutes pass and the smell of blood is in the air; bodies are piling up wherever I go, and as I hunt for the one I want to interrogate, the man leading the operation, I shoot a son of a bitch with a bullet wound in his neck, from which thick blood is oozing.

I'm not usually this generous in hastening the enemy's end, but I want to start the interrogation quickly so we can clear the place.

I bend down to close the eyes of one of my soldiers who was killed, and just as I'm about to stand up again, intuition tells me to look up at the exact moment a damned Italian points a gun at me, but I'm faster and still crouched, I trip him, knocking him to the ground.

A shot from his pistol echoes through the air, and he looks at me as I rise; I aim for his heart and pull the trigger.

As a precaution, I step on his neck until I hear the snap that tells me life has left him.

There are at least half a dozen of my soldiers down, but I don't see any Italians. And then, suddenly, almost out of the warehouse, I feel a sharp pain burst in my shoulder.

I know I've just been stabbed. It's not the first time, and the adrenaline of battle overrides the surprise. I spin around, the knife still embedded in my flesh, and fire a shot into the enemy's face.

"Boss!" one of my men shouts.

"I'm fine. Don't stop until only the leader is left."

"There's no one else. We've already taken the bastard somewhere else. We need to get that knife out, Odhran."

"Do you know any fucking first aid?"

"Yeah, I was a scout."

Despite the fucking pain, I laugh.

"And you ended up with us?"

"I didn't say I was a *good* scout."

"FUCK!" LORCAN, KELLAN, or both growl upon hearing that I've been stabbed.

"We don't have time for chit-chat. It was a knife wound, so what?"

"Are you fucking crazy?" my middle brother yells, but then makes a hand gesture. "No need to answer. It's clear you're a fucking lunatic. You should have followed protocol and stayed out of the middle of the war."

"And let my men die at the hands of the enemies?"

He doesn't answer because he knows he can't. In my place, both he and Lorcan would have done the same.

"I'll handle the interrogation," Kellan says. "You go home and take care of that shoulder."

"I'm not going anywhere until I know all the details about today's operation."

Cillian just called and said he's coming back to Boston but will leave Orla, Juno, and their child in the Caribbean for precaution.

"Our Boss will arrive in a few hours," I continue, "and you can bet that as soon as we meet, I'll have every fucking answer he needs."

Chapter 23

Odhran

"Go take care of that shoulder or Orla will be back in Boston as soon as she finds out you've been stabbed," my brother Cillian says. "I don't want her or Juno here right now."

He tries to keep a neutral tone, but I know he's utterly furious, not just because of the attack we endured, but also because he feels responsible for me.

Cillian and Kellan, I'm sure, blame themselves for not being with me when our parents died. More than once, both have tried to investigate what that did to me, but whenever they bring it up, I change the subject.

I don't like to recall that day or the look in my mother's eyes as she fell to the ground, bleeding, her arms still outstretched in my direction, trying to protect me.

Remembering my father, my dead hero, still brings nightmares to the surface after all these years.

My brothers don't need to know about that shit or that every time enemy blood—any enemy's blood—is spilled, I feel like I'm honoring our parents.

An hour ago, I finished with the Italian. By now, he's already having his first audience in hell.

The man didn't reveal anything we didn't already know: that they were sent on a suicide mission to kill as many of us as they could.

However, there's one thing he told me, after hours of persuasion, during which I broke both his legs and all the fingers on one hand, among other fun things, that I know will make both Cillian and Yerik completely paranoid once we, Lorcan, and Kellan, who stayed with me the entire time watching the interrogation, reveal it.

"I'm not done with our conversation yet," I say to my brother, who landed just a few minutes ago.

Cillian knows me as well as he knows himself and can tell from just a glance that I've discovered something serious.

"What is it?"

"They're coming after the women and heirs."

"What the fuck are you talking about?" My brother stands up from the meeting table, his face completely disturbed. "We have a fucking pact about this. They can't break that agreement!"

I watch him pace back and forth, hands in his hair, as he thinks about what to do.

"We'll have to set up a meeting with Yerik. There's no other way. If they're disrespecting the pact they made with Ruslan years ago, no one is safe."

I know what he's talking about. There isn't a single organized crime member in the world who doesn't know about this agreement.

Ruslan Vassiliev isn't just a former Pakhan of the Russian mafia; he's a legend among all criminal organizations worldwide.

In the past, his wife, Iris, was caught in an ambush. She and their adopted daughter nearly died—in fact, until recently, we were certain she was dead—but what happened was that, due to losing the baby she was expecting during that attack, she fell into a coma and then into deep depression, hiding from the world.

Ruslan let everyone believe he lost her when, in reality, she lived for years, completely removed from society.

When Iris Vassiliev was targeted, the planet went to war, and legend has it, although no one is sure, that Ruslan kept the man who attacked his wife imprisoned for years until she came out of the coma. Only then did he end the miserable life of the attacker.

From that moment on, an agreement was made among all the mafias in the world.

Wives and daughters are untouchable. Male descendants, however, don't have that same privilege. Still, until now, everyone has maintained the policy of good neighborliness.

The war is fought between adults, never with children and teenagers involved. Until now, the only ones who dared to challenge this deal were the fucking *Morales*, and that's why they're all dead.

I look at Cillian and see that he can only think about the heir, Luke. Like Yerik, both firstborns of the two organizations are boys.

"Juno won't return until this is resolved."

"It could take years," Lorcan says.

"It doesn't matter. I won't put my family at risk."

"I vote for us to decimate the carcamanos," Kellan says.

"Maybe we don't need to," I say. "It's possible that the higher-ups in the Cosa Nostra don't even know about this order regarding the deaths. Let's keep everyone on high alert for now until we meet with the Russians, but this plan might not have come from the top. They also have a lot to lose. If they break the agreement, they will become an organization against all others in the world. For every one of our heirs they take, we'll kill two of theirs."

"It won't come to that," Cillian says. "I'll arrange the meeting with Yerik as soon as possible. They're not expecting us to organize ourselves so quickly, but I already have a plan."

"What are you thinking?" Lorcan asks.

"We'll strike all the seconds in command of the Cosa Nostra. A coordinated attack. We kill them all in the same night, and our message will be sent."

"And if they don't back down?" I ask.

"Then they'll be decimated."

I DISMISS, WITH A NOD, the soldiers who followed me to my building to ensure there were no more traps.

I ended up being away for two days because there was much to resolve with the Sicilians.

I know there are more of my men on the fire escape and at the back exit of the building. I had them stay here to look after Elaine and the boy.

I don't like elevators. I actually don't like any small spaces, so I take the stairs.

With each step, the stitches from the fucked-up former scout pull, and all I want is to get under the shower and wash the grime from my body.

No. What I really want, for now, I can't have.

If I gave in to the desire, I would go to the apartment across from mine, where I had it installed.

Is Elaine sleeping at this hour? Of course, she is. She's safe, as is Jax, and for some reason I can't understand, the thought gives me a sense of peace after these days filled with death.

On my floor, I reach out to enter the code on the panel that will open the door, but before I complete the movement, a noise behind me makes me turn, the gun already cocked to blow the enemy's head off.

"It's me!" she says, pale, as I stop with the revolver, purely out of reflex, aimed between her eyes.

I think any normal woman would run in this situation. However, she welcomes the danger and instead of backing away, even though I haven't lowered the gun yet, she comes into my arms.

I put the gun away and twist her hair in my fist, forcing her to tilt her head back and look at me.

"Don't ever do something like that again. If I had shot you, it would haunt me for the rest of my days."

I see fear and confusion in her eyes, and it breaks my self-control.

Her sweet scent, a mix of soap and skin, fills my nostrils, and I don't think about what I'm doing when I pick her up, forcing her to wrap her legs around my waist, and take her mouth in a deep kiss.

Chapter 24

Elaine

Minutes Earlier

I pace back and forth in the apartment's living room where we've been brought.

It's already early morning, two days have passed, and after tossing and turning in bed for hours, I've finally made peace with the fact that I won't be able to sleep as long as I'm not sure that Odhran is alive.

I could lie to myself and say that the fear I'm feeling, that makes my stomach twist in knots, is because if anything happens to him, Jax and even Hestia and I will be lost, but I know that my fear has nothing to do with us. We're safe.

It's for him that I'm anxious.

Keiron, besides making sure we arrived here without any risk, arranged for enough food to feed a battalion.

Every night, the bodyguards looking after us show up with a special dinner, but they don't give me what I want most: news of Odhran.

A few hours ago, Jax woke up excited by the smell of pizza, tonight's dinner, and after eating a ton of carbs, went back to sleep. Hestia went to keep him company and if I had any sense, I should follow their example, but I can't because the thought of Odhran being shot or worse makes me sick with fear.

I walk to the window and, as if by cosmic alignment, see several vehicles approaching the building, and somehow, I'm certain it's him.

"Don't go there, it's the worst thing you could do," the voice of reason advises, but I know that at this moment, I'm a hundred percent emotion.

I just want to be sure he's okay. Then I'll go back and finally be able to rest.

I walk to the door and press my face against it, listening for the slightest sound on the other side, and when the silence is finally broken by the sound of footsteps, my heart races.

I unlock the door without even knowing if it's really Odhran who has arrived, but when I see the broad back covered by the leather jacket, and the well-defined ass and thighs in jeans, I let all the anxiety I've been feeling surface and move towards him.

I take just one step, and then, I'm breathless when I see him aiming a gun at my head.

Adrenaline floods my body.

Until now, I've avoided Trevino because I knew he was evil incarnate and dangerous, but I never imagined how I would feel on the day a gun was pointed at me.

"It's me!" I say, feeling my whole body trembling.

Odhran still doesn't lower the gun, perhaps because I've caught him by surprise, but what shocks me more is the fact that my legs, as if self-commanded, walk towards him.

But it's not enough and I embrace my particular monster, trusting my intuition that he would never hurt me.

He puts away the gun and wraps an arm around my waist, keeping me pressed against him, and with the other, grabs my hair so tightly it stings with pain.

He forces me to look at him.

"Don't ever do something like that again. If I had shot you, it would haunt me for the rest of my days."

The tremors in my body increase and now I'm not sure if part of them is due to fear of Odhran.

I try to pull away, I want to retreat, run. I'm good at that, but before I can move, he lifts me up, kissing me as if the taste of my mouth were his sustenance.

I grab his hair, pulling him closer, the need pulsing in every part of my body, and when several minutes later, he pulls back so we can catch our breath, a smile as wicked as it is sexy spreads across his lips.

The attraction I feel for him is uncontrollable and Odhran knows it. His eyes, usually a deep blue, are almost black, and despite his mouth still smiling, his body is tense with rigidity.

"I should run."

"You came into my arms. Too late, princess."

I know he's dark and by intuition, wild in bed as well, but I don't want to leave. For the first time in my life, I'm sure that I'm in the right place and that leaving will be the biggest mistake I could make.

Odhran

I'M NOT MYSELF WITH her.

Elaine brings out things in me that no other woman has.

I want to rip her clothes off and take her standing up, against the door of my apartment. At the same time, I also want to savor her slowly, tasting every inch of her body that belongs to me.

"For a set period of time," a voice warns, but I ignore it, possessiveness and lust coursing through my blood in massive doses.

"It's just sex," I tell myself.

So why, when the conversation today turned to the Sicilians hunting Syndicate heirs and women, was all I could think about tearing the head off anyone who dared touch a hair on her or Jax?

Violence has been a longtime companion, but this territorial feeling, this animalistic urge to mark and protect her, is not something I've ever experienced before.

Did she notice that I brought her to my apartment?

"Do you know where we are?" I ask, our lips still pressed together.

"In your place."

"I'm giving you a chance to escape, princess. If you want to lie to yourself and deny what your body wants, now's the time."

"You're right. I'm too scared to admit it, but don't stop touching me, because with you, I feel alive. I don't know if I was ever alive before having your hands on me."

Elaine

ODHRAN DOESN'T SPEAK and for several seconds, just looks at me in the semi-darkness of the apartment.

Insecurity threatens to surface.

Did I give him more than he was expecting?

God, why did I say something like that?

Because it's the purest truth.

Embarrassment hits me from head to toe, but suddenly, like a wild animal suddenly freed, he starts kissing me with even more passion than before.

The hunger with which he devours me makes me feel completely overwhelmed by his intensity.

His tongue enters my mouth, tasting me with such sensuality that I feel my sex pulse in anticipation.

The kiss is carnal, challenging, and obscene.

It's as if he's telling me with his body that after him, all others will be erased, mere sketches compared to his perfection.

Chapter 25

Odhran

Her skin burns in my hands and I can't stop kissing her. I grip her thighs and position her barely-covered sex against my cock, feeling how it makes me hard.

I lay her down on the first surface I find, the dining table in the living room, and turn on the light.

I throw my jacket and then my shirt on the floor.

I feel my wound pulling again, but nothing could stop me now.

I lean over her, kissing her mouth again, and Elaine wraps her thighs around my back.

She is delicate, soft, pure silk, and I love our contrast, even though she has to spread her legs wide for me to settle between them.

I lay my body over hers, letting her feel my weight against her softness.

Elaine moans into my mouth, bites me, scratches my back, calls my name.

She digs her nails into my forearms, and I sense it's because she doesn't know how to handle her own desire.

I grind my cock against her pulsing pussy, but when she arches, looking fucking gorgeous, needy and fully surrendered, my lust reaches a breaking point and I tear her pajama top, destroying it completely.

I lower myself and lick her nipples, eager to taste her. I suck her breasts with such hunger that I'm sure she'll have hickeys on her silk skin tomorrow.

I pull down her shorts and panties, and a rough groan escapes me when I look down and see her pussy dripping with excitement.

I run my thumb down from her clit to her entrance.

"Fuck, you're so hot!"

I dive into that paradise, hungry to taste her nectar, and thrust my tongue into her tight entrance, while my thumb makes her scream as it moves over her hard clit.

I use my free hand to squeeze her breasts. I don't remember ever feeling such urgency for a woman.

I want to be inside her everywhere, possess her completely, showing Elaine that every part of her belongs to me.

"I'm going to fuck your mouth, your ass, and your pussy. I'm going to make you come so good you'll never want anyone else."

Elaine

I FEEL HIS ROUGH HAND touching my breasts and abdomen as his tongue dives deeply inside me.

With every part of me that Odhran touches, he sets my body on fire, as if my flesh is being consumed by traces of flames.

The way he touches me is urgent. It's not about inexperience; it's a deliciously rough caress from a man who knows what he wants and what he needs to do to get it.

His lips consume mine, the pressure of his mouth combined with his stubbled face driving me absolutely wild.

I feel the orgasm building in my lower belly; the tension, born from need, making me beg for more.

"Scream for me, Elaine. Tell me what you want, baby."

"Everything, Odhran. Anything, as long as it's with you."

"*Only with me,*" he growls, and now he's feeding on my sex with his mouth open, his cruel tongue not giving me any rest.

I arch my back, leaning toward him, and my feet use his shoulders so I can offer myself more and more to my Irishman.

Without any warning, my climax explodes in his mouth and I scream his name as the most libidinous pleasure spreads through me.

The orgasm is so intense that I don't know how long I keep my eyes closed. When I open them again, Odhran is looking at me in a way I can't decipher.

Odhran

FOR TWO YEARS, I REMEMBERED her as the most beautiful woman I had ever laid eyes on.

I was wrong. Elaine isn't beautiful; she's perfect, my personal goddess.

So beautiful that she makes me feel filthy, coming from my world of decay, and if there were a single good bone in my body, I'd send her home and still keep my word to protect her, but now that I've tasted her, there's no chance of that happening.

I won't back down from the deal. She is mine for as long as I want.

I kiss her again and hold both of her breasts in my hands. As I massage her nipples with my thumbs, she almost jumps off the table.

I lower myself to inhale her female scent and go down on her again because my hunger is far from satisfied.

She comes again, and I don't stop sucking her until there's not a drop of her arousal left.

"I want you in my bed, Elaine. Don't leave tonight."

"Hestia..."

"She's safe, as is your son. Tonight, you're all mine."

I pick her up and carry her to the bedroom. I lay her down on my bed, and for a moment, I'm confused by how perfect she looks there.

I don't bring women home. Sex and intimacy are not synonyms. I've never spent the whole night with one either, but tonight I know I'll break every one of my rules.

"Don't move."

"Where are you going?"

I hesitate about telling the truth, but I'm not one for sugarcoating things.

"I need to take another shower. I've done it in the office, but..."

"What?"

"Don't panic, but I got stabbed. I don't want to risk bleeding on you."

"*Stabbed?*"

She stands in front of me, completely naked, perhaps forgetting she's exposed. The way she feels comfortable with her own body excites me even more.

"It wasn't the first time. It won't be the last."

"Where?"

"Almost on my shoulder. It's already fine. I had stitches. It was two days ago."

She moves to my back, and I hear a sound like a wounded animal when she sees the bandage.

"My God!"

Her voice trembles, and I pull her forward against my body.

"That's what I meant when I asked if you knew what it meant to be part of my world, Elaine."

"I'm not part of your world. I'm temporary."

I've killed and tortured over the past two days. I've been stabbed and seen my men die, and none of it has made me lose my mind, but now, the possibility that she might be saying goodbye while I feel my blood and senses saturated by her is enough to bring my madness to the surface.

"You're not running away," I say, reaching my limit. "Temporary or not, you're mine."

Chapter 26

Odhran

S he bites her lower lip as if she's controlling herself not to say something.

"Did you hear what I said?"

"No protection deal would make me be here if I didn't want to. I would never want such an arrangement with Kellan or Keiron."

"Because you know you're mine, woman."

I make her walk backward until she falls onto the bed.

Still standing, I pull her thighs over my shoulders, leaving her lying diagonally.

Looking at her, I touch her clitoris until I feel her getting wet again.

Elaine moans but can do nothing but that. She's completely at my mercy.

"What do you want?"

"Please."

"*Please, eat my pussy because I'm dying to come again?*"

Her cheeks turn very red, but she doesn't deny it, and in a move that catches her off guard, I spin her around, putting her on all fours.

I lick her sex and the entrance to her ass.

"I'm going to take every piece of you, princess."

I lower myself to suck her, but stop, take some of her nectar with my thumb, and press my finger into her ass.

She goes rigid, but when I start sucking her again, it isn't long before she's pushing back, giving herself to me entirely. This time, I don't let her come.

I turn her back around, laying her on the bed.

I finish undressing and, standing in front of her, I slowly masturbate my cock.

"Spread your legs wide, Elaine. Let me see that pussy. I'm dying to bury myself deep inside it."

She spreads them, not completely, but I grab her ankles and place them at the distance I want.

I lean over her and pinch one of her nipples, tweaking it as punishment for disobeying me.

Instead of complaining about the rough touch, she makes a delicious sound, and I take in a whole breast.

I swirl my tongue around the nipple and insert one finger, then another, between the slick folds of her arousal, never taking my eyes off her face.

She moans and traps me inside her body, tight and warm.

Pulling my fingers out, I use my thumbs to spread the lips of her pussy.

I invade her with my tongue while teasing her clitoris, rubbing my teeth against it.

Her hands come to my hair.

She's so sensitive that with every movement of my tongue, she whimpers loudly, begs, pulls my head, asking for more.

I continue sucking her clitoris even as she comes, and she's caught between pushing against me because I believe she's overwhelmed with sexual tension, while her thighs close around my face, forming a prison.

I kiss the inside of her thighs and pull them apart, rising up.

Climbing up her body, I give her a deep kiss, fucking her with my tongue, swallowing her breath while I squeeze both breasts.

She wraps her legs around my waist.

"No. The temptation to fuck you naked is strong, but I don't think we should take risks, and if you keep writhing under me, I won't be able to resist."

I never fuck without a condom because I'm far from being a monk, but today, I wish I could throw that rule out the window.

"You'll take the pill when we're together. I'll get any tests you want, but I need to know what it feels like to fill your pussy and ass with my cum."

"I didn't say I'll..."

"You will. You're going to let me fuck you everywhere, Elaine. I'm going to mark you on every piece."

I know, from the way she looks at me, that she wants a fight, and she's right, because my words require a longer time for both of us than I initially thought, but now I'm sure it will take a few weeks, maybe months, before I'm satisfied with her.

I don't let her retort. I never claimed to play fair, so I kiss her again until that beautiful body is writhing under me once more.

The kisses meld together as neither of us wants to stop, because since we first touched, we've become a necessity to each other.

I suck on her tongue, and she returns the intensity even more.

I kneel on the bed and bring her sitting up.

I grab a handful of her hair.

"I want that pretty mouth on my cock."

She gets on her hands and knees, and I guide my hard shaft to her lips, rubbing the slick head against her mouth.

"I want to fuck your mouth. Not just suck, but really fuck it, like I'm going to do to your pussy."

She tests me gently at first, but after the initial contact, she opens her mouth and starts sucking.

"That's it, suck it good."

I hold her face with one hand and push my hips forward. She's so small compared to me, and only half of me fits in.

I start to fuck her mouth slowly, so she can get used to it.

I go deeper; she gags, pauses for two seconds, then takes me in again, almost all the way.

I tighten my jaw when I hit the back of her throat. My legs are losing strength, overwhelmed by the lust I feel.

I keep going deeper and deeper, holding her hair tightly in my fist.

She has no choice but to let me in, but I'm attentive to her face, making sure it's what she wants.

She moans, whimpers for more, greedy and dirty.

I want to fuck her like this all night, but I need to be inside her pussy the next second or I'm going to go crazy.

"I need to feel you squeezing me, baby. I want to bury myself balls deep in you."

I've never put on a condom so fast in my life.

"Tell me how you want it, Elaine, because I'm on the edge of losing control."

"I want you, Odhran. Your way, like you've been doing so far."

"Promise me you'll tell me if it hurts, because I don't want to hurt you, beautiful."

She's so wet, but I run a finger between the lips of her sex to make sure she's ready for me.

I position the head of my cock and begin to push inside.

Elaine is slippery, wet, sucking me in, though with difficulty, into her body.

I need to force my way through because her pussy is very tight, and her walls close around me.

I pull out and rub the thick tip between her lips.

She calls my name softly and spreads her legs wider, an invitation I can't resist.

I hold her face, looking at her, pull out entirely, and then thrust back in, taking her completely.

I grit my teeth, the desire to fuck her roughly driving me to the brink of insanity.

I capture her lips and kiss her.

I pull out, and when I enter again, she digs her nails into my shoulders, almost on top of the knife wound.

"Sorry," she asks.

"Touch me wherever you want, Elaine. I'm yours."

The pleasure of owning her is wild, impossible to compare to any other sexual experience I've had.

She moves under me, her body writhing, swallowing me with her tight pussy.

The feeling of her squeezing me is delicious. Her breathing is ragged, and her sex contracts in small spasms, as if she's close to coming again.

I grab her hair, forcing her to look at me.

"You're not going to sleep tonight."

I don't know how long she will be mine, but I'm sure I won't be able to let her go anytime soon.

I bury myself in her body, riding her without any restraint now.

Hard and deep.

She trembles, but doesn't ask me to slow down. Using my shoulders as leverage, she lifts her hips, forcing me to give her more.

Her pussy is so wet that the sounds every time I pull out and thrust back in are driving me insane.

Elaine receives me with difficulty but asks for more.

I touch her clitoris, and the contraction around my shaft increases.

I change position, bringing her onto my lap, impaling her on me.

She wraps her legs around my neck and I suck on her breasts, which offer themselves to my mouth as she rides me.

Each rise is torture; she grinds as she rides me, and I hold her, keeping her still on my lap, burying myself balls deep and caressing her clitoris.

The moans are desperate.

Pulling out of her body, I put her on all fours.

I position myself behind her and, with my fingers gripping her hips, I bury myself in her pussy.

I touch her clitoris while I fuck her.

I move inside her with a hard pounding.

I lean forward to caress her breasts, which makes me penetrate her even deeper.

She whimpers as I pinch her nipples. I think they're sensitive from my sucking.

I hold her hair with one hand and increase the speed with which I finger her clitoris, lifting my body to thrust hard.

"Come," I command, fucking her like an animal.

I enter and exit faster and harder until she screams my name, squeezing me inside her.

My cock grows even thicker, and I pound deeper inside her.

I follow her into an intense orgasm, and I'm out of breath for a few seconds, all my senses caught up in the sensation of being buried inside my woman.

"Fuck, baby..."

I kiss her spine and carefully pull out.

I discard the condom and scoop her up in my arms, walking to the bathroom.

"Does it hurt?"

"I still feel you," she says, blushing.

"Tell me if it hurts, my sweet, because I want more, Elaine. I'm starving for you. You have no idea what you got yourself into by entering this arrangement."

Chapter 27

Odhran

"**W**hat's wrong?" I ask as I return to the room and see Elaine standing, wrapped in a sheet.

I kept my promise and spent the entire night savoring every inch of her body, but not because I wanted to prove something to myself, but because she's my addiction.

I left the room about an hour ago. There was a message from my brother asking me to call him because he wanted to update me on the arms shipments that had been made this week in South America.

"Nothing. I just want to leave," she says, without looking at me.

I grip her chin, forcing her to make eye contact.

"Did I hurt you in any way?"

"No."

"I'm not a sensitive guy and I can't read between the lines, Elaine. I'm not going to guess what the hell I did wrong, no matter how hard I try, so could you make things easier for us and tell me the truth?"

She pulls away from my touch and takes a step back.

"I feel like a prostitute."

"What?"

"I'm giving you my body in exchange for protection."

"I'm not paying for it. We have something that interests each other, but just like I didn't force you to come all night, I won't force you to keep having sex with me. I thought we were both together all night. My mistake. Forgive me if I imposed myself on you in any way."

The idea is repugnant to me regarding any woman, but with her? It makes me feel like a scoundrel.

Is that what I did? Did I force her to stay?

Confused as hell, I try to rethink the whole night, but I can't recall a single moment when I wasn't sure that it was as pleasurable for her as it was for me.

Elaine

HE SEEMS GENUINELY offended, and I feel embarrassed. At this point, Odhran is right. He gave me the chance to stop from the moment he touched me for the first time, back in the warehouse office. He didn't just assume I wanted him; he was careful, he asked me. I wanted him. I still want him, so why does what we did feel so wrong?

Because this Irish mobster is a risk to your heart, fool.

Deep down, I always knew that.

I didn't just run away from Odhran when I left Boston. I ran from him from the moment I arrived in the city, when I didn't even know Juno yet, because deep down, I knew that what happened today was inevitable.

"I'll accompany you to your apartment."

"I don't need that. I can go alone."

"As you wish."

"What are you thinking?"

"And what does it matter what I'm thinking? You've made a decision. I don't think there's more to be said," he says, and at this moment, he's not the guy known as Mad Lion, famous for his volatile temper and cruelty. Nor is he the playboy whose women practically throw themselves in front of him as he passes. He looks like Cillian. Serious, with a completely rigid expression, no trace of humor in his features.

Once, Orla told me there was something in common among all her boys, as she calls the three O'Callaghans and Lorcan: that each of them inherited the most important trait of their people, Irish honor. Now I see it firsthand.

"You didn't hurt or force me. I'm just confused."

"Didn't you want what happened?"

"I shouldn't want it."

"Why?"

"Because you're a bad choice."

"I never denied that or tried to pretend otherwise."

"I know. I just don't want to feel like a one-night stand."

"You won't be a one-night stand. We have a deal with no end date yet. Or we did."

"I don't want to break the deal."

"I don't understand, Elaine. I'm many things, but not an abuser. I thought you were with me, enjoying yourself too."

"I enjoyed every second. I just don't want to feel used."

"I don't see you as an object, if that's what you're thinking. Right now, you're the only one I want." He pauses. "For a long time, you've been the only one I want."

"But you let me go."

"Because I didn't want to hurt you."

"And what's changed?"

He takes a step forward, and the urge to pull back is almost uncontrollable, because every time he touches me, I forget how wrong we are for each other.

Odhran tucks a strand of my hair behind my ear.

"I'm tired of fighting my desire for you. You deserve more, and that's why I wanted you to hate me that day at Juno's wedding. The bad news is that that was my quota of generosity for this incarnation. Any good man would let you go. I'm not a good man."

"So we still have a deal, then?" I say, convincing myself that I'm only thinking about Jax.

"No, if fucking me is an obligation or a form of payment."

I bite my lower lip so hard that I don't know how it doesn't bleed.

"It's not forced, but don't hurt me or lie to me. Tell me it's over, but don't parade a woman in front of me."

"Why not?"

"What?"

"It wouldn't matter because the moment I did that, you'd send me to hell, getting rid of me for good. So tell me, princess, why shouldn't I parade another woman in front of you?"

I lift my chin.

"You said I'm yours, even if temporarily. It's mine too. You don't know the concept of fidelity, Irishman, and I don't know the concept of betrayal."

"You're wrong. I know the concept of fidelity. My parents were crazy about each other."

"Then I don't..."

"I will never leave the woman who loves me or my children crying for my death at home, Elaine. I'm not good husband or father material. I'm a killer."

He's showing me an Odhran who is even more irresistible to me than the cruel mobster.

"I'm not going to break the deal, and you, Mad Lion, are going to be faithful to me."

"I don't want another. I'm obsessed with you right now."

I ignore the last part, even though doing so is reckless and stupid.

He presses me against the wall and, with just one hand, holds mine above my head, making the sheet slide to the floor.

"Are you sure this is what you want? Am I what you want?"

"I'm obsessed with you *right now*," I say, emphasizing the last part and giving him a taste of his own medicine.

He nibbles my neck and then licks the same patch of skin.

"Are you sore?"

"In a good way."

He unzips his jeans, and I see he's not wearing boxers, his sex completely hard.

"I'll grab a condom in a moment, but I want to feel you. I'm not going to come."

He slides his rough fingers between my legs, and I close my eyes, my head tilted back.

"I'm obsessed with feeling your pussy without protection."

"It's risky."

"No. I'll be careful. I haven't finished with you yet. I fucked you for hours; now I'm going to take you slowly, savoring every bit of you."

He teases my sex until I feel myself melting for him, and when he lifts me, he doesn't enter me all at once but makes me slide slowly along his length.

The sensation makes me dizzy with pleasure.

The rigid skin is smooth as silk, but Odhran is big and thick, and I hold my breath to manage taking him all in.

Chapter 28

Odhran

I fuck her for several minutes with her thighs clamped around my forearms, lifting and lowering herself on my cock, swearing to myself that I can have some control when it comes to her, but it's a lost battle.

I knew how delicious being inside Elaine was. I spent the entire night possessing her, but when I feel her honey dripping down my cock without the barrier of a condom, my arousal no longer allows any restraint over it.

I start slowly, sliding in without haste, feeling her hungry pussy swallowing every inch of my length, but when Elaine embraces me and kisses me passionately, I know I need more.

I take her to the bed, keeping her legs in the same position over my forearms, as when we were standing, and so, eye to eye, I penetrate her deeply and slowly.

All the while she looks at me, I feel as if an invisible line is connecting the two of us.

It's not just the arousal, it's the smell, the warmth of her skin.

It's her.

Much later, I bring her onto my lap.

She is now riding me. She came twice, and I've been delaying my pleasure because I don't want to leave her pussy.

Beautiful, she throws her head back, surrendered to me, without barriers.

I quicken the pace, fucking her with more greed, pumping inside her, confused by the way I'm feeling, with an overwhelming sense of something nameless spreading through my chest.

I thrust for a long time and she pulses around me. The thrusts become almost cruel, and her moans make me lose control. Until the last second, I take her, but I know I need to stop, and after giving her one last kiss, I rise, coming on her abdomen.

Elaine is with her eyes closed, like a sated goddess, and for several minutes, I watch her.

Two years.

How could I have kept her away for so long?

Kellan was right in saying that I'm not the ideal man for her, but now, sending her away is no longer an option. Not while my hunger remains.

However, even trying to reduce everything to sex, I know that we started something unknown, that neither of us has experienced yet, and that Elaine is as confused about labeling us as I am.

I lie down next to her and turn her perfect face towards me so that I can kiss her.

I feel the intense beating of my own heart as she responds affectionately, her hand touching my jaw.

Elaine opens her eyes and looks at me silently.

"Tell me how to act."

"What?"

"I wasn't lying. I don't know how to be casual, Odhran. Everything with me involves feelings and emotions. You, on the other hand, are an expert at just enjoying and then walking away without looking back."

"Not with you. What happened between us was not a one-night thing."

"But it's not real either."

"It's fucking real."

She sits up, turning her back to me, her long brown hair covering her bare back.

What the hell have I done now? It's the first time I feel something for a woman that isn't purely sexual, and when I put it into words, she goes crazy with me?

"Can you give me a deadline?"

"Deadline?"

"We both know that soon you'll move on. Why don't we agree on an end date in advance?"

"No."

Her refusal makes her get out of bed, and I try to focus on the conversation and not on the round, pert ass that, thanks to its owner, is slipping away from me.

I get out of bed and go after her.

"Do you always run away when a discussion starts?"

She still doesn't turn around. She's standing at the bathroom door.

"What do you want from me, Odhran? I'm fulfilling my part of the deal. You have nothing to complain about."

I grab her shoulders and turn her to face me.

I don't know what I expected to see on her face. Anger, challenge, a thirst for blood—my blood?

Instead, what I notice is fear.

"I can't set a deadline."

"Why not?"

"Because I don't know when I'll get tired of you." She nods and says nothing, but even for me, who am a brute, I know I spoke bullshit. "I don't know if I'll ever get tired of you, Elaine, but I'm sure if it happens, it won't be anytime soon."

She parts her lips and I see she wants to deny what I just said, but I don't allow it, kissing her until her desire for a fight fades.

I hold her neck while taking her mouth, but when I move my hand to the base of her scalp, I feel a thick scar on her head.

Elaine shudders when I slide my finger over the wound and tries to pull away.

"What the hell was that?"

"An injury from the past."

"It's not just a simple injury from the past. Let me see."

"No. Didn't you ever fall when you were a kid?"

"I was the same kind of demon when I was young as I am now, but what I felt on your scalp wasn't just a simple injury. Show me."

She closes her eyes for a moment and then turns her back to me, as if giving me permission to check.

I push her hair back with both hands and when I see the scar I felt earlier, I'm sure it wasn't a simple fall.

"How did this happen?"

"It's the past," she repeats, still with her back turned, but I can see her shoulders trembling. "I'll take a shower before going back to my apartment, okay?"

If she were any other woman, I would agree without a second thought. I've never been involved in the lives of my partners in anything other than what happened between us behind closed doors, but with Elaine, I just can't let it go.

I pick her up, but instead of returning to the bed, I take her to the shower.

"Let's take a shower together. Afterwards, we'll eat something and then you can tell me the story behind this scar."

Even though my desire for her never fades, I don't allow myself to have her again. I wash her body and hair, taking care of her, which is new for me.

All the while, Elaine's eyes never leave me.

"Why are you doing this?"

"Because I can't stop touching you," I explain as best as I can.

Elaine

"I SHOULD GO. AT THIS point, Jax is probably awake."

Odhran lent me a pair of boxers and a T-shirt of his, and now, I sit waiting on a bench in the kitchen island while he prepares our breakfast.

During the night, with the various showers we took, his bandage came loose and now I try to hide a shiver when I see the extent of the knife wound he took.

He's covered in tattoos, but still, I can see unmistakable marks revealing that this man, who is temporarily mine, is not exactly the fairy-tale prince.

He has other scars which I assume are from knives and also one that I think might be from a gunshot.

"I'd like to see him," she says, bringing me back to reality.

"Today?"

He shrugs.

"You want me to pretend he's mine. We need to have some connection to make it seem real."

"Not *that* real."

"What?"

"Don't make him think you're permanent in his life."

Chapter 29

Elaine

I see his expression darken and I don't understand why. Isn't this exactly how he lives his life? No ties or desire to stay?

"He's just a boy, Odhran, and he's never had a permanent male figure in his life."

Instead of my explanation improving his mood, it worsens.

He turns off the stove, where a pan with steaming eggs and bacon waits for us.

"And your ex?"

"I don't want to talk about it. He was a mistake."

"What kind of mistake?"

"What?"

"Was it something serious?"

"I thought we were going to get married."

Odhran

I STARE AT HER, HOPING she's joking, but when almost a minute passes and Elaine looks at me with a neutral expression, I understand she isn't.

"Married? You were going to get *married*?"

At the moment, I don't care that I'm acting like a territorial jerk, but the truth is I can't — or don't want to — imagine Elaine living with another man in a permanent context.

In any context, fuck!

"Yes."

"Were you in love?"

"He was good to me, or at least that's what I thought."

"Tell me more."

"No. It has nothing to do with us."

"Bullshit it doesn't."

She stands up and lifts her chin to confront me.

"Can I ask you about every woman you've slept with in the last two years?"

"I never thought about marrying any of them."

"So what? I don't want to be just a fling in the lives of several men. One day, I will find the one I'll live with forever. I want ties and a home."

Does she realize how much she's revealing and that, for the first time, she's letting me see beyond the goddess façade that fears nothing?

"Why is this important? There are many single mothers who are happy."

Now I'm pushing her on purpose because something tells me that Elaine will never let me see beyond the surface unless she's forced to.

"Because it's everything we didn't have. Because my mother had terrible taste in men. Elysia's father was an alcoholic and mine..."

she pauses as if there isn't enough air in the world to fill her lungs "mine was a bastard who, when bored, used me, the stepdaughter, and Mom as punching bags. You asked about that scar, Odhran? I was thrown by him, like a rag doll, onto a glass table when I tried to protect my sister from a beating. And look, it wasn't the first time, only the one that left a permanent mark, but it's nothing compared to what I have inside here," she says, touching her own chest.

"Elaine."

"I hate you for making me remember," she says, running from the kitchen, but I catch her before she reaches the living room.

"Let me go."

"Let me hold you."

"Why? You don't care. You want my body, and I think for today, the payment has been made."

"Don't talk bullshit like that, damn it! What's happening between us has nothing to do with payments or deals. It was that way when you walked into my office, but from the moment I took that pussy for the first time, I'd chase you to hell if I had to."

"Why? There are plenty of women available."

"I don't want women. I want *the* woman. *You.*"

"Sex."

"Yes, but not just that."

She struggles in my arms.

"Go to hell with your promises. Don't fool me. We are nothing!"

"What do you want from a relationship? Because I've never done this shit before... Laugh if you want, but it's the first time I've had breakfast with a woman. You're the only one who's ever been in my home."

"What?"

I look at her and see millions of questions in her eyes, but before I can respond, the intercom rings, breaking the mood.

"Answer it," she says.

"No, if it were important, they'd call my cell."

"I need to get back home."

"Eat first."

"I've lost my appetite."

This will never work in the long run. I can't even feed her without her wanting to kill me.

Not knowing what to say, I go to answer the intercom and less than a minute later, I return to find her.

Elaine hasn't moved from her spot.

"It was one of my men. Hestia was looking for you and they told her, to calm her down, that you were with me."

I see her face turn tomato red.

"Oh!"

"Did you think you could hide something like that? For me to take on Jax, our relationship will have to become public."

"I need to talk to her first."

"Use the intercom and tell her you'll be there in a minute." I offer my hand in a peace gesture, something unprecedented for me. "Eat with me."

She hesitates and, like a little animal aware of the danger it faces, approaches slowly.

"Don't ask about the past anymore," she pleads, hiding her face in my chest. "I don't like talking about it."

"I saw my parents die. I know all about scars that aren't visible, Elaine. I don't mind learning about yours."

Elaine

I RAISE MY EYES TO meet his.

"Tell me."

"I was there and almost died too. There isn't much to say about it," he says, but I'm sure the opposite is true.

Just like me, Odhran has a side he doesn't show anyone.

"I don't mind learning about yours either," I borrow his words, and to my surprise, he kisses my forehead.

"I want to try something more than the deal, even though I know I shouldn't bring you into my life."

Our minds are selective because the only thing I absorb from what he says is the first part.

"How much more?"

"Let's live. Be mine without the obligation of the deal we made."

I know I'm on the edge of a cliff. I can even see what will happen to me if I fall, if what I'm starting to feel for him isn't reciprocated, and yet, I hear myself say:

"I want more from us both."

"How much more?"

I take a deep breath, panicking because I've never exposed myself so much, but what if he is my only one? What if the man I've been running from, whom I always thought was wrong for me, is my destiny?

"Everything," I confess, taking a leap of faith. "I want a real relationship."

I wait, feeling my heart pound in my throat, not knowing how he will react.

The Odhran I remember from the past two years would laugh at my proposal, but the Irishman in front of me holds my face with both hands.

"I want you. I don't know what to call this. It's new to me, but I know I want you in my life; but you need to know we are in the middle of a war."

"I've always been in a war, Odhran. Maybe not like yours, with guns and knives, but still a war."

"I'm not talking in emotional terms, Elaine, but about real enemies. I will protect you, Jax, and your friend, but the life you've lived until now will cease to exist."

"I know. And still, I will stay."

"Out of fear? Out of the need for protection?"

"For us both. For not wanting to stay away from you."

Chapter 30

Elaine

"I would be lying if I didn't tell you I'm worried," Hestia says as Jax grabs Odhran by the hand and leads him to the bedroom to see his collection of toy cars.

I don't think he remembers the Irishman or anyone else from the past because when we left, he was only two years old and we were away for a long time, but as soon as he saw Odhran, he smiled and started talking as if they were old friends.

I came to find Hestia before Odhran entered our apartment. I asked her to give me some time to explain that we were together, and the Irishman agreed.

I didn't have the courage to say, though, that until a few hours ago, what we had was an indecent arrangement, and now, something unnamed, but Hestia assumed Odhran is my boyfriend and doesn't seem at all pleased about it.

She's already told me about her past. I know she was married twice and that her first husband was abusive. The second one, however, from what she revealed, was a good man who made her happy.

I could see the distrust on her face when I told her about my relationship with Odhran.

"I didn't plan this. I went to the warehouse yesterday looking for protection, but now..."

"Are you in love with him?"

152

"I don't know if..."

"You don't have to answer, Elaine. I know you. I've been around you for years."

"It's stupid of me to fall for him."

"Why?"

"Aside from who he is, he doesn't do long-term relationships."

"My ex didn't either."

"The abuser?"

"No, the good man, my second husband."

"Oh!"

"He was a womanizer and at first, I gave him a hard time. It wasn't on purpose or because I wanted him to chase me, but because I was hurt from my previous relationship. We were together, but I told him not to think in terms of a future for us."

I laugh.

"A phrase men love to say."

"Yes. The fact is he didn't give up. I spent the first year waiting for him to fail me. I almost wished for it because the alternative, thinking I had found the love of my life, was terrifying. I didn't believe that handsome man could be crazy about me."

"But it didn't happen. He never failed you."

"No, and giving him a chance was the best decision I ever made."

"I would have made a gigantic mistake if I had married Claim. And it's not because he's a coward I don't admire, but because he didn't make me feel anything, he couldn't even make my pulse race."

"In that case, I agree. It would have been a huge mistake. Most people say marriage is more friendship than anything else. I disagree. It can be friendship too, but there needs to be fire, passion. You need to look at the person after a while and see that you would still want to be with them if you had the chance to start over."

"I don't think Odhran is a *forever*. He doesn't stay in relationships."

"You can't know that, Elaine. Claim seemed like the perfect man and turned out to be a coward. Maybe your reluctant Irishman, who for no logical reason agreed to pretend to be Jax's father to protect him, is your destiny."

"If that's true, life made me take many turns and come back to the same place."

"I don't believe that. I think things happen when they're supposed to. Did you know I lived two houses away, in my childhood, from my second husband, and we never met?"

"Really?"

"Uh-huh. Only years later, wounded and with no faith in love, did I meet the man who was destined for me. Would we have been together if it had happened sooner? I don't know. Maybe it wasn't our time and we needed to go through everything we did so that when we met, we would have the connection that formed instantly between us."

"Destiny."

"Yes. I believe in it and also that everything happens at the right time. But still, being an old fool and romantic, I'm going to ask you to take care of your heart."

"Maybe it's a bit too late. I can't deny or confirm that I'm in love, but I've never felt anything even remotely like this before."

Odhran

"WHY DO YOU HAVE DRAWINGS on your skin? It looks like a painting."

Jaxton, or Jax as Elaine calls him, is standing in front of me, and I'm sitting on his bed.

"And what do you know about paintings?"

The kid is a character. If Cillian's son is as talkative as Jax when he grows up, my brother is screwed. He talks non-stop, without a break to breathe.

"Mommy has taken me to a place with lots of them. Paintings," he says, pointing to some drawings that I think he made, stuck on the wall near the bed.

"These on my body are tattoos, not paintings."

"I don't have tattoos, but I want to draw too. Can you ask my mom? Will you take me to get a drawing on my hand? Can I get more than one?"

Jesus, if Elaine finds out that in the first interaction with her son after years, he's asking me to give him a tattoo, she's going to kill me.

Jax doesn't give me a chance to answer, apparently already distracted by a scar on my hand, between my thumb and index finger.

He runs his finger over it, feeling the raised surface.

I remember when I got it. I was stabbing a son of a bitch, and the blade slipped, causing the cut.

"Did you fall?"

"No, I cut myself."

"By yourself?"

"What do you mean?"

"I have a scar too, but I didn't fall, a doctor made it on me."

He takes off the shirt he's wearing and points to his chest. For a few seconds, I'm at a loss for words, seeing the cut about ten centimeters long in the middle of his chest.

What the hell is this? Did someone hurt him? I'm going to kill the bastard who did this, damn it.

"Who did this to you, kid?"

"The doctor. It doesn't hurt anymore. I'm just like you. I have a hurt too."

Damn!

"Jax, what are you doing?" Elaine suddenly enters the room, and her voice shows that we're both in trouble.

Apparently, however, the kid knows how to handle his mother better than I do because he gives her a huge smile and runs to hug her.

"Showing my superhero scar to my friend, mommy. I'm just like him," he says, pointing to the healed cut on my hand. "Can I get a painting on my body too? I want to be like Odhran."

Chapter 31

Odhran

"**W**ho did this to him, Elaine?" I ask after we leave the room, barely able to control my fury.

Hestia, the nanny, friend, or whatever she wants to call herself, has come to stay with Jax, and now we're in the apartment's kitchen, while I try to keep my voice low so as not to scare the boy.

"Calm down, it's not what you're thinking, Odhran. Jax was born with a heart condition called pulmonary valve stenosis."

"Explain it to me."

"The pulmonary valve regulates blood flow from the right ventricle of the heart to the pulmonary arteries. Jax was born with a narrowed valve. This condition can be hereditary or congenital, but in his case, I think he inherited it from my sister, as Elysia had the same issue. She never needed surgery, but my son did."

"Why? Is the boy at risk?"

"Not anymore. About six months after I left Boston, he started having trouble breathing, fatigue, and he would put his little hand on his chest, saying his heart was beating too fast. It was palpitations. That's when the doctor decided to operate on him," she says, and I see her eyes well up with tears. "I noticed something was wrong when he was still a baby because Jax had trouble gaining weight, got tired very quickly, and couldn't even run a little without getting out of breath. The doctor I took him to said those were some of the symptoms."

"Did Juno know about this?"

"Yes. I told her. That's why it was a blessing when she asked me to work at the bakery. We got health insurance, and I didn't have to worry about medical expenses anymore."

Damn!

"Did you go through hardships? You told me he needed surgery, but you no longer had the job at the bakery."

I immediately understand that the fear Elaine felt, which made her run away, was very real, and not just the fear of losing custody of Jax. From what I know of her now, she would never put her child's life at risk if there was an alternative other than leaving.

"I saved money. That's how I paid for his surgery."

"I will arrange health insurance for him."

"I'd like to say it's not necessary, but I've exhausted all my savings with the surgery and then fleeing for all this time, so I'm swallowing my pride at this moment. Thank you."

I feel incredibly awkward. I have no idea how much doctors or surgeries cost. I've never had surgery, except for a few patch-ups on my body, and always at the Syndicate's underground clinic, but I imagine what she spent is just a drop in the bucket for me.

I don't want your gratitude or for you to feel obligated to be different with me because I'll keep both of you comfortable.

"You don't need to thank me. I don't do things halfway. We're in this together, Elaine, and even if you hadn't asked me to pretend to be Jax's father, he would still be mine to take care of. How often does he need to see the doctor?"

"Now, every six months, only."

"There's no more risk to his life?"

"No. In mild cases, the child only needs regular check-ups with a cardiologist. According to what the doctor told me, Jax's surgery was successful, and he will grow up leading a normal life, although occasional evaluations are necessary."

"You didn't leave Boston just because Trevino Cabrera wanted custody of Jax."

"What?"

She's as pale as a sheet of paper, and I realize I've hit the nail on the head.

"You told me that working for Juno, you had health insurance for Jaxton. When you fled, you were on your own. You wouldn't put his life at risk if you weren't terrified. The game is up, Elaine. I want to know the whole truth. Why the hell are you so afraid of that son of a bitch?"

"I'm afraid to tell you."

"Why?"

"He's a trusted man of your brother."

"You're not hiding anything from me. If we're going to do this, I need to know even the smallest detail, so right now, you only have one option: either tell me the whole truth, or I'll find out by force."

I give her the illusion of choice when, in fact, there's no turning back. She's mine, and I'll protect her even against Satan himself if necessary.

"It's not a short conversation."

"I'm not in a hurry."

"Let's go to your apartment. I don't want Hestia to hear us. She doesn't know all the details. I thought it best not to tell her to protect her."

I take her hand and lead her to my house.

When we get there, she pulls away from me, sitting in the chair as far from where I'm standing as possible.

Elaine

"I NEED TO TELL YOU from the beginning. Since when my sister wanted to run away. Elysia was dating a guy, as I already told you, but she never told me he was married. I don't think she knew."

"But did she know he was part of the Syndicate?"

"I'm not sure. She only talked to me about him in general terms, without mentioning his name or anything more. At first, he showered her with gifts. For a young woman working as a barista, receiving bags and shoes that cost more than a month's salary must have been quite a temptation, but I'm sure she was in love too. However, even without knowing the man, I was certain that when it happened, I wouldn't like him."

"Why?"

"Because that honeymoon phase didn't last even a month. She would come home after spending the weekend with him very upset, and when I asked about it, she said she didn't know when she would see him again. I think Trevino was lying to her, and because he was married and also lived abroad, his visits weren't regular. Now I know why he never spent special dates with my sister. He had a wife and children."

"Continue," he says, but I can feel the disgust in his voice.

"I think the breaking point was when he only showed up two days after her birthday. Elysia had been acting strange, more and more down, and when, according to her, he didn't even give her a call to wish her a happy birthday, I believe it was the beginning of the end. On the day he finally came to see her, she came home with swollen eyes from crying. There were marks on her skin, on her neck and arms. A cut lip."

"Do you think he abused her?"

"Yes."

I decide to skip the part where I thought my sister wanted to leave because she discovered something related to Trevino, the Salvadoran mafia, and Janice's disappearance.

The man, being a Syndicate lawyer, couldn't have any relation to the "M" of Muerte.

"That same night, she said we needed to run away. I thought he had beaten her and couldn't accept the end of their relationship. We left. We lived in hell for months because she was pregnant and very scared, but my sister was a warrior, and gradually, our life returned to normal."

"How could she have died of an overdose then?"

"I don't believe that for a second," I say, gathering the courage to continue. "I think Trevino killed her."

"Because he couldn't accept rejection?"

"No. Because he thinks Elysia stole from him."

Chapter 32

Odhran

"Explain yourself, Elaine."

"I haven't told you the truth about my encounter with Trevino in the Caribbean, but I will now. However, you need to know something first: my sister wasn't a thief, Odhran. She was needy and had terrible taste in men, but she was never a thief. Whatever Trevino thinks Elysia stole, he's mistaken. It wasn't her."

"I'm listening, Elaine."

"You know when you asked me if I thought my sister was murdered by Trevino? The answer is yes, I do think so."

"What?"

"Elysia never used drugs in her life, and then one day, she goes out to work and dies of an overdose? I'll never believe that. Her father was an alcoholic. That was more than enough lesson for her to stay away from even a regular cigarette, so no matter what the autopsy report says, I'm sure she was murdered. If there were drugs in her system, they were injected into her."

She looks away, her voice coming out with difficulty as if it pains her to talk about it.

I don't know anything about her sister, but I know enough about Elaine to understand that she believes in this theory.

"And do you think it's related to the alleged theft Trevino accused your sister of?"

"Yes. He was probably robbed by someone, and since the rope always breaks at the weakest point, he blamed her, but I know he's wrong. When we met in the Caribbean, he told me, exactly with these words, *'I took a long time to find you, Elaine,'* and something about them finding me through facial recognition. He certainly didn't know I worked for the Syndicate's fights."

"Would your sister have mentioned that?"

"I don't think she said much about me, if she said anything at all, just as the opposite was true. She didn't talk about her boyfriend. Maybe she didn't even mention having a sister, because in the Caribbean, he told me he 'discovered' that Elysia had a half-sister. The fact is, this man thinks she stole from him and now I have the proceeds of that theft, Odhran. On the night of the wedding, he threatened me. He left a note under the door of the bungalow."

"You should have come to us."

"And say what? *'Look, the Boss's right-hand man thinks my deceased sister stole from him and now he's come after me because of it.'*

"Do you think I would have allowed them to hurt you?"

She stands up.

"What did I know about you, other than the fact that you wanted me? Oh, right, and the desire wasn't even that intense, because you left the damn wedding with a blonde!"

I know what she's doing. I can smell the fear from a distance and understand that Elaine is bringing up her anger towards me as a way to protect herself.

"Let's not revisit that. We weren't together back then. Now, we are, and I'll investigate what you just told me."

"So you believe me?"

"I believe you are certain of the truth of what you've told me, but I am a man who has much more reason than emotion inside him, Elaine."

She nods, not looking at me.

"I need to get back to Jax. I also have work to do. I need to find new clients."

"Work?"

She still doesn't look at me.

"I had a profession and I'm good at what I do."

"What?"

"Bridal bouquets. I had built up a good client base before I had to flee South Dakota. It was the place where I lived the longest."

I feel my jaw tighten with tension.

"Was that where you met your fiancé?"

"Yes."

"Why did you break up?"

"You don't want to know."

"I do."

"He broke up with me after someone destroyed the car dealership he owned as a kind of 'message' to me."

"What a cowardly jerk."

"Who can blame him? I'm not worth the risk."

I walk over to her and, even knowing she's angry, pull her into my arms.

"You are worth the risk, and I would never leave you just because someone threatened me if I stayed by your side."

Finally, I have those beautiful eyes focused on me.

"You didn't believe what I told you."

"I've already said: I believe you *think* it's true."

"But..."

"Shhh, my feisty kitty. I'm giving you my word that I will investigate this until I know every detail about Trevino's relationship with your sister and why Elysia fled."

"Really?"

"By my honor, Elaine. I'll get all the answers, but regardless of why Trevino came after you, he won't get near you again. I promise."

"The last time I fled, he or someone under his orders left a blood-covered flower."

"Tell me everything."

She recounts the incident, and I wonder what the hell this son of a bitch thinks Elysia could have stolen that is so important.

Documents? Money? Information?

No, if it were information relevant to the Syndicate, he would have already told Cillian, because it would be a risk to all of us.

"I'll sort this out soon," I say as she finishes, but without letting her go. "So you coming to me had nothing to do with Jax?"

"I don't think he knows about Jax, but I fear that if he finds out, he might harm my son, since he's the product of an affair, or take him from me through the courts to blackmail me."

I don't tell her that this would never happen. It's more likely that Trevino would take her and torture her until she confessed to things she didn't do.

The thought drives me absolutely insane.

"You can't step outside for now. All your outings, as well as Jax's and Hestia's, will need to be authorized by me."

"Because of Trevino?"

I don't like sharing Syndicate information, but to protect her, she needs to know that the danger she's in is real.

"No, because we're at war with another organization. One of their men stabbed me. This isn't a game or a joke, Elaine. They've threatened our women and children. Do you understand that?"

"I need to work. I..."

"No, what you need is to stay alive until I say you're safe. Give me your word."

"Alright."

Chapter 33

Odhran

"**B**efore we talk about the meeting with Yerik, there's something I need to address first."

"Is it about your girlfriend?" Cillian asks.

I had no illusions that both he and Lorcan and Kellan didn't know Elaine was with me when we were attacked and that I had her taken to an apartment in my building.

"Can you just explain how Juno's former employee ended up in your bed?"

"She's mine now," I say simply, and I see the surprise on everyone's faces.

Besides my relatives, Rourke and Keiron are also here.

"What I want to talk about isn't my relationship with Elaine; it's something much more serious."

It takes me almost twenty minutes to explain in detail about her life with her sister and the reason for her disappearance two years ago, but without revealing the name of the man who forced her to vanish.

"Who the hell is he?"

"Trevino Cabrera."

"What?" Cillian almost jumps out of his chair.

"I saw them talking at Juno's wedding," Lorcan interjects. "At the time, I thought Elaine looked very scared, but she assured me that Trevino was just bothering her, hitting on her, and that she could handle it. I walked her to the bungalow, and the next day, she rode with me on the boat to the neighboring town."

"We've never had any complaints against Trevino Cabrera until now," Cillian says. "Up until now, he's been loyal to the Syndicate."

"Elaine isn't lying. She's certain that her sister's death is connected to him, or rather, caused by him."

"And all because the girl supposedly stole from him?" Kellan asks, and I see he's already fiddling with his phone.

"Yes. I want him investigated. I wouldn't do this behind your back, Cillian, but besides the fact that until we clear this up, Elaine won't be safe, I need to know what the hell he's so interested in. What does he think her sister stole that's worth him chasing Elaine and Jax across the country?"

"And what about the kid?" Kellan asks. "You said he's Trevino Cabrera's son."

"He doesn't want Jax. I will take him as my own, for all intents and purposes."

This time, even Lorcan, who's unflappable, looks shocked.

"Are you sure about that?"

"Jax is four and a half years old and has been through more shit than most adults have in their entire lives. He didn't live with his biological mother beyond a few months of life and, because of Trevino Cabrera, he's had to move constantly. He has a heart condition that, although it's been corrected, requires regular supervision. Elaine is crazy about the boy. The son of a bitch doesn't know about him, and even if he did, I doubt he'd want him, except to hurt her. I don't know what the hell will come out of the investigation into him, but if there's one thing as certain as the sunrise, it's that he won't be taking the boy anywhere."

"I have a plan," Kellan says. "Get him to come to the United States, Cillian. With the shit going down between us and the Sicilians, he won't suspect a thing."

He says all this while still looking at his phone and suddenly looks up at us.

"What's up?" I ask.

Kellan gestures at the phone he's holding.

"It won't even be that hard to bring Trevino here. He's either in the country or was until the day before yesterday."

I see the expression on my older brother's face harden, and I know it's because doubt has now settled in. And one thing about the O'Callaghans is that once we catch a scent of blood, we don't stop until we reach the end of the line.

"Bring her too."

"What?"

"We'll set you two up in a room with cameras. You'll receive him, Odhran. Let's surprise Trevino by having him find you and Elaine together. Put on a show for him," Cillian says.

"Why?"

"What could be so important that he's been looking for it for two years, Odhran? What could Elysia have supposedly taken that's serious enough for the son of a bitch to be hunting a young woman for so long?"

"Not just money," Lorcan says.

"Information," Kellan concludes, which I think we're all thinking.

Our older brother nods in agreement.

"That's not the issue, though," Cillian continues. "If the information Elysia stole would put us at risk, why wasn't I informed? I would have sent someone to hunt her down myself, if necessary."

"Maybe he didn't want to show he was an idiot and left Syndicate information within anyone's reach. He knew what you'd do if you found out," I say.

"Yes, that explains something, but the girl is dead and it's been a long time, given that Jax is over four years old. This information hasn't been used, which could mean either he was mistaken and Elysia didn't steal it, or Elaine has no idea she possesses it. Her sister might have hidden it. Either way, it doesn't justify Trevino's obsession with her," the Boss continues.

"Unless the information was so valuable that no matter how long it takes to surface, it poses a risk to his life," I conclude.

Cillian nods and picks up his phone.

He dials a number on the screen, and I'd say it barely rings twice before Trevino Cabrera answers.

Cillian puts the phone on speaker.

"Boss?" we hear a voice with a strong accent ask.

"I heard you're in the U.S. Why?"

There's a reason why the lawyers dealing with the illicit parts of our business need to stay off the radar. It's not in our interest for them to frequently set foot in the United States, and they know that. At least one of the rules, we're sure Trevino violated, as if he had an affair with Elysia, he was constantly coming to the country without my brother knowing.

Now we need to find out what else the bastard was up to without us suspecting anything.

Several seconds pass before he responds:

"I'm not there anymore, but when I was, I was going to look for you. I had to return home due to an emergency."

"I wasn't in Boston until yesterday. Don't lie."

Another silence, and I'm sure if we could see him, the lawyer would be sweating.

"Alright, boss. Let's just say I had personal matters to attend to and didn't think it was necessary..."

"You're not paid to think, and you have no personal matters on U.S. soil. Your wife and kids are in Santo Domingo. But since you like the United States so much, I want you to come for a visit."

Trevino Cabrera knows it's not an invitation, it's an order.

"One of my children needed emergency surgery. You can check, Boss. I'm telling the truth. I need to stay with my family for a few days. Would you be generous enough to postpone this meeting? I've always been loyal to the Syndicate."

"You know I'll verify this information," Cillian says.

"I swear on everything sacred, boss. My boy was hit by a car."

Kellan nods, still typing on his phone, probably because he checked and found out that, at least this time, the bastard didn't lie.

"You have ten days. Come to the headquarters building at noon next Friday."

"Yes, sir."

Chapter 34

Elaine

❚❚ *Why didn't you ask me for help?"* Juno asks in a video call *"And what's this story about you and Odhran being together? When you left here, you hated him!"*

I'm not sure how secure this cell phone Odhran had one of his men deliver to me this morning is, but I don't think I have anything to worry about; otherwise, the boss's wife of the Irish Syndicate wouldn't be speaking so openly.

"How much do you know now?"

"*Are you alone?"*

"Yes. Jax is in the other room with Hestia."

"*I know everything. Both that he's not your biological son but your nephew, who his father is, and that he was also stalking you.*"

I was sure that Odhran would share the information with Cillian because, before being his older brother, he's the boss of the Irish Syndicate.

Trevino is a trusted man of the Boss, so there was no chance Odhran wouldn't reveal everything to him.

I believe in the promise he made me that he won't stop until he discovers the truth about Elysia and that we are protected with him, but until now, I hadn't stopped to think about the mess it would be to explain our relationship to the rest of the family.

"And what do you know about me and Odhran? No, forget it, you must know everything" I conclude, based on the first thing she said when I answered the video call.

"*Yes, although I can't connect the dots yet.*"

"I went to ask him for help."

"*Why?*"

"Neither you nor Orla were in Boston."

"*Did you tell him that? Does Odhran know he was your last option?*"

"Yes, I was a hundred percent honest."

"*Oh, boy! That must have bruised his ego.*"

I laugh. Juno is so cheeky.

"Can we really talk safely on this device?"

"*Yes. My brother-in-law Kellan has a hacker's soul; we are safe. Besides, as soon as we end this call, this line will cease to exist.*"

"Alright, so the truth is that when I arrived at the warehouse, he made me an indecent proposal. Protection in exchange for belonging to him."

"*God, that's so typical of the O'Callaghans. They're all cavemen. I'd almost apologize if my husband wasn't just the same. Now tell me: did you accept?*"

"I told myself there was no way out."

"*Technically, you didn't.*"

"I ran away for two years. I could have continued doing the same until you came back. The truth is, I wanted to literally play with fire, but after we were together..."

"*What?*"

"I'm in deep trouble, Juno. He far exceeds any fantasy I had. Not only is he delicious in bed, but Odhran is affectionate and protective. For all the time I worked for you, I refused to be with him because I didn't want to be an object, but he doesn't make me feel that way; he makes me feel precious, adored."

"Jesus, Elaine, I can't deny it. You're really in trouble."

"We've been sleeping together for a short time, and I feel like I've always belonged to him."

"Well, you're not sleeping, right, if what you're saying is true..." She laughs. *"And what's going to happen now?"*

"I'm going to keep pretending I'm stuck with the deal. He told me there's no deadline for it to end, but Odhran's history with women isn't good."

"On the contrary, his history is great."

"He's never dated, Juno."

"Which means he's never cheated, never betrayed. I admire singles like him and Kellan, who don't tie themselves to anyone but don't lie. My mother was a traitor" she says, for the first time bringing her past to light. *"She cheated on my father with Syndicate members, subordinates or superiors, without distinction."*

"Jesus!"

"I hate traitors. I despise them and don't think there's any excuse for betrayal. No one forces you to cheat. End the damn relationship if you're not satisfied and then move on, but cheating is unforgivable to me."

"And do you think Odhran wouldn't cheat on me?"

"I'm sure he wouldn't. I'm not saying there's no chance you'll get hurt in this story, Elaine. What do we know about other people's hearts? No one can guarantee a relationship will work, but just the fact that he agreed to this crazy protection plan, made a counterproposal, and insisted that you be his... I've never seen Odhran act like this with any woman."

I keep thinking about what she just said, and half an hour later, when I hang up, her words are still on my mind.

"Was everything alright?" Hestia asks.

"Yes, it was. She invited us to spend a few days in the Caribbean. What do you think?"

"I'd love to."

Jax runs into the room and hugs me around the waist.

"Are we going to spend a few days at the beach with Mommy's friend, son?"

His eyes light up with joy.

"With Odhran? I like him!"

Hestia looks at me, and I see the worry in her expression.

Jax shouldn't get attached to the Irishman because he'll be devastated if, suddenly, Odhran never contacts him again.

"It'll be me, you, and Hestia. There's a baby there, Juno's son, and you can play with him."

"But what about Odhran?"

"I don't know, Jax. He works here, in Boston."

"Can I call him?"

"Hmm..."

"Hmm" is a yes, Mommy?

"Hmm" means I'll think about it.

Odhran

I GO STRAIGHT TO HER apartment upon arrival.

It's two in the morning, and I'm exhausted because we had to redo the entire security setup for the Syndicate. Phones were changed, and some members had to move.

We can't leave any gaps. We know that the Sicilians will attack from above, never with a soldier. Those son of a bitches want the elite. It would be the only way to force us to negotiate.

I enter Elaine's room, and she isn't in bed, so I move to Jax's room.

There, I see only the sleeping boy. Neither he nor the nanny lying in the bed next to him notice my presence.

Jax is clinging to a stuffed bear that is clearly quite old, but the boy has an arm protectively draped over the toy.

I leave the room, and after searching the rest of the house, I head to my place, knowing it's where I'll find her.

Elaine hasn't left the building, or my men would have notified me.

I gave her the code to enter my apartment from the first night she was there, and told her she could come and go if she wanted.

I walk straight to my suite, anticipating the pleasure of touching her and kissing that mouth, but as soon as I step into the hallway, a scream of pure terror paralyzes me.

I draw my gun and move carefully, alert to everything. I'm almost at the room when another desperate scream is heard.

I kick the suite door open, gun in hand, but there's no one but her.

Elaine is in bed, crying and thrashing, begging not to have her child taken away.

In her nightmare, she has no one. She has to fight alone.

Chapter 35

Odhran

Death is a part of my world. Witnessing the enemy's fear is too, but seeing it in her, knowing Elaine is like this because of the terror of losing Jax due to Trevino Cabrera's pursuit, makes me swear right now that this shit will end, whatever the outcome of our meeting.

I put the gun down on the dresser and move toward her. Elaine is still thrashing, her face, illuminated by the bedside lamp, completely pale with panic.

"I'm here," I say, hoping this is the right way to comfort her. It was what Orla did for me when I would wake up reliving the death of my parents.

As soon as she feels my arms, she stops fighting, surrenders, and hides her face in my chest while a damn voice screams inside my guts.

Mine.

"I'm with you and no one is taking Jax away. He's yours."

"Odhran?"

"Yes, it's me, baby, and you're safe."

Elaine

IT TAKES ME A FEW SECONDS to believe his words because the nightmare was too real.

In my horror film, I had been stabbed and was bleeding on the floor while that bastard took my child away from me.

Jax was calling my name, crying, and I could do nothing but watch him go.

Remembering this makes my crying start again and I cling to Odhran's body, the desperation hitting me so deeply that I can't fight against being engulfed in this wave of fear.

"I'm here, Elaine," he repeats, as he strokes my hair.

Slowly, his powerful body calms me down, and I remember where I am, the fog of sleep giving way to reality.

Odhran's embrace is unparalleled. For someone who lives a life of hurting people and punishing enemies, he is unbelievably affectionate.

I inhale his masculine scent and my body reacts violently to his presence.

The adrenaline from the panic has not subsided and a raw need clouds rationality. Primitive desire winning by several bodies' advantage over reason.

I straddle him, spread my legs, and sit on his lap, in an invitation that leaves no doubt about how much I need him and that I can't wait.

He looks at me as if he's unsure.

"You're still crying."

"I want you. I need you."

I bite his chest, neck, jaw, lips, and when I slide my hand between us and feel his thick erection through his jeans, I moan and beg him to make me his.

Odhran

SHE PUSHES ME ONTO the bed and pulls down my jeans just enough for my cock to spring free.

"Elaine..." I groan as I feel her small hand wrap around my shaft, but I still try to dig for the last gram of self-control. "Baby, I don't think that..." *"Fuck!"*

Her soft, warm mouth sucks eagerly on the head of my cock, swallowing the pre-cum.

My hand goes to the back of her neck and I force her to take all of it, thrusting my hips up.

"Breathe through your nose. I want to fuck this mouth."

I turn her body, laying her down, and straddle her torso, one leg on each side of her beautiful face. I brace my hands on the mattress, my legs stretched out like I'm doing push-ups, and thrust my cock deeply into her throat as I would into her cunt.

I fuck her this way for over a minute until the desire for the warm, wet heat of her sex makes me rip her clothes off and pull her up onto me.

Holding her close, my hands on her shoulders from underneath, I make her sit down hard.

She doesn't ride me; I fuck her hard and give her no choice but to take it all.

My wife's moans of pleasure mix with my own.

The kisses we exchange don't seem enough, and teeth come into play, combining bites with sucks in an insatiable devouring.

She opens her eyes, stops kissing me, letting me see her desire and surrender.

Her hard nipples brush against my chest, and her cunt, completely filled by my thickness, tightens in a warning that she's close to climax.

The way I take her is brutal, my cock leaving no space inside her. I pull her by the neck, my tongue exploring her delicious mouth.

The visceral need to show her she's mine makes me possess her cruelly.

My brain is a mess because this madness that hit me after we fucked wasn't part of my plans.

The tension and urgency, the hunger that only she can satisfy, make me forget anything but this connection.

It's a brutal fuck, but Elaine seems to love every second, as she begs for more.

When she comes, a primal sound escapes her throat.

Heat and a shock of pleasure explode inside me and I follow her, filling her cunt with my cum.

It's the best feeling on the fucking planet, and I know immediately why.

We forgot the condom.

I hope the desire to push her away kicks in, but it never comes, so I lie down and bring her with me.

For a long time, we lie in silence as I stroke her back, and I know the exact moment she realizes what just happened as she tries to get up.

"Oh my God!"

"I know."

"Jesus, I need to..."

"What, Elaine? There's nothing to be done."

She pulls away from me.

"You don't want kids!"

I don't deny it. I'm not a liar.

This time, when she tries to get up, I let her go.

I watch her run to the bathroom and throw an arm over my face as I hear her turn on the shower.

The problem is, with Elaine, I can never let it go, and after finishing undressing, I follow her into the water.

She doesn't move when I hug her from behind.

"I messed everything up."

"What?"

"I'm the one who seduced you, Odhran."

"I wanted you. I still do."

"I need to go home," she says, pulling away and facing me.

"Because living on the run is part of who you are," I accuse, but she ignores my irritation.

"What are we going to do if it happens?"

"What do you want to do?"

"I can barely take care of Jax, protect him." She shakes her head, as if she can't believe this happened. "Let me go."

"No. We have to decide what we'll do if it happens."

"It's none of your business."

I turn off the shower.

"What the hell are you talking about? How is it not my business? If we've made a baby, it's mine too. The fact that I don't want to be a father doesn't mean I can't love my child."

"There is no baby. It was an accident and nothing will come of it. That would be really bad luck."

"Bad luck?"

"What else can I call it—getting pregnant by a man who says he'll never want children? The same man who just repeated it? Please, let me go. I need to think."

"What do you mean?"

"There are still options."

I know what she's talking about. I'm no fool. I know all about the female reproductive system and contraception.

"Are you thinking about taking the morning-after pill?"

"I don't know. I need to be away from you for a bit to decide."

I look at her, and my cynical side tries to see if she's bluffing or what Elaine expects from me, but all I see is fear and doubt.

"Don't take the pill." I hear myself say, as if my brain and heart are disconnected.

Reason screams that I'm the worst choice to be a father, but thinking that I might have made a child with her makes me sure that despite swearing I wouldn't have heirs, I want him.

"You're not serious. It's a child, Odhran, not a toy you can just abandon when you get tired of it, like you do with your women."

"Toys are for boys, Elaine. I'm a man. If there's a child of ours inside you, I want him."

"And I'll never let any of you go," I finish silently.

Chapter 36

Elaine

"Will you be able to handle this?" he asks me, while keeping me sitting on his lap.

It was the plan, and yet, I, who never considered myself shy, am dying of embarrassment because since I arrived, Keiron and Rourke have already seen me like this.

I still haven't recovered from the issue of my possible pregnancy, but everything else at the moment is overshadowed by the knowledge that soon, Trevino Cabrera will walk through that door.

After I calmed down the night we made love without protection, I told him I needed to go, but to my surprise, Odhran put on a sweatshirt and followed me home. Without any embarrassment, he came into my room and settled into my bed, and even when I went to check on Jax, the Irishman didn't hesitate to follow me.

I had put him and Hestia in the same room, but talking to Juno, she explained that since there is enough space in the apartment, as it has four suites, I should let my son sleep alone to see if he adjusts.

"Elaine?"

"Do you want me to lie or tell the truth?"

"Always the truth."

"I'm not ready to deal with Trevino. Maybe I never will be, because this man has been my boogeyman for years."

Odhran

AT FIRST, EVEN AFTER Cillian's advice, I thought about meeting him alone, but then I concluded he was right. It's better for Elaine to face the bastard once and for all.

I want to see his reaction when he finds out she's mine now.

Regardless, it's a trap.

We know for sure that Trevino has lied to us for years, as he's been to the United States several times without reporting it to Cillian.

"He won't do anything to you. He values his own life too much to dare make a move."

"He won't believe that we're together. No one will. You don't stick with the same woman, let alone have a child with her. My God, Trevino will put the pieces together, find out everything, and take Jax away from me!"

She's on the verge of a hysterical breakdown, and I know she's not faking it. Elaine is desperate just at the thought of losing Jax.

What she doesn't know is that, regardless of whether Trevino believes we have a child together or not, even if he discovers that Jax is his and that he wants to be a father to the boy, he will never take him away from Elaine, not if I have to kill him to stop him.

Even if it's proven that his visits to the United States were innocent, I wouldn't spare him if he tried to take Jax away from Elaine.

"Calm down. Remember what we agreed to discuss? I didn't claim him before because I didn't know about Jax. You didn't want to tell me he was mine because I'm a player."

"He doesn't look like you or me. He resembles *very* much the biological father."

"That doesn't mean anything. Besides, if you know what's good for you, Trevino won't doubt what I say. Isn't that why you chose me in the first place? Because I'm the damn king everyone fears?"

She smiles as I expected and wraps her arms around my neck.

It's the first time she's acted spontaneously since we had unprotected sex about ten days ago. Until now, Elaine has been tense, and even sleeping with her every night hasn't made her relax.

"You say that as if I had come up with a wicked plan."

"No, I know you wanted to seduce me and found the perfect excuse," I tease.

"How can you be so calm? I can't lose you, Odhran. Jax is my life. It doesn't matter that he didn't come from inside me, Jax is my child. When Trevino finds out about him, he will use it to blackmail me about whatever he thinks Elysia stole from him."

"No one will take him away from you."

"Why are you doing this?"

"Doing what?"

"Why did you agree to pretend to be his father?"

"Isn't it a bit late to ask that?"

"Did you say yes just because you wanted to get me into bed?"

"I didn't need an excuse for that."

"Maybe I found the perfect excuse so you wouldn't run away from me later because I wanted you naked in my bed indefinitely," I admit silently.

"And now?"

"What?"

"Why am I here? I didn't need you to find out what Trevino thinks Elysia stole from him. I'm sure you Syndicate people can be very persuasive."

"I want him to know that she's mine."

"Why?"

"Because if I need to kill him, he'll be sure of the reason."

"And you wouldn't kill him without a reason?"

"Let's not discuss this, Elaine."

For over an hour, Keiron has told me that the lawyer was already outside.

We're in the office of one of our warehouses, and I wonder how much cold sweat is accumulating on that bastard's forehead right now.

He thinks he's been summoned to the meeting because we discovered he came to American soil without permission. He probably believes he'll be meeting with Cillian.

He will see my brother too, but not before I assess his reaction to Elaine's presence, and more importantly, to her role in my life.

"What should I say when he comes in?"

"You're smart, Elaine, and you should know that in a psychological war, words are ammunition for the enemy."

"So you agree with the saying that silence is golden?" she asks, a hint of a smile covering her beautiful mouth.

"Yes, because silence is the wisest. Only a fool spills words into the wind that will later be used against him."

"You're not like that. I know you don't talk much, but your explosive temper is legendary among the Irish."

"I don't argue, Elaine. I kill. My wars end too quickly."

She threatens to smile, but then, realizing I'm serious, her face turns pale.

"Don't hurt women or the innocent."

"No, but that doesn't mean I'd think twice about killing those women's husbands or those same children's parents."

I watch her swallow hard, her eyes widening.

"I've asked this before, but I'll repeat it. Do you know what you're getting into by agreeing to be mine?"

"It will be temporary," she says, avoiding eye contact.

"Look at me, Elaine, and tell me if you really believe that. From now on, you and your son will be under my protection."

"I won't be around forever. We're temporary."

"You might be expecting my child, and that will be *forever*. Besides, even if that's not the case and you move to China, I'll still be keeping an eye on you and Jax."

"Do you think you're threatening me? All I want is to see Jax safe. You don't need to worry about me, but if you give me your word that even if something happens to me, you'll take care of Jax, Odhran, I won't have enough days left on Earth to thank you."

"Being under my protection might make you both a target too."

"I know, but I've been a target for a long time, and I'm tired of running. Jax has to start school soon. He should have been in one already, to be honest, but my wandering life doesn't allow for that."

"We'll deal with that when you get back from the Caribbean."

When Elaine told me about the invitation from my sister-in-law to visit her on the island, even though I didn't want to be away from her now, I immediately knew it was the ideal arrangement.

The war with the Italians has already begun, and it's only a matter of days before shit hits the fan.

"She and I have already talked about it, but..."

"What?"

She turns red.

"I don't think the schools Juno will put the child in are the same ones I can afford."

"Don't worry about that."

"You don't need to pay for his school. At some point, I'll go back to work. I can handle it."

"You're not going back to being the girl from the sign."

She rolls her eyes.

"Jealousy has no place in a relationship like ours."

"I'm not joking. You won't be flaunting that pretty ass in front of those bastards anymore."

"I don't feel like showing off my backside either. I was talking about going back to work on my bouquets and..."

She doesn't finish speaking because there's a knock on the door.

Soon after, Keiron asks if he can come in.

The tension that had eased returns, and Elaine almost jumps off my lap.

I grab her thighs, preventing her.

"Quiet. I've never publicly claimed a woman before. Now that you're mine, you'll learn what that means. You can't run away every time I touch you."

"The lawyer seems anxious," Keiron says.

"Let him in."

Five minutes later, he's back with our "visitor." To be honest, I didn't remember his face very well, but now that we're face to face, his resemblance to Jax is undeniable.

"Trevino Cabrera," I greet. "You can start by telling us what was so important that you had to set foot on American soil about a dozen times without authorization in recent years."

Sticking to our agreement, Elaine leans back against me.

"Aren't you going to introduce us, baby?"

"Do you want me to?"

"It's proper etiquette," she pouts.

"Elaine, this is a lawyer who works for the Syndicate," I say slowly. "Trevino, this is my wife, Elaine Ramsey."

Chapter 37

Elaine

It's automatic. As soon as I'm face to face with Jax's father, even before he can open his mouth to respond to Odhran's mocking greeting, my arms go straight for the Irishman's neck, because the lawyer's gaze terrifies me.

I don't need any proof that he was the one who killed Elysia. I can see, in his eyes, that this Trevino is the concrete embodiment of evil.

It's no small thing, considering I've been involved in Syndicate fights for years, a place where I'd say ninety percent of the attendees are murderers.

There's something more about Cabrera, however, that tells me I should never let Jaxton near him if he wants custody of the child.

I mask a shiver as I remember the last nightmare I had with him. *He doesn't know about Jax, Elaine. Calm down.*

Another chill of pure terror sweeps over me as I imagine my son in the hands of this monster.

Never, even if I have to kill him myself, will Trevino Cabrera get near Jax.

"Now that we've gotten past the formalities," Odhran says, "start explaining what you were doing in the United States."

The tone he uses is icy.

I became somewhat obsessed with this man two years ago, before I had to flee, and I started to notice everything about him. To an unsuspecting observer, the monotone delivery might sound almost bored, but I can sense the contempt in it.

What's really going on here? From the way he ordered Trevino to explain his visits, it's clear he wasn't summoned here just because of me.

I watch, satisfied, as the man pales.

It's not so great when there's someone above you on the food chain, is it, asshole? Scaring women is easy, but going up against someone who can turn you inside out without even losing sleep is a real game-changer.

God, I'm so angry at him I could punch his face in, but I know I need to stay calm. Odhran is playing a game with him, and I won't ruin everything by acting impulsively.

"I didn't know you were married," he says, but I see him quickly remember who he's talking to. "I didn't mean to be offensive, boss."

Boss? Odhran told me he barely remembered his face.

Cowardly brown-noser.

"Elaine is the mother of my child, so what does a fucking piece of paper matter? Married or not, she's mine."

"Child?"

Now I can see that his surprise has turned into panic, and I think I know why.

I can almost see the gears in his brain turning. He's probably thinking about how deep a hole he's in for having pursued and threatened the woman of one of the bosses.

And even more so, for having killed—because even though I have no proof, I know it was him—the sister-in-law of Odhran.

"Yes, Jax is my son. I'm going to ask you one last time: is there any particular reason you left your post in Santo Domingo and appeared in the United States without notifying us so many times?"

I notice that even after making him wait for over an hour before receiving him, Odhran still doesn't make him sit down.

Trevino Cabrera is around fifty years old, according to the research I did on him, and he's still a handsome, fit man. I can understand why my sister fell for him, but could it be that Elysia didn't notice the coldness in his gaze? He seems to have no soul.

"Every time, I came to visit my wife's relatives. Family above all, boss," he says, and I have to say that for a lawyer, he lies badly. Even I, not being an interrogation expert, know that his answer is a blatant fabrication.

My heart, which had finally started to return to a normal rhythm, starts racing again when Odhran says:

"Visiting your wife's relatives? In the dozen times you've been to the United States in recent years? Our records of the entries you were authorized to make only show two trips. Are you good at math, Trevino? You're missing *ten*."

"I..."

"Let me try to help you. Did some of these visits have to do with my wife?"

"Of course not, I never..."

I'm dying to mention the note he left at the bungalow in the Caribbean, or the blood-stained flower from my last escape, but I remember what Odhran advised me, that silence is golden, so I control myself just in time.

"What the hell was so important about what Elysia supposedly stole from you that made you pursue Elaine for two years, Trevino?"

I feel breathless, attentive to every detail. Despite all the fear I've had of Trevino over the years, I expected to see a tough guy who would at least try to fight back against Odhran, but what he does next is utterly disgraceful.

He tries to run, turning around towards the door, only to find Rourke and Keiron waiting outside.

"You need to go," Odhran says only to me.

"Why?"

"You know why, Elaine. From now on, you can't witness anything more, baby."

I nod, even though I want to stay and hear him admit he killed my sister, because I'm sure, with Odhran's *prodding*, he will confess.

"I don't know what time I'll be back today. Or even if I'll come back, but don't think shit. I just want you," he says.

He stands, lifting me into his arms, and sets me on my feet.

"You don't need to come with me."

"Cillian is in the next room. That's where I'm taking the bastard... for now, but first I want to make sure you're safe inside a car, on your way home."

Trevino remains standing at the entrance. No one has touched him, but the lawyer has his back to us.

There's enough space for me to pass, and feeling exhausted, I silently pray that this will be the last time I see this man.

Maybe this wish makes me a terrible person because I know if it happens, it's because Odhran killed him, but if his death is the price for Jax's safety, I hope my Irishman tears the bastard apart.

I'm almost through the threshold when I feel Odhran a few steps behind me as my arm is grabbed tightly.

"You bitch! I should have killed you in the Caribbean!"

I'm thrown against the wall, my head hitting with such a loud crash that I fear I've broken some bones.

I see the room spinning for just a few seconds before Odhran slams his elbow into Trevino's nose.

"Get this son of a bitch out of my sight!" he roars and, the next second, he's crouched near me. "Talk to me, baby."

"I'm tired."

"What the hell happened here?"

"Call a doctor for her. Now, Cillian! The bastard hit her."

And then he focuses all his attention on me.

"Don't sleep. Can you do that for me, Elaine? Stay awake like the good girl you are. I promise I'll slowly rip his head off and make him pay for what he did to you."

Chapter 38

Odhran

As I walk to the back of the warehouse—not the one where I received that fucking lawyer, but one even more isolated, where no one will hear his screams—the image of Elaine injured, passing out, is still etched in my mind.

Despite every instinct telling me to rip Trevino Cabrera's head off right there in the room, for the first time, my protective side took precedence over my vengeful one.

The doctor who specializes in treating the Syndicate arrived quickly.

He told us that, for safety's sake, he preferred to take an X-ray of her head, even though Elaine seemed fine. I took her to our clinic, and at least regarding the fainting, it doesn't seem like anything serious happened.

Throughout the examination, she clung to me, hiding her face against my chest, avoiding looking at anyone in the room, as my brothers and Lorcan were also present.

Rourke and Keiron took that piece of shit Trevino to where I ordered them.

Seeing Elaine so vulnerable, scared, knowing she is normally a warrior, a survivor, made me even angrier.

My thirst for blood is stronger than I remember feeling before.

I took her home and placed a dozen of my trusted men to guard the building.

Elaine seemed awkward, as if being hit by that bastard was somehow her fault; she spoke little to me.

I don't like her silence, especially after what happened, but we'll have time to deal with that later.

"You can't kill him until we get everything we need," Cillian warns me before we enter, as my older brother knows me well.

I keep my madness well hidden, concealed from society, but once it surfaces, I become an animal.

"I'll get all the information, but no one touches him but me."

Everyone remains silent, and I know it's because they understand how I'm feeling.

"The son of a bitch is suicidal," Lorcan says. "Attacking her in front of you can only be described as a death wish."

"He knew, the moment he walked into the office and saw her in my lap, that he was doomed. Attacking Elaine was the last act of cowardice from a desperate man, but he will regret acting on impulse."

"Why do you think the bastard was sneaking into the United States? Nothing will convince me he was just after Elaine," Cillian says. "Maybe that too, but there has to be more. He's been entering the country clandestinely in the past."

"It could be to see his girlfriend. Elaine's sister, Elysia," Lorcan argues.

"Maybe, but I think there's more to it. Anyway, we'll find out."

"Before killing him, make a mental checklist of what you need to obtain, brother," Kellan says. "Find out why he's been coming here. Get him to confess if he killed Elysia and, most importantly, what the hell he thinks his ex-girlfriend stole from him that made him so obsessed with getting it back."

"Odhran?" Cillian calls when I don't say anything.

I know that they, knowing me too well, are worried I might lose control and kill Trevino before we get our answers.

I stop walking, now with only the heavy iron door separating me from the lawyer.

I close my eyes for a moment, not yet wanting to put into words what has been haunting me since the moment I saw her lying on the floor.

"Elaine might be pregnant with my child. That bastard didn't just hurt my girlfriend, but he might have harmed an innocent she carries in her womb. My heir!"

"That miserable bastard!" Cillian roars. "Are you sure she's pregnant?"

"No, but we forgot the condom. For the past ten days, it's been a possibility."

"Fuck!" Kellan punches the wall. "And when will we know if they're both okay?"

"Only when the pregnancy is confirmed." Lorcan answers for me. "If it happened recently, we need to wait a few more days to be sure if Elaine is pregnant, but I don't know shit about obstetrics, other than the part about childbirth. Since I found out my wife was expecting our child, I became obsessed with learning everything about it so she wouldn't be at any risk."

"If she were pregnant," Cillian says, his voice sounding grim, "she might have had a miscarriage and not even realized it."

I step away from everyone because I need a few minutes alone.

Is this a punishment? Am I being punished for saying I didn't want children?

Because after the initial shock, that same night we fucked without a condom, I was already certain that if the pregnancy was confirmed, I wouldn't give up either of them.

"Odhran."

"One minute, Cillian."

"It's not your fault."

"I should never have brought her to the meeting with Trevino."

"And how the hell were you supposed to guess the bastard was a fucking suicide case?"

"My duty is to protect her and also the child she might be carrying. A baby we might never even know exists. Damn it!"

"We'll make him pay."

"And what difference will it make? We punished those who killed our parents, and did that ease the pain of missing them?"

"We can't change the past, but we can take revenge."

I make a decision.

"I don't want to kill him today."

"What?"

"I'll take Elaine to the doctor, to the best fucking baby specialist on the planet, and he'll tell me if she is or was pregnant. Only then will I decide how I'll deal with him. Until then, I'll make him regret every second he raised his hand against her."

I ENJOY THE SOUND OF breaking bones.

The red blood leaking out as well, and for an hour, without even bothering to interrogate him, I used my fists to beat Trevino Cabrera.

No matter how much Kellan called me or tried to tell me I needed to stop, I needed to hear that bastard's screams because with each one, I felt I was honoring Elaine.

Unlike my middle brother, neither Cillian nor Lorcan tried to stop me, maybe because they understand the desperation I'm feeling at the thought that a newly conceived child might have suffered the consequences of the bloody world I belong to.

No matter how many times I hit him, however, my hatred doesn't dissipate.

"Odhran, we need him alive, fuck's sake," Kellan reminds me again.

"I'm not going to kill him. I'm stopping now," I say, but right after, I dislocate his jaw with a punch.

My hand trembles with the desire to cut his throat. The knife hidden in my ankle begging to end that worm's existence.

"I don't..." Trevino tries to speak, but I grab his neck with both hands, squeezing it until he nearly loses consciousness.

"You will only speak when I say you can. Not to explain yourself. What you did can't be undone, you bastard."

"Tomorrow," Cillian finally says. "He's so fucked up that any information he gives us won't be reliable."

"I'm not finished yet."

"You're done, cousin," Lorcan says. "At least for now. Go back to your wife. Elaine needs you tonight."

Just the mention of her name finally calms my inner demon and makes me pull back.

"He's mine," I warn them all.

"We know that, kid," Cillian says.

Chapter 39

Odhran

I opened the front door with the hope that, as happened the other night, she would be in my suite, asleep, but all I found was silence and darkness, a representation of my life before Elaine came back to it.

I head to the shower to take another bath because I always feel filthy around her and Jax, and I plan to check on her today.

Ten minutes later, I look at the huge, completely empty living room of my apartment. Before Elaine was here, I never minded this, but now, every time I walk through the corridor and head to where the two of them are settled, it feels like stepping into a parallel reality.

There, there is life and laughter. Jax is always chatty, and Hestia is hovering around him like a mama bear.

There is, above all, the woman who came to me uninvited and who now, I don't know if I'll ever be able to let go of.

I walk down the corridor connecting the two apartments until I reach her bedroom.

I open the door slowly, expecting to find her asleep, but besides Elaine, there is Jax, awake, looking completely vigilant and protective over his mother.

The bedside lamp is on, and something tightens in my chest seeing the way he looks at the woman who has been risking her life for years to ensure he is safe.

Jax lifts his head, and when he sees me, he puts a finger to his lips, asking for silence, probably mimicking the actions of adults.

He runs his little hand over her face and then gets off the bed. He comes to me.

Without any ceremony, he takes my hand and starts walking towards the corridor.

"You can't make noise. Mommy is sleeping now."

"Now?" I ask, stopping and bending down to talk to him.

Jax is wearing a short pajama with bears. I've already noticed his fascination with the animal, as there are several stuffed bears in his room.

One of them, however, a gift from Elysia when the baby was born and with which he sleeps, is almost falling apart. Elaine said she never washed it because it had Elysia's scent, and it was the only concrete reminder of Elysia for the two of them.

She told me she never mentions Elysia to Jax except when showing him pictures of his aunt but hasn't told him yet about the real role of "aunt" in his life. She plans to do this when he is older and can understand the whole story.

"She cried because she had a bad dream. Grandma Hestia woke up, and so did I. I went to her in mommy's room. I told her it was just a bad dream. Grandma Hestia told me that bad dreams are called... nightmares?"

"Yes."

"Do you have bad dreams too, Odhran?"

I bend down to talk to him.

"Not anymore."

"I only have dreams where I'm eating ice cream." He smiles, in his childlike innocence.

"When your mom cried when she had the nightmare, was it just because of that or do you think she was in pain?"

"Pain? — He looks confused. — Did Mommy fall?"

What the hell am I doing? Can't I say a few words to the boy without frightening him?

"No, little one. Never mind."

"She's okay. It was just a nightmare." I hear Hestia's voice say as the door to her room opens.

When I brought Elaine, I tried in every way to convince her to accept a nurse to keep her company, but she refused. I had no choice but to tell Hestia more or less what had happened and ask her to keep an eye on my wife.

Jax's nanny — I don't even know if I should call her that, as she is more like Elaine's mother and his grandmother — looked at me with concern, though she said nothing.

Who can blame her? What mother would want to see her daughter, by blood or not, with someone like me, taking risks and getting hurt?

"Let's go back to the room, Jax," she calls, and it doesn't escape my notice that she doesn't greet me.

"I want to stay with Odhran."

"He will go back to his own apartment."

"I'm not going anywhere until Elaine wakes up."

"Please," Jax begs, clasping his little hands in a pleading gesture.

"Let him stay with me," I say. "I'll be in the living room. Once he falls asleep, I'll take him back to his room."

She doesn't seem pleased and is very reluctant, but I can see she understands this isn't a request.

Jax has a lot of shit to face in the future.

There's no guarantee that he won't need special care again due to his heart condition and that his biological mother was stolen from him without him ever having the chance to be with her. If it makes him happy to spend some time with a bastard like me, I won't deny him that.

I get up, pick him up, and head to the living room.

"Once you fall asleep, I'll take you back to your room. You can't stay here overnight," I say seriously, sitting on the couch and keeping him with me.

I thought it would be a matter of minutes, but about an hour later, Jax is still talking non-stop about everything and anything.

He asked again about "the paintings" on my body. If I like soccer and if I know how to skate.

He told me that he likes juice more than milk and that he hates the oatmeal porridge Hestia makes.

Gradually, I relaxed from all the madness of the night, and with one arm around him, my eyes started to droop.

I vaguely remember feeling his head against my chest and holding him even more tightly before falling into a deep sleep.

Chapter 40

Elaine

I wake up startled, not by the nightmare I had earlier, but by the realization that Jax was here with me when I fell asleep again.

With my heart racing, I leave the room, still disoriented, open the door, and head into the hallway.

I don't know if I'll ever get over this feeling of panic, that my child isn't protected.

Yes, I will, because by now, Trevino is in the hands of the Irish.

Honestly, even after my little show with Odhran in front of the monster, I still feared that the Syndicate men, not my own but the rest of the family, wouldn't believe me.

Now, I have a bump on the back of my head and my body aches, but I know that Trevino Cabrera dug his own grave.

I'm not a fool. I understood that the Irish were after him because he apparently came to my country without authorization. I think they set a trap for him, and like the idiot he is, he walked right into it.

It's funny how monsters in our dreams are far worse than in real life. I know it's likely that Trevino or someone on his orders killed Elysia and that he's been after me all this time, but that's because he considered himself stronger, because the coward was dealing with unarmed and physically inferior women.

I'd be lying if I didn't say it was satisfying to see him sweat and the fear widen his eyes when confronted by Odhran. And it's precisely because I was sure the man was on the brink of a panic attack that I don't understand why he came after me. Unless he had no doubt he was completely lost, that nothing he said would save him from being punished by the bosses.

I walk down the hallway to Jax's room, but I don't find him. I head to Hestia's room next, sure he's there, but what I see is my friend propped up against the pillows, reading.

"Jax?" I ask, now genuinely worried.

"He's with Odhran in the living room."

"I don't understand."

"I found them in the hallway about an hour ago. Jax didn't want to go to bed; he wanted to stay with his... *boyfriend?*"

There's a tone of reproach in her voice, and I know it's coming from concern. If there's someone I'm sure wants the best for me in this life, it's Hestia.

"I'm afraid for you, Elaine. Actually, for both of you."

"What happened today wasn't Odhran's fault, Hestia. For the first time, after two years of running, I confronted the man who's been threatening me. The same one I think killed Elysia."

"What?" She puts down the book and comes over to me.

I've told her almost everything, but I've been sparing her the worst.

"Odhran isn't a saint, Hestia, but today he was my hero. Without any guarantee, he took my word and confronted the man who was keeping me from living, even without laying a finger on me."

"Why didn't you tell me earlier, dear? Have you been carrying this burden alone all these years?"

"And what difference would it make to sadden you?"

"I knew Elysia didn't commit suicide. We didn't spend much time together, but I trust my judgment of people. Your sister was a good girl."

"She was. Her only mistake was getting involved with a monster. What does your judgment say about Odhran?"

She takes a deep breath as if it's hard for her to speak before answering me:

"You two are in love, and that's why I'm so worried. Because I think it's a forever."

"He doesn't love me."

"Maybe he doesn't realize it yet, but he's crazy about you, Elaine. I've known you for a long time, so don't try to deny that Odhran is your love too. I don't know if you started this story the right way. You never told me exactly how this protection deal with the Irish happened, but I know you're no longer together for mutual interests."

"I..."

"Answer me this: if everything that's tormenting you right now suddenly disappeared from your life and you were guaranteed that that monster, Jax's father, would never come after you again, would you leave Boston? Would you start over somewhere else?"

I calmly think about this scenario, where I could live free of fear but forever without Odhran.

"He isn't yours forever", reason tells me, but it doesn't help.

"No. I wouldn't leave until I was sure that what exists between us is an illusion."

"And that's why I'm afraid. Because what you experienced today isn't a unique situation. You'll be at risk for the rest of your life if you stay with him."

"Living is risky, Hestia. You're right. I fell in love with him. I didn't plan it, but it happens, and I won't run anymore. I'll stay until the end, until there's nothing left."

"And if the end never comes?"

"Then I will have found my forever."

I leave her room and head to the living room. I knew they were together, but I wasn't prepared for the scene I find.

Odhran is lying on the couch, wearing only black pants, shirtless and shoeless, with a completely asleep Jax on top of him.

I can't contain how my heart fills with emotion seeing them like this. I approach slowly, not wanting to disturb them, but I observe every detail. My son holds one of Odhran's fingers, his other arm around the broad neck, and his head resting against the tattooed chest.

My boy's angelic face radiates peace.

Odhran holds him against his body, as if in a silent promise to protect him from all harm, and even while asleep, he shows strength.

I know it's dangerous to get used to this, this feeling of being at home, but I can't help but feel complete.

Odhran shifts, as if even asleep, he's alert, aware that he's being watched. I'm not surprised when his eyes slowly open and meet mine.

The dim light from the lamp highlights his striking features.

Beauty and ruggedness in a package of muscles.

Brutal and protective.

Wild and loyal.

Beautiful and *mine*?

For now, yes, he is mine.

He carefully stands up, keeping Jax asleep in his arms, and comes to me.

He takes my hand, and together, we head toward my son's room.

He doesn't say anything; it's as if a special connection, different from anything we've had so far, has formed.

He lays Jax on the bed, and for a few moments, I watch him sleep. I kiss him, and before I can take a step, Odhran picks me up and carries me to my suite.

Chapter 41

Elaine

"I want our son," he says as we reach the bedroom.

Odhran has held me all the way, as if carrying something precious in his arms, and lies down on my bed without letting me go, positioning me over his body.

"What?"

"I'm not a good choice, Elaine, but I'm crazy about you." He shakes his head as if trying to understand himself. "I can't explain."

"Try," I whisper, not believing this is happening. My breath catches and my heart races. "Maybe you need to say what you're feeling as much as I need to hear it, Odhran."

Odhran

ELAINE LOOKS AT ME with her beautiful eyes shining for me, because of me. Her mouth slightly open, as if searching for air.

I lived thirty-one years thinking I was immune to the damn disease that seems to attack much of humanity because when my parents died, a part of me did too.

I know, though, that I can no longer suffocate the violence of the feeling Elaine has stirred within me, because it no longer belongs to me; it is hers.

I think about what happened today, which was nothing compared to what could have happened if Trevino Cabrera had reached her before she got to Boston and asked for my protection.

The mere possibility makes me feel like a dagger is tearing through my chest, creating a wound so deep that no doctor could mend. Along with the pain comes the certainty that I would die before allowing anyone to harm her.

"I am the darkness, pure evil, but I can't give up your light," I begin. "Near you, with you, I can see something beyond the death that surrounds me. I almost feel human."

"You are human."

"Most of the humanity in me is lost, Elaine. I'm a killer and I'm okay with that." I touch her face, feeling the warmth and softness of her skin. "Today, at this moment, is your last chance to escape. If you decide to stay, you will be mine forever."

"Because I might be pregnant? Is that what caused this change?"

"No. I want you and I want the baby, if there is one, but I also want what I have no right to desire."

"What?"

"Everything."

Her face softens in a way it never has in my presence. I've seen Elaine smiling and playing with Jax, but with me, she seems in a constant state of alert.

Not today. Not now.

At this moment, she is entirely mine.

"I love you, beautiful."

Her face becomes serious again.

"Don't say that if it's not what..."

"I love you. I didn't think I could go this far, to feel so much, but this feeling that warms my chest every time I see you smile... it has to be love."

"Odhran."

"I'm not a prince and I don't know how to say sweet words, baby, so I'll show you in the way I can just how much you are mine."

It's as if our bodies react before our minds do, because in an instant, I'm opening a heart I didn't even know I had to the one I'm now sure is my destiny.

In the next moment, the sexual tension between us becomes so intense it's akin to a volcanic eruption.

"I need to fuck you more than I need to breathe, woman."

We almost tear each other's clothes off. The desire, now unrestrained and reckless, taking the forefront, forgetting the past and the risks.

The good that exists in her and the evil rooted in me.

We're not opposites. We're complements.

"I need to bury myself in you and kiss you for hours. Mark you so you never forget who owns you."

"I don't have an owner."

She looks at me, breathless, when only after testing her with my fingers to make sure she's wet, I penetrate her fully.

"I'm your owner. Your master, as you are my queen."

It's as if our skins are interconnected in a connection where we don't know where one starts and the other ends.

"Why me, Odhran?"

I withdraw from her and then sink back into her honey, her tight pussy clenching around me, pulsing.

"Because it could never be anyone else. Because it's always been you."

I devour her mouth, no longer driven by the urgency of desire, but to show her how crazy I am about her.

"You're never leaving. If you try, I'll hunt you down. I'll bring you back until you understand that your destiny is with me."

Elaine

THE PRESSURE OF ODHRAN'S mouth on mine is ravenous. His hands grip my hips with such force while he takes me that I know I'll be marked all over, but I don't want him to stop.

"Am I hurting you?" he asks when I bite my lip to keep from screaming.

"No. Keep going. Harder."

"Don't you have any sense, woman? Don't you realize that I have no control around you and that provoking me like this is dangerous?"

His voice is harsh, telling me that he's struggling to keep his inner beast restrained but is losing the battle.

"I'm not afraid of you. You might be a monster outside, but not with me."

He grabs my hair and crashes our mouths together roughly, plunging his tongue deep into me as his hips thrust harder and harder, making me moan, completely lost in pleasure.

I open my eyes and he's staring at me. There's something frightening and dark about Odhran that makes him irresistible to me.

Odhran

POSSESSING HER IS MY compulsion. With Elaine, my most primitive side emerges. The hunger I feel for her will never be satisfied.

She wraps her arms around my neck, pulling me closer. The need for each other consuming us.

My cock is like steel as I thrust in and out of her pussy, fearing I might hurt her.

"Tell me if it's too much."

I almost pull out entirely, and when I enter her again, she screams. I silence her with my tongue, fucking her like that too.

Elaine is on the brink of orgasm, writhing beneath me, trying to extract everything she can from our pleasure.

My hidden monster is tamed while I'm between her thighs.

Does she know that she possesses me like no other has?

I give her pleasure and pain, lust and brutality, but above all, I'm giving her my love.

Elaine arches beneath me, gasping, and murmurs my name as an intense orgasm robs her of her strength.

My thrusts inside her are relentless, my cock traveling the tight path of her pussy without pause, our pelvises colliding.

"I want to come inside you."

I touch her clit, determined to bring her with me again, and when I hear her moan and start to writhe once more, I increase the pressure on her pleasure point and the speed with which I fuck her.

"Come with me, Elaine. I love you."

"I'm afraid to love you."

"I'm not giving you an option. You belong to me."

My words have a catalytic effect on both of us, and with our eyes locked on each other, we come together.

I've never felt so connected to another human being in my life, and I lower myself to kiss her again because I don't want to lose her warmth just yet.

When I pull away slightly to let her breathe, she caresses my hair.

"I'm giving you my heart, Irish. Take care of it, don't break it."

I'm still inside her, and her unexpected declaration makes me hard again, but when I resume moving, it's slow, in a deliberate and undeniable possession.

"I've spent my whole life finding you. I will never hurt you."

Chapter 42

Elaine

"**M**ommy, I did something really bad," Jax says, his eyes filled with tears.

I left the room mortified because Odhran stayed here, but unlike other times when he left before Hestia and Jax woke up, he didn't seem worried about being seen.

In fact, he wore clothes that he had left here last week, which I had washed and forgot to return.

The moment I see the sadness on my son's face, everything else loses importance, and I kneel down to talk to him.

"Hey, it couldn't have been that bad."

He wipes away a tear.

"I spilled hot chocolate on Giggle and Grandma Hestia had to wash him. Now the bear will lose its smell of love."

I feel a lump in my throat because, yes, the bear will lose the scent of Elysia after being washed. It was the only real thing left from my sister, and I had hoped that when I told Jax about his biological mother, her scent would still be on the bear.

"My love, it was just a little accident. We all spill things all the time."

"You too, Odhran?" he asks, looking over my shoulder.

I look back and see that the Irishman is seeking my help. He doesn't handle children very well, which makes it incredible how much Jax adores him.

"He spilled water on me yesterday," I say, smiling at my man and begging him to play along.

"He did. And Elaine once dropped my cupcake," he says, giving me a wink and reminding me of the incident.

I was at Juno's store, and one of the customers was fawning over him. Instead of getting revenge on the woman, I accidentally dropped the last chocolate cupcake of the day, his favorite.

"Revengeful," he whispers so only I can hear.

"So you're not angry?" My son seems more relaxed.

"No, love. It's all right."

"Good morning to you all." Hestia joins us, looking like she's holding something in her hand. "Actually, I think the accident turned out to be a good thing. You were probably wondering where this went. I think Jax found it, put it inside the toy bear, and forgot about it."

My son is already distracted, showing Odhran his new electric train, a gift from him. By the way, several toys arrived for Jax a few days ago.

"What is it?" I ask, confused.

"I think it's a flash drive."

She hands me a white device.

"Yes, it is, but it's not mine. I've never stored anything on a flash drive in my life. I wouldn't have any use for it or anything to put on it."

I look at the object in my hand.

"Are you sure it was inside the bear, Hestia?"

"Absolutely. And I'm sorry to say, but I don't know if it still works because it went through the washer. I heard a metal clanging noise and decided to check. I thought it was batteries."

"No, I've always found talking bears scary and never put batteries in Giggle."

"But that's what I thought it was. I stopped the machine, and when I opened it, the noise I heard was the flash drive banging around inside. Apparently, the bear's zipper opened during the wash, so I'm not sure if it will still work. If it's not yours, then the only explanation is that it came with it."

"Impossible. The toy was new when Elysia bought it and..."

"What?"

I feel my blood run cold.

"Can you take Jax to the kitchen for a moment?"

"Yes, but is everything okay? Did I do something wrong by opening the bear?"

"No, Hestia. I'm just a little confused about the flash drive. We'll join you in the kitchen soon."

I wait for her to leave with Jax and then move closer to Odhran.

"What's going on?" he asks, probably because he sees how confused I look.

"Do you remember that Jax said he spilled hot chocolate on Giggle?"

"Giggle is his bear?"

"Yes. It has batteries, but I never put any in because..." I feel my face heat up. "I was afraid of talking toys when I was little."

He doesn't mock me as I thought he would. Instead, he gives me a kiss on the forehead.

"Until Jax's age, I was afraid of stick insects. My mom used to say I would wake up screaming, saying the tree was coming into my room to kill me."

"I want to know more about your past later."

"There's not much to say." He shrugs, and the smile fades. "I grew up in my early teens."

"Was that when your parents died?"

He nods, and I can see how uncomfortable the conversation makes him.

"I'm sorry, I didn't mean to bring up bad memories."

"Tell me about the bear."

"Hestia went to wash it and heard a noise after she started the machine. She checked, thinking it was batteries, and found this when she opened it."

I hand him the device.

"A flash drive?"

"Yes, she thought it was mine, but I've never had one. There's no way Jax put it inside the bear."

He looks at me, and I know we're both thinking the same thing.

"Do you think it was Elysia?"

"I don't know. It could just be a coincidence, having come from the manufacturer like Hestia suggested, but Elysia was the one who bought the bear for Jax. Do you think there's a chance she hid this flash drive in the toy, and it's what Trevino has been looking for all this time?"

"Yes, it could be."

"In that case, the monster was right. She stole it. My God! How could she do something like this? Is there any way to check what's on it? Hestia said it got wet."

"I'll try. I'll go to my apartment for a moment to call Kellan."

"Will you tell me what's on it?"

"If it's Syndicate business, no."

"But what if it's about my sister?"

"Then I will tell you."

He's already heading towards the door, but I hold his arm.

"Elysia wasn't a thief, Odhran. If she took this, whatever it contains, it was like a kind of insurance."

I hate how shaky my voice sounds.

"Don't be like that."

"How can I not be? You said it might be Syndicate business. What if Cillian doesn't believe I ever knew the flash drive was there before?"

"If that were the case, why wouldn't she have used what was on it for her benefit? Or even handed it over to Trevino?"

"I didn't know about it, Odhran. You have to believe me."

"I believe you, Elaine, and my brother will too. No one will accuse you of anything. You have my word. Now, I'll see if I can access the contents of the drive; if not, I'll give it to Kellan. He'll find a way to check what's on the flash drive."

Chapter 43

Odhran

As soon as I step into my apartment, my phone starts ringing.
"Kellan?"

"Where are you?"

"At home. I found something."

"I'll explain later. The men have noticed unusual activity on your street. An attack could happen within minutes. You need to get Elaine and Jax out of there immediately. Use the fire escape. There's an armored car waiting for you. Keiron is driving. Try not to draw attention. We want to catch them by surprise."

"I'll put Elaine, Jax, and Hestia in the vehicle, but I won't leave with them."

"No, you will. It's Cillian's orders. You're going with them, and tell your wife they'll be heading straight to the Caribbean. It's no longer safe for them to stay on American soil. Lorcan and Rourke have already sent their wives there as well."

"Are they Sicilian?"

"We don't know yet, but we'll find out. Lorcan has just given Trevino a *little push*. He'll start talking soon. We're sure he was betraying us with another organization, now we just need to find out which one."

I know that by *little push,* he means the truth serum, and I also know that Lorcan's brother-in-law, Maxim, used the same method when he had to interrogate a traitor from the Russian brotherhood.

"Is there a plane waiting for them?"

"Yes."

"Odhran?"

"What is it?"

"Stay alive."

"That's the plan. How serious do you think the situation is?"

"On a scale from zero to ten, eight. Now, get your ass out of there immediately."

"WE HAVE TO LEAVE NOW."

"What? But Jax is still eating and..."

I can see from the way she looks at me that she's scared and that her mind is in denial.

I hold her face.

"Elaine, we're about to be attacked at any moment. Just grab documents; I can handle everything else, but we need to leave the building in the next few minutes."

"Trevino?"

"I don't know. It could be someone working for him. Now, move, baby. We don't have time for explanations. Trust me."

"I trust you, but I'm scared for Jax."

"Do what I say, and nothing will happen to you. I'll die before I let them touch a hair on your head."

Elaine

I FEEL SO NAUSEOUS that I'm about to faint.

Just one look at Hestia, and she understands that something serious is going on. We've been on the run for years, and she's more than used to not wasting time on questions that are much less important than our survival.

So, when I enter the kitchen where Jax is having breakfast and tell her to grab the basics for the three of us, as well as documents, she doesn't question me.

"Mommy, aren't you going to eat? It's so good!" my son says, taking a bite of a pancake.

"How about this? Odhran called us for a plane ride, so why don't we put the leftover pancakes in a container and eat them on the way?"

"A *plane?*" he repeats, his eyes sparkling and already forgetting about the meal.

"Yes, and then we'll arrive at an island. It's going to be a lot of fun. Now, we have to go, sweetie."

I thank God that Hestia has already dressed him and put on his shoes for breakfast.

I hold his hand, hoping he doesn't notice how much I'm trembling, because Jax is very sensitive and can tell when I'm not okay.

"Odhran, are you going to take me for a plane ride?"

The Irishman exchanges a look with me.

"I'll take you to my plane, and you and your mom will have a nice trip."

I understand that this means he won't be coming with us, and my heart tightens with worry as I imagine a very real chance that something could happen to him.

My eyes blur with tears as, after Hestia returns with our bags, I let Odhran guide me out of the building, where Keiron is waiting for us in the back.

Hestia shows as much concern as I do. Only Jax seems completely oblivious, chattering away in his typical only-child monologue.

I have no idea if we'll actually make it to the island, but I trust Odhran and am sure we'll be safe.

I look out the darkened window of the vehicle, wondering if my fate will always be to run. And if I'm expecting a baby? Depending on the age, a child can't just leave their life behind, suddenly moving to a new city and country.

And wasn't that exactly what you subjected Jax to in recent years?

I'm confused, scared, and exhausted, and I lean my head back against the vehicle's seat.

"You'll be fine," Odhran says in a tone meant for only me to hear.

I open my eyes and look at him.

"And what about you?"

"It's not my first time, Elaine."

"I know, but you're not immortal."

"Nothing will happen to me, you know why?"

I shake my head, embarrassed at being so emotional. I've never considered myself the needy type or someone who cries in corners. I've never had time for that, as I've been too committed to surviving.

He wraps an arm around my shoulder and pulls me closer. He lowers his head and whispers in my ear:

"Because you're mine. I'm not going to make you available to the world, woman. You'll be my wife. I'll fill our home with heirs."

The promise sounds like a threat, given our current situation, but his words calm me because they mean he's making plans. I know more than ever that when we have something to fight for, we become practically invincible.

"I'll hold you to that, Odhran. Don't you dare let them catch you."

His face grows even more serious.

"I'll come back from hell to protect you, Elaine. I wasn't joking when I said you're never getting rid of me now. We belong to each other. Take that as a promise or a threat, the choice is yours, but nothing will change the fact that in this life, I'm yours forever."

Odhran

ABOUT AN HOUR LATER, I finally manage to calm down as I see the three of them boarding the plane that will take them to Cillian's private island.

As she reaches the last step of the stairs, just before disappearing from my view, she looks back.

She doesn't say anything, but she doesn't need to. I know what she's silently asking of me.

Come back to me.

What she doesn't know is that not even Satan incarnate could stop me from doing that.

Chapter 44

Elaine

I don't know what I was expecting when I finally set foot in the Caribbean, on the same island I fled from Trevino almost two years ago, but it wasn't for my chest to swell with intense emotion when Juno and Orla came to meet me and, without saying a word, enveloped me in a hug.

For a moment, I allow myself to stay that way and relax, feeling calmer.

"You're never getting away from me again," Juno says, in a tone of false threat.

"I've heard that line more times in the last few days than I can remember."

"From Odhran?"

I nod, agreeing.

"So it's really serious between you two?"

"Yes. I'm terrified, but I'm not running from how I feel anymore. I'm here to stay in his life."

"That's what I'm talking about!" Orla interjects. "My boys need strong and determined women."

"I don't know if I'm strong," I admit. "I've never had the option but to keep fighting. Why would I give up now that I'm in love?"

Odhran's aunt's smile widens, but then she says, touching my face:

"I'm sorry for what happened, dear."

I have no doubt she's referring to the assault I suffered from Trevino.

"Do you know everything?"

Both nod their heads in affirmation.

"Let's go inside," Juno says. "I'm being the worst hostess in the world, but I can't believe you're really here."

I notice, from my peripheral vision, a tall blonde and a slightly shorter brunette watching us from a distance; I assume they are the Russians Odhran mentioned would be here. He told me the other day that they've been added to the Syndicate, one being Rourke's girlfriend and the other Lorcan's wife, but I don't know who is who.

Rourke's girlfriend...

I look at the blonde woman more closely now and immediately recognize her. She's the same girl I warned at the bar, the only time I came to Boston after I fled, to be careful of the Irish who seemed to be watching her.

Both women hesitate before approaching us.

"Elaine, these are Tulia, Rourke's girlfriend" she says, pointing to the blonde and confirming my intuition "and Taisiya, Lorcan's wife. Girls, this is my runaway friend, Elaine. I hope you get along because I don't know how long we'll be isolated here."

I shake my head, smiling. Only Juno could make something as serious as a forced quarantine sound like a joke.

But what do I really know about her? For Cillian to choose her as his wife, she's surely familiar with the mafia. From the beginning, she seemed very comfortable with orders concerning her safety, as well as with the restrictions she's been under, which, of course, must be expected from the First Lady of the Irish mafia.

"Nice to meet you, Elaine" Taisiya is the first to speak and without the slightest formality, approaches and hugs me. "I was curious to meet the woman who tamed Mad Lion."

"Don't be indiscreet, Taisiya!" Tulia pretends to scold her, but she's smiling as well.

"Did I say something untrue? One by one, all the filthy Irishmen are being taken down."

Tulia doesn't offer any contact other than a handshake, and it takes me two seconds to realize that I'm facing a woman who is slow to trust people.

"The pleasure is mine," I say, unsure how to continue the conversation.

The circumstances of our reunion couldn't be more bizarre.

"I'm so happy to see you again, my daughter!" Orla says, but as soon as she kisses me on the forehead, she rushes over to where Jax is.

I see that he looks confused when he sees her, probably because he doesn't remember her, but Odhran's aunt wastes no time, getting straight to the point.

"Do you still like cupcakes?"

I watch a smile spread across my son's face. Perhaps his memory of our past in Boston doesn't let him recall the details, but he always talked about the cupcakes "from that aunt" Juno.

"I love sweets, ma'am," he says politely, and my heart swells with pride, "but I don't know if mommy will let me have one because I just had my breakfast and then it's lunch."

There's a chorus of "aww" from all the women present, and Hestia and I exchange a knowing look, pleased to see that we're doing a good job. But I know it's not enough. Jax needs a normal life. To make friends and go to school. To have his schedule respected, and not live like a fugitive, constantly moving cities, changing rooms, altering his daily routine within months or, sometimes, even weeks.

"How about this," I hear Lorcan's wife say, perhaps sensing that I need to talk with Odhran's relatives, "we go inside to unpack, and then decide if we'll have lunch or eat some cupcakes. What do you think?"

She gets a brighter smile from my boy than the sun, and I feel calmer seeing that Jax hasn't been too affected, at least on the surface, by our abrupt departure from Boston.

We start walking toward the house, but the cellphone Odhran handed me when he said goodbye starts ringing.

I show the phone to them, indicating that I received a call, and step away.

"Did you arrive safely?" I hear the gruff voice, but the one I most want to hear right now, say.

It means he's alive. Safe.

"I'm sure you already know the answer," I say, a bit annoyed with myself for feeling so emotional.

"Stay like this, waiting for me, beautiful. When I get there, you won't be sleeping."

"Are you coming?"

"Don't you doubt it? As soon as everything is over, I'll find you, Elaine. Your place is by my side."

I hesitate before responding, my heart pounding in my chest.

"I love you," I finally say. "Don't you dare get stabbed or anything like that, Irishman. You're mine."

"I am, and I'll come back to you, baby. I'll always come back."

Chapter 45

Elaine

"**I**'ve been a terrible friend," Juno says, surprising me, as soon as we're alone together. This time, I won't be staying in the bungalow like at the wedding, but in the main house.

I had forgotten just how large Juno's residence on the island was.

A huge floor-to-ceiling window lets us see the ocean in all its glory.

It was through this window that I was staring, distracted, when her declaration brought me back to the conversation.

"I'm not sure I understand."

"First, tell me: are you hungry?"

"A little, but I'd rather talk first."

The two of them look at me as if they're worried.

"We know," Orla finally says.

"Know what?"

"That you might be pregnant."

"Jesus! How could he...," I start, feeling my face flush with embarrassment, but then I remember that we repeated the same "slip" last night, and this time, consciously. "Why did he tell? We still need to wait a few days before I can take the test."

"The main reason is that there are no secrets between us, Elaine," Odhran's aunt declares. "And it's not because we have issues with privacy concepts, but because keeping important information like this goes against security concerns."

"Security concerns?"

"Sweetheart, you are not just... and when I say 'just', it's not to belittle you, but because relationships can go very right or very wrong, so don't take it personally. The fact is, now you are not *just* Odhran's girlfriend but might be the mother of his heir. Bringing an O'Callaghan into the world means your child will be protected like a little prince would be if..."

She stops speaking.

"If what?"

Juno holds my hand.

"If something were to happen to my brother-in-law, Elaine. It's not what we want. I pray every night for God to have mercy on our family, and I can't be sure He even hears me, given our men's 'business branch,' but I do it anyway."

"I also pray for Odhran, even though he told me he doesn't get along with God."

Orla shakes her head.

"You know what he told me when he witnessed his parents dying? That God didn't like him, or He wouldn't have allowed that. I think that was the moment he stopped talking to the Creator."

Despite having spoken superficially with me about his parents, I sense intuitively that the episode affected him much more than he admits. So much so that until recently, he didn't want to have a child.

"The fact is that being married to someone in the Syndicate means uncertainty about the future," Juno continues, "but one thing you will never need to doubt: whatever happens, you and your child will always be ours."

"I'm not married to Odhran."

"He will bind you forever, my dear. If you have any illusions about that, wake up to reality." Orla smiles.

"I don't want to leave. I don't intend to go far because I love him."

"Even knowing what we represent?" the matriarch asks.

"My life and Elysia's wasn't a fairy tale."

"I assume not," Juno says, sounding awkward. "I never tried to delve deeper because I thought if I did, you'd ask me about my past as well, and I wasn't ready to talk about it."

"Was it really that bad?"

"My mother let Syndicate men abuse me, beating me. After a while, she started asking them to..."

"Jesus, I will never hear that without wanting that bitch to come back to life so I can kill her again," Orla says, her eyes welling up with tears.

It's the first time I see her show any vulnerability, and it tells me that Juno's life story must be much worse than she's letting on.

I understand Orla's sentiment. I never knew Juno's mother, nor do I know her name, but I want to strangle her. The duty of a parent is to protect their child, not expose them to harm.

"They..." I start, unable to continue.

"No," my friend replies, and for the next half hour, she tells me everything she remembers about her childhood, up until the day Cillian rescued her.

Her life was a horror movie, and anyone who sees her now, strong and confident, can't imagine the hell she went through.

Juno's story is the greatest proof that you can't judge a book by its cover. I would never have guessed she survived a mother who, if she weren't dead, would deserve to rot in jail for the rest of her life.

"Your turn," she says. "And I swear I'm not asking out of curiosity, but because I want to truly get to know you."

"You already know that Jax isn't my biological child, but my nephew." They both nod, as I've already discussed this with Juno at least. "Elysia and I are daughters of different fathers. Hers was an alcoholic, but despite the illness, a good man. My mother left him and took Elysia with her. She remarried. My father wasn't a drug addict, but he was an abuser of women who beat us all."

"My God," Orla says.

"There was nothing we could say to make her leave him, so one day, when we were old enough, Elysia and I left home. Mom stayed with him until the day they both died."

"He killed her?" Juno's voice quivers, turning into a near-whisper as she asks.

"No. It was an accident. A short circuit in the wiring of the building they lived in. In total, four families lost their lives. We kept in touch with her, loved her, and advised her as best as we could, but she always found excuses to stay with the wretch."

"It's very hard to leave toxic relationships," Orla says. "I was lucky to have a good man, but I had friends who suffered like hell at the hands of their husbands, and they never left them. Physical abuse, betrayal, verbal disrespect. It's like being sick and not being able to walk to the cure, which in this case would be distancing oneself from the bastards who made them suffer."

"My mother used to say that dad was good at first. I don't know if that's true or if that beginning lasted a month or two. The fact is she lived stuck in the past, in the illusion that he could go back to being someone who only existed in her head."

"Maybe what she remembered as 'the phase when they were in love' was the honeymoon period that couples experience when they don't know each other well enough."

"Yes, that could be," I agree with Orla. "The fact is Elysia and I wanted something different. Especially Elysia. I'll try to shorten a long story. After a few disastrous relationships, she finally seemed in love, until, after the initial phase passed, she started coming home in tears with red marks on her arms."

"Are you telling us that this boyfriend, who we now know was Trevino, was hitting your sister? The same son of a bitch who attacked her yesterday?" Juno asks.

"Yes, the very same. But there's much more to it. I think he killed Elysia."

Chapter 46

Elaine

"I don't understand anything," Juno says.

"Let me try to create a timeline. I think it will make it easier. You won't remember because you weren't in the United States yet, but maybe Orla does. Do you remember Janice, a fight staff member whose sister was kidnapped by Salvadorans?" I ask Odhran's aunt.

"Yes, I'll never forget her sister's story. The poor girl committed suicide, and Janice disappeared shortly after. All the women in the Syndicate talked about it for months."

"I think they *disappeared* her."

"What?"

"I became friends with Janice. She told me in detail about the ordeal her sister went through until she couldn't fight anymore and committed suicide. And that's why, knowing my coworker relatively well, I'm sure she didn't just leave, as if she were running away from those bastards. She never collected her belongings from the apartment she was living in or even the last paycheck she was owed from the fights. I think the 'M' of Muerte killed her because she did everything to ensure justice for her sister."

I see Juno shrink back, as if feeling a shiver.

"You're right, Elaine. I wasn't here when it all happened, but Odhran told me the story of the girl who threw herself into a crocodile-infested swamp to escape the Salvadorans. He did that so I would understand that the threat from those bastards against me was real."

"Threat?"

"The boss's nephew, a jerk named Joe Pineda, tried to grab me once on the university campus where I was studying. I got away from him and the bodyguards protected me, but he swore he would get revenge. He even sent someone after me in the college bathroom, but Odhran... um... *resolved* the problem."

I know that this *resolving the problem* means Joe Pineda is no longer with us, and I'm relieved to hear that.

I researched the 'M' of Muerte because Janice's sister's story left me negatively impressed by the brutality of the Salvadoran mafia members. They don't respect women or children. They don't even have a code of loyalty among themselves, and several have been sentenced to death in Texas.

"Does Cillian know about this?" Juno asks. "I'm referring to Janice's disappearance."

"I don't think so. In New Jersey, the general belief is that she simply left because she couldn't handle her sister's death. I never believed that."

"I don't understand. But what does this story have to do with your sister or Trevino Cabrera?"

I sigh.

"I don't know. It's just that as soon as I told Elysia about Janice's sister's death and then her disappearance, she told me that we needed to move. Actually, leave the state. At the time, I thought that her secret boyfriend, whom I didn't even know was Trevino Cabrera and certainly didn't know was part of the Syndicate, had something to do with the fate of the two sisters. It was very immediate: as soon as Elysia heard the story, I could see on her face that she was scared, and the next day, she wanted to drop everything and move."

"But that doesn't make sense," Juno says. "Trevino Cabrera is a high-ranking Syndicate official."

"A trusted man of Cillian's, otherwise he would never have set foot on this island at the wedding," Orla says.

"When I found out he was a Syndicate member, that's what I thought too. Now, I'm not so sure. He confronted me at the wedding. Said my sister had stolen from him. He chased me for over two years saying that my sister had stolen from him, although I had no idea what he was talking about."

"And now do you?" Orla asks.

"No, but this morning, Hestia found a USB drive inside Jaxton's favorite bear. A gift my sister gave him when he was born."

"My God! Do you think there's something on that USB drive that Trevino Cabrera wanted?"

"Yes, and we'll find out soon because I handed it over to Odhran."

"What could be on it?" Juno asks Cillian's aunt.

"For him to have pursued Elaine for so long? Either evidence that he was stealing from the Syndicate or some other form of betrayal, as Elaine initially thought, like being connected to the Salvadorans or even another mafia. In any case, I wouldn't want to be in his shoes when my boys find out."

I don't tell her what I think: that regardless of what they find on the USB drive, I think Trevino will be killed.

Odhran is a man of his word and he knows that I will only be safe with the lawyer out of the game.

I never wished anyone dead, but I know that he ended my sister's life, preventing my nephew from growing up with his mother. He turned our lives into hell, and for that, I'll be glad when he's no longer breathing the same air as us.

ABOUT TWO HOURS LATER, when we're all having a late lunch prepared by Juno's housekeepers, I approach Tulia.

"You didn't follow my advice, girl. Ended up stuck with one of the Irish," I say, ensuring only she hears.

"I thought you didn't remember me. I was so embarrassed when I saw you arrive."

"I rarely forget a face, and when I found out Rourke's girlfriend was Russian, and then saw you here, I put two and two together. So, in the end, did you manage to pick just one?"

There's a story that's always circulated behind the scenes of the fights about a "deal" between Keiron, Rourke, and the women in the past. I know both are straight, but I suspect they used to share partners.

"I love Keiron, but as a friend I'll keep in my heart forever. Rourke is my life. My man."

"I never thought I'd live to see this day."

"Rourke taking a woman seriously again?"

"No, I never met his first wife. In fact, I didn't have any close connections with Syndicate members. I only worked the fights. I'm talking about having two Russians mingling with the Irish Boss's wife."

"It's a long story," she says, smiling.

"I love a good love story. Go ahead and start talking."

Chapter 47

Odhran

Days Later

I've always been fine with the darkness and filth of the places where we usually take our "guests."

The smell of blood, the screams of pain, the fear of others—none of it bothers me, but at this moment, I'm done with this shit. I just want to wipe the bastard off the face of the earth so I can join my brothers and Lorcan to discuss the alliance we're forming with the Russians against the Sicilians.

"You're going to talk, you son of a bitch!" I punch Trevino in the face, but he remains silent.

Even the "truth serum" didn't work on the bastard.

His face is disfigured, and several parts of his body are missing. We managed to keep him lucid by injecting drugs into him.

I've already had my revenge. I beat and tortured him so much that my arms are numb from exhaustion, but I can't kill him until I get what I need.

I got him to confess that he killed Elysia, but not because he was obsessed with the supposed stolen material he accused her of stealing.

He admitted he went after Elaine, which is an unnecessary confirmation I didn't need, but no matter how much I hurt him, he won't mention the damn pendrive, which now, more than ever, I'm sure is the key to everything.

The adrenaline still controls my body, making me feel like I've taken some energy drink.

The attempted invasion of my building came from the Sicilians and ended with seven of them dead.

Cillian ordered the bodies be chopped up and delivered in trash bags to the Cosa Nostra.

"You're going to kill him and he still won't talk," Kellan says.

"How can you know that?"

He shows me the pendrive I gave him a few days ago. He's facing away from Trevino, so even if the bastard is still thinking clearly, he won't be able to see what my brother has in his hand.

"Did you find out what was on it?"

"Yes. Part of it was lost, but I think what I accessed is more than enough."

"Are you sure?"

"No, but there's nothing more to be done. It seems to have been partially damaged. I'll try again later, but my head is already boiling from this shit."

"What's on it, Kellan?"

"Not here. It's something that can only be discussed in private, and Cillian needs to hear it too. Don't kill him," he warns the men in the room with us. "Come with me. Our brother is waiting for you with Lorcan. We have a lot to discuss."

"WAS THAT BASTARD STEALING from us?" my older brother roars.

"Yes, in more ways than one. Besides selling our routes, several of our men were killed during the delivery because of him. There's much more. He also embezzled around a hundred million dollars from us."

"I promised I'd let you kill Trevino, Odhran, but I'm the one who will finish this. It's a good thing Juno isn't in Boston. I won't be going home today."

"I don't care," I say. "I've gotten what I wanted from him, and to be honest, I'm tired of drawing blood from the bastard, but I want to understand how he could operate for so long without anyone realizing it."

"Now, the million-dollar question is: why the hell would he risk it this way?"

Kellan spins the pendrive between his fingers.

"This doesn't just explain the whole operation. It's the key to recovering our money. The passwords for the offshore accounts are encrypted. That's why he was so desperate to find Elysia and then Elaine. He's been stealing from us for years, risking his own neck for nothing when the pendrive disappeared."

"The idiot stored all the information in the same place?" I ask.

"If you ask me, he doesn't know shit about information technology, and it's not the kind of thing you can just share. Hiring a hacker to steal from the Syndicate? He was risking not only being robbed by that guy but also being exposed if the hacker decided to betray him."

"So, in the end, we didn't suffer any loss?" Cillian asks.

"As far as money goes, no, we'll recover everything, but we don't know what information Trevino passed on or to which rival organization."

"We need to find out," Lorcan says.

"This," Kellan shows us the pendrive "doesn't just contain offshore accounts and their respective passwords. Not even our routes that he sold... There's proof that Trevino was associated with another criminal organization. I think, combined with the fact that he was pissed off for not being able to get his hands on the stolen money, what kept him silent, no matter how much Odhran tortured him, was knowing that if he told us anything, his secret associates would come after his family."

"Do you think it was the Sicilians?"

"I assume so, but jumping to conclusions is premature. Part of the pendrive was lost. We'll recover the stolen money, but I'll keep working on the device to try to uncover the rest. Maybe we have a secret enemy we haven't suspected."

I know what he's saying makes perfect sense. Any organization Trevino was spying for, passing information about us, wouldn't want the bastard to turn them in. If they suspect he did, they'll decimate the lawyer's family as revenge.

"So, in the end, it was about the money, but also because the bastard feared for his descendants?" I ask.

"I believe so. Anyway, the fact is that since we have the pendrive, Trevino is of no more use to us. If my theory is correct, he won't reveal anything we don't already know, no matter how much we continue to slice him up while he's still alive. I'll work on the pendrive to recover the rest of the information."

He glances at Cillian, who stands up, indicating that the meeting is over. I know he'll go straight to settle accounts with Trevino. Like all of us, my older brother has his demons to exorcise.

"I'm heading to the Caribbean," I say, without elaborating, and despite the mess we're in, they all laugh.

"To see your wife," Cillian says.

"Yes. Elaine called me earlier today. Orla is worried about the assault she suffered because of the possibility of being pregnant," I say, my words scratching my throat, as thinking that our child might have been harmed by that bastard drives me mad again. "Juno and Taisiya's doctor is flying out there. He will examine her and do the pregnancy test. I want to be present when it happens."

"Come back in time for the meeting with Yerik," Lorcan warns. "I asked Ruslan to arrange everything to move it up. We can't afford to wait so long to reaffirm our agreement with the Russians against the Sicilians. They are determined to strike, and now, with the gift Cillian sent them" he continues, referring to the chopped-up bodies of the soldiers that the Cosa Nostra has already received "we can expect retaliation at any moment."

Elaine

"YOU'RE GOING TO CRACK the floor," Juno says.

"I'm nervous. I think the doctor's visit is an overreaction."

"It's not, dear. You might be pregnant, and confirmation is necessary, especially after what you've been through." She sighs. "We both know that's not why you're feeling so anxious, but because Odhran is supposed to arrive soon too."

"What's going to happen?"

"What?"

"If I'm pregnant, I don't want him to marry me just because of the baby. My mother married for love twice, and both relationships went very wrong. What can happen with a union formed out of duty?"

"Do you hear yourself?"

"I don't understand."

"Elaine, we're talking about Odhran 'Mad Lion' O'Callaghan. Can you imagine your man doing something out of obligation, without truly wanting it?"

I think about what she's saying and also about the last night we spent in Boston.

"No."

"He would take on the baby if any other woman had become pregnant, but if he asks you to marry him, it won't be because of the child, but because he wants you."

"He said we are forever."

"Then what's tormenting you, dear? I know your life example was terrible, but if I had only followed my parents' relationship, I would never have married either. You know what I learned, Elaine? The past serves as a learning tool, but it's not the whole book. This is your story. Rewrite it according to what you want. Don't let fear stop you from being happy."

Chapter 48

Elaine

I asked him to leave.

I'm too nervous about the possibility of an unplanned pregnancy to handle everything at once. I noticed, from the way he looked at me, that he didn't take it well, but he didn't want to argue, which tells me he must have talked to Orla, Juno, or both.

When he arrived earlier today, after a quick chat with everyone, Odhran, without the slightest embarrassment despite our "witnesses" and the laughter from Jax, who found it *very funny* when he picked me up, took me to the room where I'm staying and for about three hours, made love to me.

It wasn't sex. I felt the difference. The lust was still there. He's filthy, has a dirty mouth, and knows how to drive me wild, but this time, there was something more.

He seemed determined to make me fall in love.

As if I wasn't already...

Later, he talked about the future. He didn't use the word marriage, but he talked about us—yes, he used the plural—moving to a big house and mentioned again about putting Jaxton in preschool.

And still, with all these "guarantees," I'm terrified.

I watch intently as the doctor takes the pregnancy test out of his bag. He asks me a few questions, like the date of my last period and if I've been feeling any different symptoms lately.

I answer, trying to control the anxiety that grows with every passing second.

"Will the test give me certainty?" I ask, I think for the fourth time, and the doctor looks at me without showing any sign of impatience.

Either the man is an excellent actor, as he doesn't seem annoyed by my insecurity, or he's so used to anxious women like me that it's part of his daily routine.

"Yes, we will have certainty, but I'll also take a blood sample, and by tomorrow morning at the latest, I'll have the answer, because the Beta HCG test leaves no room for doubt."

I was surprised to see that he brought a complete mini-laboratory with him, and I think it must have been a requirement from Odhran. Aside from the doctor who examined me at the Syndicate clinic on the night I was attacked by Trevino, I haven't consulted any others.

About twenty minutes later, I'm waiting for the urine test result, pacing back and forth in the bathroom, and only while obsessively staring at the object in my hand do I realize that despite all the current downsides, I really want this baby. And when, after looking away for a few seconds, the confirmation appears, I can't contain my emotion.

I leave the bathroom seeking validation from the obstetrician and swear I can feel my heart beating in my ear. The fear doesn't go away, but the desire to be a mother, the certainty that a small part of me is being created inside my body, overshadows everything else.

He takes the test from my hand when I offer it to him, and I might be going crazy, but I think he hides a smile. He looks for just a few seconds before saying:

"Congratulations, Miss Ramsey, you're pregnant."

My heart leaps with pure happiness.

After asking me to sit in one of the armchairs in the room, he begins to explain the next steps, confirming the need for the Beta HCG test, as well as an ultrasound in the future.

I ask a question or two, avoiding the one that frightens me the most, but I know that if this man will be taking care of me until the delivery, as is likely to happen, there can be no secrets between us.

Besides, he's Juno and Taisiya's obstetrician, which means Cillian's family trusts him.

"I have the feeling that you want to tell me something and don't know how."

I nod in agreement.

"A few days ago, I was assaulted," I start, and I feel angry for feeling embarrassed. No woman should fear revealing something like this. That coward would beat me even with just one arm, given our size difference. "Does that pose any risk to my baby?"

"What kind of assault are we talking about?"

I see in his expression that although he tries to remain neutral, he fails. Then, I'm horrified as I guess what he's thinking.

"It wasn't Odhran. He would never lay a hand on me. It was an accident with a... um... stranger," I explain carefully, because whether he's a Syndicate doctor or not, I'm not sure how safe it is to reveal this.

"I didn't say it was," he quickly defends himself.

Despite appearing upset at the fact that I might have been assaulted by the father of the child I'm carrying, apparently this displeasure isn't enough to make him confront the Syndicate elite, in case it was Odhran who hurt me.

"It's alright," I say, fearing the man might have a heart attack from fear "with that cleared up, can you please answer my question? The man I told you about pushed me. I hit my head. I passed out, but I was examined by a doctor at the time."

"Did you have any tests done?"

"Just a head X-ray."

"Well, Boss told me today that a clinic will be set up on the island in the coming weeks."

"Are you sure about that?"

"Yes. So, I'll be able to do all the tests calmly, since you can't... um... return to the United States for now."

"Alright, but are there risks?"

"Beta HCG levels begin to decrease immediately after a miscarriage and usually return to baseline levels within a few weeks. However, in cases of incomplete miscarriage or ectopic pregnancy, beta HCG levels may remain elevated for a prolonged period. I'll be more reassured when we do the imaging tests."

"Thank you," I say, feeling my heart sink. "So, I just have to wait? The positive result from the test we just did might just be because the beta HCG levels are still high, but maybe I've had a miscarriage?"

He looks at me sympathetically.

"Yes, I'm sorry."

He leaves the room, and after being alone for half an hour, I know I can't keep hiding.

I asked Odhran not to attend the consultation, even against his will, but he has the right to know the truth.

Chapter 49

Odhran

"Another castle, Odhran," Jax asks, and Luke, my nephew, along with Nikita, Lorcan and Taisiya's adopted daughter, a little girl my cousin rescued, clap their hands, although I'm sure they have no idea what they're celebrating.

I never thought that playing in the sand could be relaxing, but after nearly an hour with the three of them, the tension that was dominating every cell of me when Elaine kicked me out of the medical appointment has diminished.

Being with her is like entering a new universe, and it's not poetic at all; it's because I had to control my temper like I don't remember ever having done before when she told me to leave the room.

I have the controlling gene in my DNA, if such a thing exists. I'm not good at delegating tasks, especially when it comes to those important to me, and the woman who just dismissed me, the one I intend to put a ring on and show the whole world is mine, represents the pinnacle of my universe since she came back into my life.

A wave crashes on the beach, filling the castle moat with water, and the three little ones cheer.

I smile at their happiness.

Living in our world is like living in hell, with Satan himself as a neighbor, but I intend to keep the innocence of Jax, Luke, the little girl, and however many more come, for as long as possible.

"Mommmy!" Jax calls, looking over my shoulder.

Finally!

I turn to her and feel my chest tighten when I see her face. The eyes, especially.

Elaine is crying.

"Hey, guys, shall we go in to see Grandma Orla?" I suggest.

"Grandma!" Luke shouts, and the other two laugh.

I scoop all three of them up simultaneously and walk towards her.

"Do you want to come in or stay out here?"

I know something is very wrong, and it can only be the doctor's answer about the pregnancy.

"I'll wait for you."

After leaving the boys with Hestia, I'm back in five minutes.

"I..."

"Shhh... We'll talk later," I say. "I want to hold you for a bit first."

I pick her up and start walking along the water's edge. At first, she resists relaxing because I think she's fought alone for so long that she doesn't know how to trust her peace to someone else.

She says she wants my protection, but I know I still have a long way to go before making Elaine believe that she's the only one for me, my everything.

"The first time I saw you, what I thought was that I had never met a more beautiful woman in my life."

She had laid her head on my chest but lifts it to look at me.

"No need to play the seducer, Irish. I'm already won over."

"My father used to say that when we O'Callaghans set our eyes on our one and only, we know immediately it's her. I always knew it was you, but I didn't want to get married."

"Because you liked being single?"

"Not for that reason. I'm thirty-one, baby. I'm past the stage where bodies attract me just for being perfect. After a while, you don't remember names or even what happened. The pleasure is instant, it doesn't last. Pure physical satisfaction."

"So it's about what happened with your parents?"

I nod, indicating yes.

"We grew up inside the Syndicate. We went to family meetings, parties, and you know something I always noticed? My father never looked at another woman. If my mother stepped away, he followed her with his eyes. The world began and ended with her. He was a tough man. He saw as many deaths as I now have, but when it came to our mother, he never stopped telling her how much he loved her. In a world where death and blood were our everyday, at home, we had our own little universe."

"Odhran..."

"We were taught never to share information. My father had many enemies, and saying where we were going, whether to a bakery or a vacation, represented danger for everyone. The day my father died was my birthday."

"My God!"

I don't look at her because if I do, I won't be able to finish, as I can tell from her tone that she's about to cry.

I want Elaine to understand what she means to me, and I'm going to open up like I've never done with anyone before.

"I spent the whole week talking to my friends, all children of Syndicate members, that on my birthday, we'd go to a special place. I was starting to play drums, obsessed with it, and my parents promised to get me the best one money could buy. We spent an hour inside the store. On the way out, shooters killed them. I only escaped because a bodyguard saved me."

"It was a tragedy, my love."

"It wasn't. The ones who killed them were the parents of two of the children to whom I told where we would be that afternoon. I broke a rule. I shared our location with anyone who would listen, and that's why they were killed."

Elaine doesn't say anything. She wraps her arms around my neck, and when I sit with her in the sand, she cries, holding onto me.

"I know it's pointless to say, but I'll say it anyway. It wasn't your fault. If your friends were children of Syndicate members, they should have been keeping an eye on your father for a long time."

I look out at the sea.

"You're right, it's pointless to talk. My brothers have tried, but I'll never stop blaming myself."

"So why did you choose to open up today?"

"To tell you that I'm in love with you, Elaine, and it's not something that will end tomorrow. I hesitated to get involved because I knew, from the very first second I saw you, that once I touched you, I would never let you go. I don't deserve you. I know it was my fault Trevino reached you that day, and if the doctor told you that it caused you to lose our child..."

"It wasn't anyone's fault but that monster's, Odhran. He was closing in on me. If I hadn't gone to find you, I don't know if I'd be alive today."

I close my eyes and press our foreheads together.

"I have the feeling you're going to leave at any moment because you think what I feel isn't serious. I've messed up a lot in my life, but I've never failed to keep a promise, and I'm swearing to you today that my heart is yours, baby. I want you and I want our children, as many as you want to have. I want to adopt Jax."

"You want to?"

"Yes. He's mine, just like you are. Now, tell me why you were so sad when you left the house."

"He did the urine test, and it came back positive."

I look at her, unable to believe it, feeling incredibly happy, but soon realize that something is wrong.

"What else?"

"He's not sure if I'm still pregnant. — She sniffles. — He took my blood, but even with that test, he can't be certain. Only with the passing weeks and when we can do an imaging test."

"An ultrasound," I say, remembering that Lorcan's wife always gets one, and Juno did too when she was pregnant.

"Yes."

"And when will it be done?"

"He said around two or three weeks from now, when I'll be six weeks pregnant."

"Why can't it be determined from a blood test?"

"Because in some cases, beta HCG levels remain altered afterward..."

She doesn't continue, and I understand immediately. I pull her to my chest, holding her as if in a protective dome.

"I want this baby, Odhran. I know we didn't plan for it, but I really want it to still be inside me."

I kiss her hair and say nothing. I hold her in a way that, I hope, shows all my love.

I could put the world at Elaine's feet, but I can't give her back the life of our child if it was taken, and that drives me completely mad.

"Marry me."

"And if I don't..."

"I'm not asking because you're pregnant. I want you to be, and I want to leave you with a full belly of my children every year, but my request is for you. I love you, Elaine. And I will love you until the day I die."

"That man killed my sister and may have killed my child too. I don't know if I'll be okay if the miscarriage is confirmed. Just the possibility makes me desperate."

"I don't want just your good days, little one. I'll take everything from you and be whatever you need."

She looks at me for a long time, crying. Then she says what will seal her fate forever:

"I accept."

Chapter 50

Odhran

Meeting of the Irish Syndicate and the Russian Organization

We learned our lesson.

The last time we met, in a warehouse, we were attacked by the Cosa Nostra.

At the moment, we trust no one except our closest allies, and the location of the meeting was only revealed an hour before.

For months, we have been working together, quietly fighting our common enemy with planned actions, but now both Yerik and Cillian know that we will have to plan and put an end to these threats once and for all.

We don't delude ourselves into thinking we'll wipe out the Sicilians, but we will eliminate the one who, for now, wants war.

There was no reason for it to have started, except if the idiot who gave the orders to attack us intended to wipe out the leadership of both organizations by catching us off guard.

The meeting where we suffered the ambush had been orchestrated by Ruslan, because with Lorcan's wife pregnant, an unprecedented link was created between us and the Russians, as the baby would, in a way, be the heir to both organizations.

A permanent bond would be formed between the Syndicate and the Russian Brotherhood.

Perhaps that frightened our enemies. We'll never know for sure. We didn't ask for this shit, but now we'll only get out of it when we have the head of the current Cosa Nostra Counselor, who we've learned gave the order for the attack, on a platter.

The room is filled with a heavy atmosphere of tension, where every exchanged glance between the members of both organizations is laden with distrust and hostility.

A few years ago, if you had told Cillian and Yerik they'd be gathered here, they would have killed the damn joker, but the truth is, on the day of the attack, one saved the other's life by simultaneously shooting at Sicilians who were positioned behind them.

I doubt it's something either of them will ever forget. Both are honorable men.

We are opposites in everything. The Russians are cold, we Irish are explosive.

Today, however, no one is trying to mark their territory. The only thing we want is to eliminate the threat that has been hovering over us.

"I don't want to wait." Ruslan, Lorcan's grandfather, Yerik's grandfather, and the current advisor to the Russian mafia, Grigori, is the first to speak. "I think our response needs to be immediate."

Although he is no longer the Pakhan, he is respected by criminal organizations worldwide, making the Cosa Nostra's action even more suicidal.

There are other mafias waiting for a signal from us to join the war, but forging alliances means owing favors, and if that's the case, at least it's with the Russians, whose interests align with ours at the moment.

"They're not respecting women and children. Because of that shithead, our wives are prisoners on a damn island," Cillian says.

Yerik nods, and I have no doubt that the Russians have also hidden their families for now.

"What do you suggest?" I ask Ruslan, but Grigori answers.

"Eliminate the Cosa Nostra counselor. For months we've been dancing in hell. There have been more deaths in the three organizations during this period than in the last five years combined. But the attack they tried to organize at his house, possibly knowing his girlfriend and stepson were there" he continues, and I'm not surprised they know about Elaine and Jax "cannot be met with any retaliation less than death."

"In any other scenario, I'd say we wouldn't need to go that far," Dmitri, one of Yerik's trusted men, says "but if they're not capable of honoring a damn pact, leaving our wives and heirs out of it, there's no alternative."

"I also suggest small-scale attacks," Lorcan says. "The death of the counselor and, on the same night, the extermination of about a dozen second-tier men. We won't touch children or women."

"And if they don't back down?" Leonid, another Russian, asks.

"Then there will be no alternative," Ruslan says. "We will be the protagonists of a bloodbath."

The meeting stretches for four hours because everything must be carefully planned. Flawless logistics; otherwise, we'll return to our women in coffins.

The coordinated attacks will occur in five American cities, but we know the Cosa Nostra counselor is not in the United States, but in Europe.

"He requests two or three prostitutes per night," Ruslan says. "One of them will drug him with an undetectable poison. I've used it before. It takes three days to take effect."

"Why not do something spectacular?" my middle brother asks.

"Because there's an exact point to which you can push your enemy. If you push him less, he'll seem weak. If you push him too much, there's a chance we'll all die. We don't want to humiliate the entire organization, but to show that we will never forgive an attack, and more than that, we will eliminate those who ordered it. Once we kill the other second-tier men on the same day as the counselor, they'll get the message."

The first attacks will occur within a week.

The deaths of the second-tier men won't be as simple as that of the counselor.

Stabbings, hit-and-runs, shootings, hangings. We'll be creative to make the greatest impact possible and leave no doubt that we could do the same to any of them.

In addition, we will destroy two drug refinement labs and sink a ship with their arms smuggling.

"That will be enough," Ruslan says.

"How can you know?" Maxim asks.

"Because we are assassins, but above all, we are businessmen. No one likes to lose money. Like us, the Cosa Nostra is not a single man; it is a whole, and when that whole is threatened, they will retreat."

Chapter 51

Odhran

We're all wearing bulletproof vests right now. Cillian was adamant about it.

Normally, we wouldn't be on the field. For a long time now, Lorcan, Kellan, and I have been banned from participating in battles where the chances of not coming out alive are high. The loss of any one of us, or all of us simultaneously, represents a greater risk than death itself—leaving our Boss exposed, as Cillian would be without his most trusted men—the family.

Today, Kellan, Lorcan, and I are tasked with hunting down and eliminating three of the most important men in the Cosa Nostra's second tier, as decided in the meeting with the Russians. Each of us is in a different city, about to send our target to hell.

The car I'm in is armored, as are the vehicles of my men, who form a three-car convoy. They're not flashy at all. Nothing like the latest models that those fucking Mexicans like to use, but something that would never attract the attention of the authorities. Indeed, two patrol cars passed by me while I was heading to the property where my target is, and they didn't even slow down.

We have a significant part of the country's police on our payroll, but there's always the risk of running into real cops, like that bastard Joaquín Oviedo, who has always been waiting—and perhaps still is—to lock my older brother up and throw away the key.

As we approach the property, I hear the sound of tires on gravel while the vehicle moves slowly down the deserted road at this early hour of the morning.

I can already see the entrance to the property when, suddenly and without any warning, the battle begins.

Were they waiting for us?

Maybe yes, maybe no. But that doesn't matter in the slightest.

When we leave here, there won't be a single Sicilian left alive. Without stopping the cars, which continue in convoy inside the property, we retaliate.

The sound of gunfire fills the air, and when we finally get out of the vehicles, all we can see are enemy bodies scattered around.

Ten minutes later, we're inside the residence, and I have my target at my feet. The gun is pointed at his head, but the decision was to use creativity in eliminating the second tier.

The man is still breathing, though with great difficulty, as the shot I gave him in the abdomen is bleeding profusely.

He won't last much longer, so I need to decide how to end his shitty existence.

I pull the hunting knife from inside my boot. I like to use it for this kind of mission.

I cut his throat from ear to ear, but not enough to kill him yet.

My men know what they're supposed to do, and immediately, the Sicilian's blood begins to be collected and spread across the walls and ceiling.

I crouch near the man who is still trying to speak, even though he's only minutes away from leaving this planet.

"Do you know who I am?"

— *A fucking Irish...*

"That's right, smartass. I'm a *fucking* Irishman, and we're going to take out your associates, just like we did with you. But you don't have to worry about that anymore. Tell the Devil, when you meet him, that he doesn't need to thank me for sending another asshole his way."

I hold the knife with both hands and drive it between his eyebrows. He will be photographed like this, and the image sent to the Don.

I can't deny that the work is a masterpiece, and his eyes, wide open with terror, add a final touch to my mission.

I stand up knowing we need to leave, but the thrill of the hunt, of war, still pulses through my veins.

ABOUT FORTY-EIGHT HOURS have passed, and after receiving the news that the mission was a success, my brothers, Lorcan, and I are gathered.

"Is it over?" Kellan asks.

"The Russians did their part, we did ours, but it will never really be over. It's just a break so we can catch our breath," Cillian asserts.

"Ruslan told me that the Don of the Cosa Nostra contacted him, proposing a negotiation," Lorcan says.

"Why not with Yerik, but with the former Pakhan?"

"Yerik refuses to speak with him for now."

"He's right," Cillian says. "Let them shit their pants in fear first. Keep them on edge, not knowing when the next attack will come."

"Yes, my grandfather refused to meet with him at this time. The Don said he wasn't aware of his advisor's actions."

"That's a fucking lie!" Cillian growls. "Or he's a piece-of-shit leader who doesn't deserve the position he holds. If he can't control his own men, he doesn't deserve to be the Don."

"I don't buy that story either," I say, standing up. "But since we're on a break, I'm going back to my wife."

"The clinic I had set up on the island is ready," Cillian says. "Though, if our actions bring a positive result, the women and children won't need to stay there much longer. Elaine could come here to Boston for the exams she needs."

They all know about our situation concerning her pregnancy confirmation: that the doctor who examined her on the island said her beta HCG levels are still high, but that he won't provide a precise diagnosis until she undergoes imaging tests.

"I don't want to wait. Hestia told me she hasn't been sleeping well. I'm heading there right now. Whatever the result of the test, my place is by her side."

Chapter 52

Elaine

I thought I already knew the exact definition of fear. After all, that's what I felt fleeing from the moment Elysia died.

The fear that haunted me back then, and even when I was with Trevino Cabrera in the Syndicate's office, was a malevolent presence hanging over me. I knew that the one causing it was someone flesh and blood, but somehow, my mind found mechanisms to turn the man into a bogeyman, the villain of a horror movie, who would disappear if I closed my eyes.

We humans always find a way to keep surviving even under threat, as long as we have hope rooted within us.

To be someone better, richer, more beautiful, immortal.

I feared Trevino, but I was certain I would defeat him because I would never give up.

The terror I feel now, however, is not from my bogeyman, but from fate, from God, and from the fear that my body might no longer be carrying the child I already love, even without being sure if it's alive or not.

"Let's begin," the doctor says, and I feel Odhran squeeze my hand.

I've seen various facets of him.

The angry version, the passionate, sexy, arrogant one.

I've never seen him suffer, though, and when I look at his face, I know that's what he's feeling now, even though he's being strong for me and for us.

When he arrived earlier today, surprising me—because Odhran is many things, but not a romantic—he knelt at my feet in front of the whole family and put a huge diamond ring on my finger. Then, with his ogre-like passionate manner, he declared for anyone who wanted to hear, without even waiting for my "yes" or making an official proposal, that we were engaged.

"Can you give us a moment?" I ask the doctor and the nurse from the clinic Cillian had installed on the island, which rivals any regular hospital.

It's frightening that in a place that's supposed to be a vacation retreat, they had to set up something like this, but at the same time, I know that the recent war wasn't a one-off event and that, in the future, we might need to stay here on other occasions.

"I love you," I say as soon as the doctor leaves and closes the door behind him. "No matter what the test results are, I love you, Irish."

He bends down and kisses my forehead.

His face is tense with anxiety, but he seems to relax when he pulls back to look at me.

"I wish I had the power to guarantee that our baby is still there."

"I know, but let's leave it to God's will," I say, trying to sound stronger than I feel.

"He doesn't get along well with me. Maybe He doesn't even remember who I am anymore."

"He does know. For a while, I was angry because I couldn't accept that He allowed my sister to be killed, but then, when He continued to protect me and Jax, I regained my faith. Let the doctor in, Odhran. I can't wait any longer. I'm too anxious."

Five minutes later, I have my nails dug into his palm, the nervousness drowning me in its waves, but when the machine emits the most beautiful sound I've ever heard, I finally let the emotion I've been holding back come out in tears.

"Everything is fine with the baby, we have it here," the doctor says, pointing to the screen, but it's as if no one else is in the exam room.

Odhran looks at it in awe, then at me.

"He's strong like his mother," he says. "A fighter, or a fighter-to-be."

"Our son or daughter," I say, unable to hold back the tears.

The doctor said we would only know the sex at the next exam, if the baby cooperates.

After the technical explanations about what we're seeing and how the baby's development will proceed from here on, the entire team leaves again, probably sensing that we need to be alone.

"I will never stop protecting you, Elaine. Not you, nor our family. I can't promise you we'll live in paradise, without risks or danger, but I swear that if any son of a bitch comes near you, I will take you back. I will die before I let them take you from me."

Odhran

WHEN WE LEFT THE EXAM room at the island clinic, I was fucking surprised to see our whole family, including Rourke and Keiron, gathered in the hallway.

Only Elaine and I came, as even though she's very close to Hestia, she asked me to stay with Jax because the boy had been restless since early morning, probably sensing our tension.

So, I didn't think they'd come, and only now that I have everyone here do I realize how good it feels that they did.

Cillian is the first to approach, and after kissing Elaine's forehead, he holds my face.

"I don't need to ask you the result because I can see from your expression that everything is fine. I'm not sure if I've told you this before because I'm not good with words, but I feel your pain, brother, and your joy is mine as well. I'm glad you've finally managed to move past the past. I can't wait to see another O'Callaghan in the world."

Have I moved past it? I don't know if that will ever happen, but I won't stop living with the woman I love, or filling her womb with my children, because of the guilt I still feel.

I will never forget what happened to my parents, but I have two children and the woman who is my world to honor and protect.

"I plan to do my part, filling this hellish planet we live on with many O'Callaghans."

Chapter 53

Elaine

Three Months Later

"**H**e's so happy at school, my daughter," Hestia says, smiling.

I nod in agreement. What I don't explain is that it's not a regular school, but one specially designed for members of the Syndicate. Everyone inside, from the teachers to the inspectors, and even the principal, is, in some way, connected to the large family we've formed.

The school is of excellence, as Odhran explained to me, and it was Orla's idea, because it would be too risky in the future for the heirs of Syndicate men to send their children to regular schools. From what I know, the Russian Organization has something similar.

Odhran still doesn't talk to me about Syndicate matters, but I know we are going through a period of relative peace. I don't ask questions because after talking a lot with Juno and my two new friends, Tulia and Taisiya, on this specific issue, I understood that the less we know, the better.

We returned to Boston a few days after my pregnancy was confirmed, and now I know I'm expecting a boy. Jax is going to have a little brother, and when I explained this to him, he could barely contain his joy.

I run my hand over my abdomen, but I still can't see much, except for a slight rounding at the bottom.

"You're very anxious about the baby."

"I am. I can't wait to feel him move, but the doctor said it will be some time before that happens."

"Go distract yourself, Elaine, or whatever that Irishman has planned for you."

I smile, feeling my cheeks burn with embarrassment.

"Are you sure it's okay if you stay with him this afternoon? Odhran is being all mysterious with the surprise."

"I thought he was only coming back to Boston tomorrow."

"So did I, but he was away for a week, so who am I to complain if my Irishman is home earlier than expected?"

She hugs me.

"I have to confess I was wrong, my daughter. I was very afraid of your involvement with Odhran, but now, after months of seeing him treat you like a queen, I know you really did find your destiny. In fact, you're each other's destiny."

"Yes, I know. Our life won't be a fairy tale, but I wasn't dreaming of one. I don't believe anyone is a hundred percent good in the literal sense of the word, Hestia. We all feel anger, at some point in our lives, or are resentful, vengeful, and even slightly envious. It's part of human nature to be flawed. To a greater or lesser extent, we are all sinners. Odhran isn't a prince, but he's the one my heart chose."

She nods.

"And what about absolute evil? Do you think it exists?"

"I've had living proof that it does. Trevino was its embodiment. The men who kidnapped Janice's sister were too."

"You still think about her, don't you?"

"I do. We weren't even that close, yet I can't forget her face. I wonder about the families of missing persons. I think never having an answer about what happened to your loved one must be worse than knowing they're dead."

"Don't even get me started, but enough of this sad talk. Evil will always exist in the world, Elaine, and so will the death of innocents. The other day, I heard a story on TV about a father that left me devastated. He said his daughter was killed on a night out at a bar with friends. The man was crying and said he always advised the girl not to drink in public because there were men who would take advantage of the situation."

"What happened?"

"According to him, the daughter was vocal about women's rights and that, instead of parents like him teaching girls not to drink in public, boys' parents should raise their sons in a way that even if they saw a drunken girl, they wouldn't take advantage of her."

"I agree. It's not about the woman being drunk, wearing a short skirt, or even being naked. An honorable man would never exploit the situation."

"But that's the crux of the matter. You said 'an honorable man'. For most men, I believe, good upbringing and examples at home will be enough to make them respect women and not see them as objects to exploit, but every basket has a rotten fruit, or the news wouldn't be filled with headlines about rich young people who grew up surrounded by all privileges and loving parents, yet still abuse, sexually assault, and kill women."

"It's a sad view of the world."

"But realistic as well. Evil is everywhere. Men and women can suffer its consequences, but the statistics don't lie. Our gender is still, by far, the most targeted by physical and sexual violence."

I shudder at the thought that my former coworker, who fought so hard to get justice for her sister, might have endured the same kind of torture as the one she tried to protect.

The monster that killed Elysia is in hell now, where it always belonged, but there are many others like Trevino scattered around the planet.

"I would give anything to know what happened to Janice."

"I know, my dear. But some questions will never have answers. Move on with your life. Don't look back. It's the only way to keep our sanity."

I GET INTO THE CAR smiling, partially forgetting the conversation with Hestia, while wondering what got into Odhran to want to carry out this kind of fantasy.

He's very "creative" behind closed doors, but also very careful with me, so when I received a new phone earlier today with a message saying I needed to discard the old one—something quite common between us and done almost on a weekly basis—I was initially surprised.

The Syndicate soldier who handed me the phone said he was instructed to inform me that I should follow all the instructions to the letter.

An hour later, a message came through, as always, from my man, telling me what to do.

I was to bring one of the old outfits I used to wear when I was the girl on the billboard and meet him at the place that used to be the headquarters of the fights.

The only rule I broke was giving Hestia the address of where I was going. I no longer have secrets from her.

Now, however, it's not my heart mother I'm thinking about, but the handsome man who will be my husband in a month.

I open the car door, pleased that Odhran didn't make me come with bodyguards. I'd be mortified if, while I'm here, the men were left wondering what we were doing inside.

The place seems deserted, but I'm not afraid. I trust Odhran with my life. Next to him, I'll always be protected.

Chapter 54

Odhran

"**D**on't do anything until we're sure she's safe, goddammit," I warn for the umpteenth time as we leave the forest behind the old warehouse. The same one where, a few months ago, Keiron took Elaine away on the back of his motorcycle.

Finally, after years, I need to accept that against all odds, God still watches over me. Only this explains my early return to Boston, originally scheduled for tomorrow, and that just minutes after my brother showed us, in a meeting, the final content of the flash drive, Hestia called me apologizing and saying she didn't want to interrupt our meeting, but since Elaine had forgotten the new cell phone I sent her, she was worried.

It took five seconds for me to realize that something was very wrong.

I didn't schedule any meeting with her, nor did I send a new cell phone.

I don't like scaring Hestia, but this time, there was no avoiding it. I asked her to explain what happened, and she said that a Syndicate soldier had delivered a new cell phone to Elaine and told her she should come meet me at the old warehouse.

My mother-in-law also said that Elaine received instructions from me not to tell anyone about the meeting, but Elaine never hides anything from her mother, especially because she fears that something might happen to Jaxton and no one would be able to find her.

We've already found the bastard traitor who led my wife into a trap and know that she has only been inside for about an hour.

Kellan has finally managed to decipher the entire contents of the flash drive, and what he found was far beyond what we could have ever imagined.

Trevino was indeed associated with another criminal organization, betraying us, but not the one we thought—the Sicilians.

The betrayal against us came from an alliance with the Salvadorans, but the reason behind it, I couldn't guess in a million years.

Trevino Cabrera is Gómez Fuentes' father. It wasn't his heirs and wife that he was protecting by withholding information from me, but rather his eldest son, born out of wedlock, who is the leader of one of the most vile criminal organizations that deal primarily with human trafficking. There's even a rumor that they inherited the "business" from the Albanian mafia, which was exterminated by the Russians from American territory a few years ago.

"We're going to get her out of there, Odhran."

"Don't bother trying to negotiate, Kellan. Shoot to kill, especially Gómez Fuentes, if you get the chance. As much as I'd enjoy wiping that bastard out, nothing is more important than making sure Elaine is safe."

"He won't do anything to her. At this very moment, Cillian has not only invaded their organization's headquarters, but we also have Gómez Fuentes' family as hostages. Everyone, without exception, is in our older brother's custody," Kellan says.

We have three dozen men with us, but with the hatred I'm feeling, I could go in alone.

"If you ask me, at this point, Gómez Fuentes already knows we have his children and won't do anything to Elaine until you show up to negotiate," Lorcan says.

"The only negotiation he'll get from me will be a quick death. He won't leave here alive."

Elaine

"SO YOU THOUGHT IT WAS my father who fathered a child with your sister's whore?" the man with a tattooed face and the letter "m" on his right cheek, the symbol of his organization, "M" for Muerte, asks, throwing his head back and laughing.

I try to hide my fear, but I can't.

It's been about an hour since I arrived, and aside from being tied to a steel beam, they haven't done anything to me, but I have no doubt that if Odhran doesn't find me in time, my son and I won't survive.

I was wrong all along. I think he's sure I'm going to die because the man confessed every sin to me.

At least one thing I know my sister lied to me about: when she told me her boyfriend was a famous and wealthy lawyer. Rich, yes, but a lawyer who didn't live in the country? She used her father-in-law's persona, that damned Trevino Cabrera, to protect her boyfriend's real identity.

Gómez was Elysia's secret boyfriend, and not even in two lifetimes would I understand how my sister, after everything she went through, could have gotten involved with someone like that.

Now I have all the answers I've been searching for years.

I know that as I initially thought, my sister's desire to disappear really had to do with what I told her about Janice's sister's death and my colleague's disappearance.

Elysia discovered that it was the Salvadorans' kidnapping that led Janice's sister to suicide, and that was apparently the last straw for her.

Not the assaults, not the mistreatment she suffered. She needed to know what Janice's sister had gone through before she could flee.

From the beginning, Gómez Fuentes knew it was my sister who stole the flash drive, and that's how the hunt for her began. Gómez informed his father of what happened, and since both had a lot to lose, my sister became a target to be eliminated.

I also discovered—and couldn't hold back the tears when I heard the son of a bitch recounting it, smiling—that Trevino killed my sister accidentally. He wouldn't have given her a quick death, just pretending she had an overdose. He injected a drug that caused a reaction in her already fragile heart, resulting in a cardiac arrest.

I have no doubt that my sister stole the flash drive as a way to have some leverage against her child's father. Despite everything she discovered, however, she really had no idea who she was dealing with or what he was capable of.

"Jax is a good boy, sir." I keep my voice calm, and despite being certain I'm dealing with a monster, I still try to appeal to any feelings he might have.

"Don't waste your time. I already have the daughters I want, with the woman I chose, not with an American whore. Now, it's time to go. We can't stay here. I have plans for you, and if it weren't for the fact that you're suspicious, I would have arranged it somewhere else, but I thought you wouldn't fall into the trap. Only an invitation to screw your Irishman would make you break the security protocol he imposed on you. If sex is what you wanted, you'll have that in the coming weeks with dozens of partners, until I end your life."

I start to cry, not believing that my fate is to die, after having a glimpse of happiness, at the hands of one of the demons I've been fleeing from for years. But then I remember Odhran's promise on the beach.

"I will never stop protecting you, Elaine. Neither you nor our family. I can't promise we'll live in paradise, without risks or danger, but I swear if any son of a bitch comes near you, I'll get you back. I'd die before I let them take you from me."

At this moment, I have nothing left but my faith, so I close my eyes and pray.

Chapter 55

Odhran

I know this is no longer just a mission; it's the mission of my life. The one that will determine whether I have the right, even if I don't deserve it, to a life filled with the light of the woman I love and my children—I formalized the adoption process for Jaxton a week ago, with a "nudge" to the government agencies to expedite the action—or if I will plunge once and for all into the depths of hell.

I move carefully, every step knowing that the salvation of my wife depends on this.

The warehouse is surrounded, and the Salvadorans who were guarding it are dead.

We have considered every way to breach the place where Gómez Fuentes is holding Elaine hostage, and I decided that while Lorcan and Kellan, along with the other men, will enter through the doors and windows, I will surprise him from the glass ceiling.

I'm not wearing a shirt, just jeans, and I have a gun and a knife with me.

I can already see her, tied to one of the iron posts, and apparently still well.

And *still*, for me, is the key word. There's no time to waste.

From where I am to the drop, it's about five meters, and there's a good chance I'll break a leg on the way down, but it's the only way to catch him completely off guard. If we entered through the door, the chance of that bastard shooting Elaine would be high.

I heard the last part of their conversation and how she tried to negotiate, bringing up some humanity in the bastard by mentioning Jax, but it was of no use.

I also saw the exact moment he took the call informing him that we had his family, and the despair any normal man would feel did not show on his face. He looked pissed, but not remorseful like any father would be if his five children were in the enemy mafia's hands.

Once we eliminate him, we'll send his wife and children out of the country. They are all daughters and will be sent to El Salvador. The mother will receive a warning—the only one—not to set foot on American soil again.

Because there will be nothing for her here. The mafia known as "M" for Muerte ends today.

In every city in the country where there are cells of theirs, as well as in the prisons, they will be exterminated.

I see Gómez Fuentes looking around the warehouse, seeming paranoid. There are four men with him, and I have no doubt that they are all in Kellan, Lorcan, and our soldiers' sights.

He's not standing still, but walking in circles. Occasionally, he points the gun at Elaine but then turns away, as if expecting an attack.

Too bad for him that he never looked up.

I aim for his hand. I need to hit the one holding the gun, and I know I have only one chance before hell breaks loose.

For a few seconds, I close my eyes and pray.

"Show me that you are still with me, God. I don't have much faith, but Elaine does. Help me save her."

I've never hesitated in my life, but at this moment, as I prepare to shoot him, I feel a slight tremor in my hand, and even so, I pull the trigger.

And then, a second later, I see Gómez Fuentes stagger and drop the gun.

I stand up and leap onto him, shattering the glass ceiling and feeling several pieces cut into my flesh and my blood flow. I feel no pain, there is nothing within me but the desperate need to save her, to ensure she is protected.

I fall on top of Gómez Fuentes, and even caught off guard, the bastard fights back.

I hear gunshots and the Salvadorans' bodies falling as my brother shouts orders to our men.

"You made the last mistake of your life, you son of a bitch. No one touches my family."

I shove the gun into the bastard's mouth and pull the trigger. His head explodes in front of me.

A muffled scream comes from Elaine, and when she sees the dead man under me, she faints.

I get up and release her arms and legs. Elaine falls unconscious into my arms.

Without looking at anyone, I scoop her up and carry her out of the warehouse. Maybe what happened will change something between us. Elaine witnessed my worst side. She saw the killer she calls love in action, but none of that matters as long as she is safe now.

We are finally out of the place, which will soon be blown up. I take her to the back of a van, where a doctor is waiting.

Without opening her eyes yet, Elaine lets out a scream of terror.

"You're safe, love. I've got you, and I'll never let you go."

"Odhran?" she finally gathers the courage to look at me.

"Yes, baby. I'm here. Tell me if you feel pain anywhere."

"No. I think he wanted to psychologically torture me first," she says, and I see a tear roll down her face.

"I need to examine her, Odhran," the doctor we brought says.

"It's okay," Elaine agrees, "but don't leave."

"I'm not going anywhere, sweetheart. I'll always protect you because you're mine."

Chapter 56

Odhran

Odhran and Elaine's Wedding Day

Elaine smiles at me as if no one else is around, even though there are about fifty guests, including family.

I promised her I would give her everything she ever dreamed of, and so it was done.

Dress, decoration, cake, sweets, bouquet.

None of this is more than a grain of sand compared to what I would do for her.

I hold her close to my chest, my lips at her ear swearing my love, while we dance to our last song before I steal her away just for me.

I look around, always alert.

I know there are five times as many security personnel as there are guests. We will never give our families a chance to be caught off guard again, no matter that the war with the damned carcamanos is on hold for now.

"I know you're tense," she says, lifting her face and touching my jaw.

"This is my relaxed version."

There's no way I can ever be a normal guy. Being on guard, waiting for the enemy, is part of my nature.

"I love you, Irish, and I must be crazy because this unique mix of fire and ice that only you have drives me wild. As much as I want you to just enjoy yourself, I don't want you to change."

"I changed when I realized I could never continue a solo flight after I touched you. I changed when I realized the possibility of us having a child. I changed when I made Jaxton my boy. I love you more than I could ever explain, Elaine, but you need to know that I will never make a promise I can't keep. I am who I am. Yours, devoted, crazy, passionate, but not part of the hero team."

"I don't care what it means to the world. To me, Jax and our Madden, who is yet to be born, you are a hero."

Elaine

Two Months Later

"MOMMY, WHERE'S MY BROTHER? Is it going to take a long time for him to come out of your belly? It's already so big!" Jax says while playing Lego with Odhran on the carpet of the room. Hestia and I laugh.

Not a blessed day goes by without hearing that question.

"He's excited," she says, while I see Odhran kiss our son's forehead, get up, and come over to me. "I think the idea of having a little brother is filling all his thoughts."

"Maybe, once this one is born, we'll need to arrange for another," Odhran chimes in with the most mischievous look in the world, not at all concerned that my mother is listening.

After giving her an irresistible dimpled smile, he picks me up and starts walking toward our bedroom.

"Lack of training won't be the issue." I feign annoyance. "You're insatiable, Irish."

"I'm in love with you, woman, and I can never get enough."

Odhran

Madden O'Callaghan's Birth Day

I LIFT HIM UP IN MY arms, to the height of my face, not believing that my son is with me now.

In the days leading up to his birth, I was as anxious as Elaine and refused to leave her side, obsessively surrounding her with care to the point that one day, after hearing Hestia say it, Jax surprised me with a "Dad, you need to relax, let's play video games?".

I looked at him, certain he didn't realize how he addressed me, but I did.

I held him close and for several minutes kept him embraced, and then I uttered the words I used to hear from my own father and thought I would never say to anyone:

"I love you, son."

Jaxton O'Callaghan smiled and laid his head on my shoulder, and that's when I understood what Elaine meant on our wedding day.

I am a monster to the world, but their hero.

Now, as I look at Madden O'Callaghan, I know that for my family, I would go to hell a thousand times and always come back, because I found my paradise on Earth.

I move closer to Elaine in the hospital bed where Jax is lying beside her. They both smile at each other, and I suspect it's because of my gooey way with our youngest.

"Come here, husband. Your place is here, with us. Always with us."

Epilogue 1

Elaine

Five Years Later

I smile as I open the door and find the house in complete silence, because I know where I'll find my three men.

I head to the kitchen to grab an apple because even though I'm missing them terribly, I'm starving, the little one in my belly begging for food after a whole day in my bouquet studio, attending clients with barely a moment for a break.

"I heard your car and came to check if you were going to eat," I hear Hestia say behind me.

I turn around and show her the apple. Then, I walk over and give her a kiss on the cheek.

"I'll be right back. I just need to greet the three of them."

"Do you know where they are?"

"I'm sure."

I climb the stairs and, as expected, as I approach the room that was specifically remodeled to dampen the sound, I can already hear some noise.

I hold the doorknob before entering, preparing for the scene I know I'll find. The last months of pregnancy always leave me very emotional.

I finally open the door and when I see Jaxton playing the bass and Odhran sitting at the drums, shirtless, with our Madden on one leg, each of them holding a drumstick and playing in sync, my heart overflows with love.

It's not just the sight of a father sharing an activity with his two boys. It's that of a man who fought his demons, overcame them, and decided to leave the past behind.

Odhran told me that since the death of my in-laws, he hadn't touched the drums again, and drumming had always been his passion.

One day, Juno, not knowing the whole story about his parents' death, gave a drum set to Madden when he was two years old.

Our son did what children do when they need help: he asked his father.

I could see the pain in Odhran's features, but I let him decide.

Several days passed and then, without any prior warning, I came home from work and found the three of them in Madden's room, improvising a "rock band."

Now, it's a ritual. They love this time they spend together to the point where Odhran had the room remodeled for "rehearsals."

"Look who's spying on us, boys!" I hear my Irish say, and as always, my body reacts to his sexy voice.

A chorus of "Mommy" followed by hugs around my legs begins, as well as a conversation with their little sister in my belly.

Half an hour later, Hestia comes to take the two of them away to leave us alone.

Odhran sits with me on his lap, one hand resting on my already prominent belly and the other holding a drumstick.

He plays a hypnotic tune and for several minutes, I just let myself lean against his chest.

"Did I make you fall asleep?" he asks, suddenly stopping.

I turn and hold his face.

"No. As always, you made me daydream, Irish. I love you, my husband."

Epilogue 2

Odhran

"**W**oman, don't forget who you belong to, or I'll have a jacket made for you: Property of Odhran O'Callaghan."

She rolls her eyes, but instead of calling me a jealous jerk as I probably deserve, she wraps her arms around my neck while I climb the stairs straight to our bedroom.

We just got back from Cillian's birthday party, and even though I'm sure of my feisty woman's love for me, I go crazy when I see her dancing with the other women from the Syndicate.

Elaine is sensual and uninhibited, and I doubt that in the minds of those bastards, except for my family, they weren't fantasizing about her.

Just thinking about it makes me want to kill them one by one.

"Don't be a caveman, Irish. Haven't you understood that I'm yours?"

Instead of answering, I throw her onto the bed and, in a split second, strip her naked. I only take off my jacket, shirt, boots, and socks before burying my face between her thighs.

Hours later, sweaty and with a drowsy Elaine in my arms, I kiss her hair, thinking that I've never felt so much peace in my life, if anyone in my world is entitled to such a privilege.

Our three children are well, and as far as possible, the constant wars between the organizations are under control.

Jaxton's heart has not caused any concern since, although we always keep up with the semiannual check-ups with the cardiologist.

We both want more children — as many as the Creator blesses us with — because hearing the laughter of the kids, along with the loving smile of my wife, is the highlight of my day.

About a year ago, I found out what happened to Janice, Elaine's missing coworker, because I'm not the type to leave questions unanswered. I knew it was something that troubled my wife, so I went after it.

To my surprise, she's alive. At least she didn't fall into the hands of those motherfuckers from the "M" of Muerte.

It wasn't easy to find her, as Janice became a nun and isolated herself from the world. I visited her once to make sure it was really her, and when she told me she was happy for Elaine's concern but was where she wanted to be and didn't wish to maintain external ties, I passed the message, word for word, to my wife.

Elaine, as I knew she would, respected her wishes.

It's one of the qualities I love most about her. My queen doesn't try to change anyone. She respects space and boundaries.

"Aren't you tired? My God, I married a mutant!" I hear the laughter in her voice.

"I'm not a mutant, you cheeky thing, but my desire for you will never fade. Now, however, I just want to hold you, woman, and have confirmation of the lucky bastard that I am."

The End!

Did you love *Indecent Protection*? Then you should read *Web of Seduction* by Amara Holt!

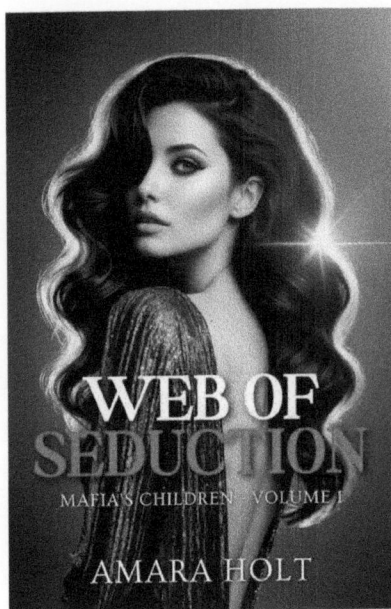

Web of Seduction is a gripping dark romance that will **ensnare** your heart and keep you turning pages long into the night.

Enrico, the **enigmatic** underboss of the Cosa Nostra, has always walked a solitary path. With power and control at his fingertips, he's never allowed anyone to get too close—especially not women. But when fate forces him to share a house with Pietra, the **mafia princess** and daughter of his boss, everything changes.

Pietra has loved Enrico from afar, her forbidden desires hidden beneath a mask of **innocence**. She's always been the good girl, the obedient daughter, but the time has come for her to reveal her **true self**. In the shadows of their shared home, Pietra's long-suppressed passion **ignites**, and she begins to weave a dangerous **web of seduction** around the one man she can never truly have.

Enrico knows he shouldn't want her—she's the daughter of his best friend and mentor, a girl he watched grow up. But the more he tries to resist, the more he's drawn into her **trap**. As the lines between right and wrong blur, Enrico finds himself caught in a battle between **duty** and **desire**.

In **Web of Seduction**, love isn't about finding the perfect prince—it's about falling for the dark, alluring **anti-hero** who breaks all the rules. Will Enrico be able to escape the seductive web Pietra has spun around him, or will he surrender to the forbidden passion that could **destroy** them both?

If you crave stories filled with **intense chemistry,** forbidden romance, and the allure of a love that defies the odds, **Web of Seduction** is the book you've been waiting for. Get ready to lose yourself in a world where **power, passion,** and **danger** collide.

About the Author

Amara Holt is a storyteller whose novels immerse readers in a whirlwind of suspense, action, romance and adventure. With a keen eye for detail and a talent for crafting intricate plots, Amara captivates her audience with every twist and turn. Her compelling characters and atmospheric settings transport readers to thrilling worlds where danger lurks around every corner.

9 798330 596713